SOME DARK HOLLER

LUKE BAUSERMAN

YOUR FREE BOOK IS WAITING

Read the fascinating history and folklore that inspired Some Dark Holler in, *Six Tales from Sixmile Creek*. You can get a copy FOR FREE when you sign up to join my Reader's Group. To get started, go to: www.lukebauserman.com/sixtales

THE DEVIL'S FINEST, 1865

Death's horse limped through the snow on three legs. A severed head dangled from the saddle horn, bouncing with every lurching step.

The rider slumped over his steed, snoring into the silver river of his beard; the black hood had fallen back, exposing hair as pale as moonlight. His cloak was draped in inky folds over the pearl-white flank of his horse. Dark trees choked the path, making way for the horseman and closing immediately behind.

A drift barred the way ahead. The horse floundered as it entered the deep snow, the stump of its right foreleg pumping in space. It snorted and reared onto quivering hind legs.

Death awoke. His head bumped a snow-laden bough, showering him in chill flakes. "Whoa, Isham," he said, pulling back on the reins.

The horse came down, flanks heaving.

Death slid from the saddle, landing thigh-deep in the drift. He wiped his eyes with pallid hands and yawned. Reaching into a leather saddlebag, he drew out an ear of corn as black as coal. He pried loose a handful of kernels and held them out to the horse.

Isham nuzzled his master's palm, raking the kernels into his mouth with fleshy lips.

Death ran his hand over the saddle and tested the girth strap. He glanced at the severed head, its frozen mouth leering around the rawhide thong worked through its jaws.

Some fool's always trying to outrun his own shadow.

Death cinched the strap tighter. The Devil had a surprise coming tonight.

Isham snorted and raised his head, breathing a great gout of vapor into the night. A ghostly limb sprouted from his legless nub, barely visible in the moonlight. He flexed the unearthly leg and stomped.

"That ought to get us to this infernal meeting a little quicker," Death said. He put his foot in the stirrup, swung back into the saddle, and clucked his tongue. Isham sprang forward, clearing the drift with ease.

The path grew thin and soon disappeared altogether. They moved through the snow-clogged bracken and creaking trees into the heart of the forest. At length, Death saw an orange light quivering in the darkness. He urged Isham toward it, and they emerged into a clearing ringed by a black wall of pines, a fire blazing at its center. The snow had drawn back from the heat, leaving a damp ring of ground.

Three figures were gathered around the flames. At Death's approach, a small, finely dressed man rose from his perch on a stump.

"Welcome, Pale Rider." He lifted a cane in greeting and removed his top hat.

Death fixed the smaller man with a gaze as cold as ice, then turned his head and spat in the snow. "Scratch, you're a thorn in my side, you know that?"

Scratch raised an eyebrow. "My, my, what a foul humor you're in tonight." He shrugged. "No matter. This won't take long. William, quick and orderly as he is, has given me two contracts already signed in blood. His own, which is due for renewal, and one for Amos, our newest recruit." He reached into his coat and withdrew two pieces of parchment and a pen. "All we need is your signature, and you won't be bothered for another seven years."

Death scowled. "Save it. I found something that belongs to you." He unhooked the rawhide thong from the pommel and tossed the severed head onto the ground. It rolled to a stop at the Devil's feet.

Scratch turned the grisly offering with his boot, examining the face. He clucked his tongue. "Henry tried to run, did he?"

"I chased him clear across Arkansas!" Death leveled a finger at Scratch. "From one side to the other. You know how long that took me? Four days to hunt him, and three days to ride here. That's seven days that I've had to abandon my duties, all on account of your failure of a servant. You know why it took that long to catch him? In every campfire the fool made, he crossed two sticks and poured salt over them." Death folded his arms. "Tell me, where'd he learn to do that?"

Scratch spread his hands in a gesture of innocence, diamond cuff links winking in the firelight. "I haven't the faintest idea. Maybe you let it slip in front of him like you just did in front of these two mortals." He pointed to the two men waiting on the other side of the fire.

Death squinted, taking in the mortals for the first time. They both wore the gray uniforms of soldiers. The first, a middle-aged man, squatted by the flames, his palms held out to catch the heat. He met Death's gaze and smirked. At his side, a gangly youth sat on a log, bouncing one knee, hands tucked into his armpits, steadily avoiding Death's eyes.

Death snorted. "If they've got any sense betwixt the two of them, they'll see just how useful that little trick was to their friend." He patted Isham's neck. "There isn't a soul on this earth my horse can't run down." He looked back at Scratch and waved dismissively. "I'm done cleaning up your leavings, Scratch. I won't be signing these deals."

Scratch shrugged. "Suit yourself."

Death pulled on the reins and wheeled Isham away from the fire. This felt good; he should have done it centuries ago. He'd been a fool to let the Devil push him around in the first place.

"How's dearest Maude?" Scratch asked.

Death stiffened, his breath catching in his throat. How did Scratch know about Maude? He pulled Isham back to face the Devil.

Scratch arched a perfect black eyebrow. "Thought you had a secret, didn't you? That's right. I know you've been holding her back from the Judgment." He wagged a finger. "Naughty, naughty."

"I make no distinction between saints and sinners." Death spoke through clenched teeth. "The Judgment is no concern of mine, and Maude is no concern of yours."

"I've never accused you of dividing the goats from the sheep." Scratch winked. "The only prejudice I've ever known you to show is your eye for redheads. But contrary to your claim, Maude is very much my concern. By the way, have you had any luck finding her?"

Death's hand leaped instinctively to the reaping hook sheathed alongside the saddle. "Scratch! If you had anything to do with her disappearance, I swear I'll—"

The Devil laughed, holding up his hands. "Whoa, slow down, Pale Rider. I don't know where your sweetheart has run off to." He paused, his eyes glinting with malevolence. "Or who *with*."

Death's nostrils flared, and he pulled the reaping hook halfway out of its sheath.

"Put it away, Death. You know it'll do you no good here. I was merely going to point out that before you took a shine to her, the girl was destined for my neck of the woods." Scratch rubbed his chin. "It had something to do with her burning the cabin down with her uncle inside." His face grew serious. "And if I find her first, well...," his eyes narrowed, "I keep a special place in Hell for pretty faces." He held up the contracts. "Then again, if I ran across the girl and you and I were on good terms... I might be persuaded otherwise."

Death released the reaping hook, his fingers balling into a fist. He bowed his head. "All right. Let's get this over with."

A grin spread over Scratch's face, erasing every ounce of menace from his features. "I thought you'd say that." He held out the pen and papers.

Death snatched the documents. A quick glance confirmed that Scratch was offering these mortals his standard contract: their "might, mind, strength, and soul" in exchange for seven years of protection from the grave. Death bit his lip as he scrawled his name, then thrust the papers back at Scratch.

The Devil accepted the documents. "Everything's in order, then."

Lifting Isham's reins, Death prepared once again to leave.

"Not so fast." Scratch raised a finger. "We have to take care of my newest recruit." He tucked the papers into his coat and turned to the gangly youth. "Are you ready for your first assignment, Amos?"

The young man stood and rubbed his palm on the patched knee of his pant leg. "Y-yes sir," he said, walking toward Scratch with jerky steps.

Scratch handed Amos a sealed envelope. "You'll be traveling north, to the lumber camps on the Great Lakes," he said. "The specifics on the boy you're after are inside."

Amos accepted the envelope with trembling hands.

"You have seven years from today to persuade him to join my service. As my servant, you'll be immune from Death. If you're successful, you can choose to take another assignment, good for another seven years free from Death. If you fail, well..." Scratch glanced at the fallen head. "You'll be subject to the Dread Horseman, just like dear Henry. Any questions?"

Amos shook his head.

"Very well." Scratch placed his hand on the boy's back and pushed him forward. "Death, remove your imprint."

Amos stumbled toward Isham's flank, quaking. Death seized the boy's shoulder and shut his eyes. Amos gasped and went rigid.

The boy's mortal imprint was a kind of long shadow that trailed from his being and connected him to Death. Every human was tagged with one from birth. It kept Death from having to personally collect each mortal when their appointed time came.

I just wasted four days hunting down one of these, and here I am creating another, Death thought. He cursed himself for his weakness. He cursed Maude for her hair, red like the sunset, and for smelling of lavender when she tucked her head under his chin. He resolved to let her go, and in the same thought, he knew he could not.

With a sigh, he detached the imprint from Amos and released him. The young man staggered away.

Scratch grinned and thumped Amos on the back. "Feels good, doesn't it?"

Amos looked back at Death and shuddered.

"On your way then," Scratch said. "No time to waste."

Amos nodded vigorously and struck out from the fire, striding with purpose.

"North is that way," Scratch said, pointing in the opposite direction.

The youth did an about-face, stammering an apology.

Scratch chuckled. "All nerves, isn't he?"

"He'll have more to worry about once I come to collect him," Death said.

The third man spoke for the first time. "Not all of us are as blundering as Henry."

Death turned in the saddle to face William. He was taken aback by the man's gall. "What did you say?"

William crossed his arms. "You talk as if the boy is sure to fail, and yet here I stand, a servant of Scratch for over ninety years."

"That's bold talk for a mortal."

"Indeed," Scratch said, stepping between William and Death. "William, it's not your place to goad the Reaper. Are you ready to earn another seven years?"

William locked eyes with Death. "Always."

Scratch produced an envelope and handed it to William. "I'm sending you after a boy named Ephraim Cutler. I'm quite eager to recruit him. Don't let me down."

William rubbed his thumb over the envelope. "Master, it only took me four years to persuade Amos." He inhaled deeply. "I'll deliver this Ephraim Cutler to you in three and a half years, in exchange for fourteen years of your protection. That's half the time for twice the reward. What do you say?"

Scratch laughed—a mocking sound. "You are ambitious, I'll give you that. But no, I'm afraid your request exceeds the bounds of our arrangement."

William's eyes flashed. "But Master, I—"

Scratch held up a hand. "That's enough, William. You're free to leave."

William swore, and stalked off into the trees.

Death watched him go. He lifted his black hood over his head. "I don't care how much time it takes, Scratch, I look forward to beheading that one."

Scratch sighed and patted Isham's muzzle. "He can be insolent, but in the end, he's only a man. William fights so hard against his fate. Death, Heaven, Hell—he isn't satisfied with any of it. But how I love to watch him struggle." He grinned at Death. "Don't be so mulish about these dealings, my friend. Recruiting mortals to do your work makes eternity pass most delightfully. You really should try it sometime."

2

PISTOL KISSES, 1872

Ephraim inhaled the cool night air. A hoot owl called from a stand of post oaks to his left. The big moon bathed the frosty creek bottom in a soft yellow glow. The thrill of the hunt pulsed through him. He glanced at the other men who made up the hunting party, a dozen in total, and each gripped his rifle in anticipation.

"It's a sixteen-shooter, seventeen if you have one in the chamber," Peyton Henson said. He held his lever-action rifle out to Ephraim and tapped the brass tube magazine.

At a head taller and two years older than Ephraim, Peyton had the air of a freshly minted dandy. His leather boots were as well-oiled as his rifle, and his hat had yet to weather a single rainstorm.

Ephraim shouldered his battered single-shot and curled his toes through holes in the soles of his brogans. "A coon hide with sixteen holes in it ain't worth much," he said.

Peyton snorted. "You don't use 'em all at once. A gun like this, you load on Sunday and shoot all week long."

Off in the trees, the hounds began to bay.

Peyton slapped Ephraim on the back. "Sounds like they found us a coon."

The hunting party waded into the forest, through the ferns and bushes, whooping to their dogs. Manson Owens, the local blacksmith, raised his lantern so high it knocked the brim of his hat sideways. "Who-e-e-e!" he shouted. "Give it to 'em, Lonnie!"

They made their way downstream and found the hounds gathered in a knot on a sandbar, sniffing around. One dog, young and gangly, splashed into the water, headed for the far bank. He came out of the creek, shook the water from his coat, and cast about, searching for the trail. He disappeared into the thick timber, and a moment later his excited voice made the forest ring. The other dogs lifted their heads and followed suit, fording the creek and crashing through the brush in a tumult of soprano howls.

"Did you see that?" Peyton said to Ephraim. "Clyde picked up the scent before all the others! And tonight's his first time trailing a live coon."

"You say he's a purebred Redbone?" Ephraim asked.

"Yeah. Pa got him for me last week, for my eighteenth birthday."

"Sure is a fine-lookin' animal."

The hunting party crossed the water in pursuit of the hounds. The whole woods rang with the sound of the chase. Peyton ran ahead with his older brother Silas, leaving Ephraim with Manson Owens.

On the far side of the creek, they encountered a steep hill. Ephraim slowed his pace to match Manson's, falling behind the other hunters. The old man reminded him of a locomotive he'd seen once, climbing the slope one steady chug at a time. He looked at Ephraim. "You ever been past the old Sherman cabin in Butcher Holler?" he asked between breaths.

"Not for a long time."

Manson nodded. "It's best to stay clear of that place, 'specially when you're out huntin' alone."

They crested the hill and came to the head of Butcher Holler. The voices of men and dogs floated up the slanted ground. Mason peered down into the bowl of the hollow. "By golly, that coon knows folks don't like this place, so he run down there!"

Leaves, slick with frost, plastered the ground. Ephraim and Manson picked their way down until they came to an abandoned cabin. Naked vines of poison ivy lined the spaces in the log walls and skirted the eaves. The door and shutters had long since given way before mountain winds.

Ephraim peered inside. Dry leaves and other woodland debris littered the floor, making the single room look like the cavity of a dead tree.

"I'm gettin' old and fat," Manson said. He leaned against a hitching post, took off his hat, and fanned himself. Beads of sweat trickled down his face; even his bushy mustache had the sheen of perspiration. He studied the abandoned cabin, his nose wrinkling. "This place gives me the all-overs. I never could figure why Ol' Wes Sherman chose to live out here on the backside of nowhere. I bet he kept a possum for a yard dog and owls in his henhouse."

Ephraim shuddered. Around Sixmile Creek, Wes Sherman was a legend. After the death of his daughter, the old man had lived a hermit's life, claiming the woods surrounding his cabin, as well as all the game in them, as his own. No one bothered the old man—until the day they found him, wild-eyed, wielding a rusty shovel over Ezekiel Birdseye's half-buried corpse. Wes said he'd caught the boy hunting on his "property."

The matter was settled without recourse to law. Wes was lynched. The Birdseye family led the execution and even provided a chicken dinner for the whole town afterward.

Some folks said the ghost of the old man still haunted Butcher Holler.

Down the hollow, behind the cabin, the hounds began keening and barking in rapid tempo.

Ephraim smiled. "I reckon they got him treed, Manson! We best get down there."

At the bottom of the hollow, they found the men and dogs gathered around the base of a large chestnut tree. Peyton had his rifle at the ready. "Clyde chased it up there, boys. This one's mine," he said, motioning for the other hunters to step back.

Ephraim forced his way through the squirming pack of dogs and lifted his lantern, casting light into the bare branches. Nothing stirred. His ears rang with the baying of the hounds. He squinted up and frowned. "You sure he's up there?"

"Sure I'm sure," Peyton said. "I wasn't ten feet behind Clyde when the coon went up."

Most of the dogs, Clyde included, were leaping up the trunk in a frenzy, but one of them remained apart from the pack. It was Manson's hound, Lonnie, the oldest dog in the bunch. He stood a few yards away from the tree, sniffing here and there.

One by one, the hunters grabbed their dogs and silenced them.

"Ephraim, you see him?" Manson asked.

Ephraim shook his head. "Just because Peyton saw him go up don't mean he's still there."

"Oh, he's up there all right," Peyton said. He shot Ephraim a squint-eyed glance, then scanned the branches.

"My money's on Ephraim," Manson said. "I ain't never seen someone hunt like he can. He can out-track a hound. And you ought to see him shoot! The boy knows how to put meat on the ground."

"I don't see Ephraim running around with his nose on the ground," Peyton said, winning a few chuckles from the group. "My money's on the dogs." He looked at Ephraim. "In fact, why don't we make a bet on it, hound dog Cutler?"

Ephraim's throat clenched. What did he have that Peyton could possibly want? Certainly not his old rifle.

"I'll climb this tree and look for the coon, and you look wherever you think he went," Peyton said. "If you find it, I'll go home with you, skin him, and tack the hide on your smokehouse wall for you. If I find him, then you have to do the same for me."

Ephraim grinned. This was a bet he could make. He spat on his palm and stuck out his hand. "Deal."

Peyton looked at Ephraim's hand, then spat in his own. "All right then." He gripped Ephraim's hand and shook.

They broke, moving in opposite directions. Peyton went to the base of the chestnut and took off his hat, his slicked-back hair shining in the lantern light. He motioned to his older brother. "Come on, Silas, give me a boost."

Ephraim walked around the tree in a circle, studying the trunk. Manson was exaggerating his hunting abilities—he'd never out-tracked a hound—but he paid attention to everything in the woods. He had never been able to afford a dog of his own, so he'd learned to hunt without one.

He studied old Lonnie, who still sniffed the ground by himself. What had pulled the old dog away from the rest of the pack?

Ephraim walked over to Lonnie. "You smell somethin', boy?" he asked, scratching the dog's back.

Lonnie pushed his nose into the fallen leaves, then peered into the darkness and barked.

Ephraim heard a faint rustle. He lifted his lantern, and for just a moment he caught the gleam of a close-set pair of eyes.

"Good boy, Lonnie," Ephraim said. The coon must have run up the side of the tree and jumped off, landing here, several yards away. In their excitement, the dogs, and Peyton, had been fooled.

Ephraim moved stealthily toward where he'd seen the eyes. Lonnie followed him, snuffling along an invisible trail. A few yards from the chestnut, they came to a collection of tombstones: the Sherman family graveyard. The stones jutted from the earth at odd angles, like broken teeth.

The back of Ephraim's neck prickled. *I wonder if this is where*

Wes Sherman is buried. He held up his lantern. Underbrush popped on the far side of the graveyard; he turned in that direction. Eyes gleamed orange in the lantern light, and the coon chittered.

Ephraim set the lantern on top of a tombstone and shouldered his rifle.

Lonnie barked, sending the coon scurrying away through the graves.

Ephraim lowered his cheek to the stock and glanced down at Lonnie. "Get him, boy!"

Lonnie dashed into the graveyard with a howl.

The coon emerged from between two graves and leaped onto a tree. Ephraim saw its shape, nothing more than a dark hump, scrambling up the trunk. He took aim and squeezed the trigger.

The rifle cracked, and the coon fell into the underbrush with a crash. In the woods behind Ephraim, Manson Owens let out a whoop.

THE CUTLERS' old sway-backed mare, Molly, poked her head out of the lean-to on the side of the smokehouse as Ephraim and Peyton entered the yard. Ephraim heard his ma's voice floating through the open window. As they neared the cabin, he made out some of her words: "—never forsake me."

His stomach twisted into a knot, and the excitement of winning the bet evaporated like his breath in the night air. Through the window he saw her, sitting in her rocking chair. She held something in both hands, brought it to her lips, and kissed it. The object glinted dully in the lamplight. Ephraim's heart froze mid-beat. She was talking to Pa's pistol again.

Ephraim glanced at Peyton. He had to make his friend leave

before he saw Ma. Folks around Sixmile Creek were already speaking of her sanity in hushed tones.

Peyton held the dead coon up by the back legs, admiring it. "He sure is a big one. How old you reckon he is?"

Ephraim looked back at the open window. Could he make it over to the window and shut it before Peyton noticed?

"You don't have to skin it for me," Ephraim said. He held up the possum he'd shot on the way home. "I got to skin this anyway. I'll just take care of both."

Peyton laughed and thumped Ephraim on the back. "Not a chance, Cutler! A deal's a deal. You out-tracked my dog." His eyes flicked to the cabin, and his brow furrowed. "Your ma left the window open. It's gettin' a little cold for that, don't you think?"

Ephraim's heart hammered against his ribs. "Uh, she believes in the benefits of fresh air. You bring your knife?"

"Of course I did."

"Good. Come on then," Ephraim said, leading the way to the smokehouse.

The smokehouse smelled of old wood smoke and briny earth. Ephraim wished he could shut the door and block Ma from Peyton's view, but they needed the moonlight to see. They set their lanterns and the dead animals on a rough-cut bench that ran along the wall.

"You goin' to the stir-off at Lester Ewing's place tomorrow?" Peyton asked. He laid the coon on the bench, pulled a knife from his belt, and cut a slit running the length of its belly.

"No," Ephraim said. He slapped the possum down and started skinning it. The sooner Peyton went home, the better.

In the cabin, Ma started singing to the pistol in a high, quavering voice. "*They stood in the moonlight nearby the gate. Goodbye my darlin', I know you'll wait!*"

Ephraim's knife slipped, and he nicked his thumb. Blood welled up. He hissed between his teeth and squeezed the cut finger.

"You all right?" Peyton asked.

Ephraim nodded. "How 'bout you? You going to the stir-off?"

"Yeah."

Ma's singing swelled. *"Oh, darlin' believe me far over the sea. Through life and death so faithful I'll be!"*

Peyton stopped skinning the coon and craned his neck to stare out the open door of the smokehouse.

Ephraim's throat felt tight. "They havin' a dance?" he asked. The last thing he needed was for everyone in town to hear about Ma serenading Pa's gun.

"Huh?" Peyton asked.

"They havin' a dance? At the stir-off."

"They always do," Peyton said, still peering toward the cabin.

Ephraim peeled the hide off his possum. He hung it on a nail protruding from a beam in the roof.

Peyton looked at the naked possum carcass in surprise. "You done already?"

"Yep. You 'bout done with that coon?"

"Not yet. I just got him cut down the back legs."

"Give it here. I'll finish it up so you can leave."

Peyton shot Ephraim an annoyed look. "You think I don't know how to skin a coon or somethin'?"

"Once more he seeks the old garden gate. But he arrives, alas, alas it's too late!"

"Give it here!" Ephraim motioned with his bloody blade.

Peyton rubbed the back of his neck. "All right, sorry if I was movin' too slow. I don't mind stayin' to finish it." He pushed the coon to Ephraim and folded his arms.

Ephraim slapped the already-skinned possum down on the bench in front of Peyton. "Take that and go on home," he said. "It's late."

Peyton lifted the carcass by the back legs. "Did I do somethin' to vex you?"

Ephraim shook his head. His face felt hot. He drew his knife through the hide over the coon's belly.

Ma quit singing, but she kept humming the tune.

Peyton shrugged and left the smokehouse. From the corner of his eye, Ephraim saw Peyton pause in the yard, possum dangling from one hand. He peered through the open cabin window, his head cocked.

Ephraim gritted his teeth. "Peyton!"

Peyton glanced back.

Ephraim pointed the bloody skinning knife at him. "I said go on home now! You hear?"

~

EPHRAIM FINISHED SKINNING the coon and tacked its hide to the outside of the smokehouse. The warm skin grew cold beneath his fingers as he stretched it; he'd scrape it tomorrow.

With the bare carcass in one hand, rifle and lantern in the other, he walked toward the cabin. Ma had quieted down. The soft creaking of her rocking chair was now the only sound coming through the window.

Josiah Cutler, Ephraim's father, had built the gaunt, two-room shack a year before his son's birth. He'd intended the structure to be a temporary shelter, a roof to live under while he built a nicer home. But scratching out a farm in the canted mountain landscape had required all of Josiah's strength, and so year after year, the Cutlers put off construction of a new home. Ephraim often wondered what life would be like if Pa hadn't died.

Without a doubt, Ma would be a different person.

In the doorway of the cabin, Ephraim paused and studied his mother. The madness had crept over her gradually, like one season changing to the next. It was impossible to say exactly when it had started. He watched her lift a quivering finger and run it down the length of the pistol's barrel. She was getting worse.

"I got a coon," he said, shutting the door behind him.

He frowned at the sight of the cold hearth. Ma had let the fire die. Then he saw the empty wood box and kicked himself. He'd forgotten to fill it before he went hunting. How could he have been so thoughtless?

He set his rifle and the possum on the table, ran to the wood-pile in the yard, and returned with an armload.

Ma looked up from her lap.

"How're you feelin'?" he asked as he carried the wood to the fireplace.

Ma smiled. "I'm fine. The good reverend stopped by to see me before sundown."

Ephraim deposited the wood, then knelt by his mother and took her hand between his own. Her fingers were cold. He warmed them for a moment before returning to the fireplace and grabbing a fistful of kindling from a basket by the hearth.

After creating a small teepee with the kindling, he struck a long match and held it to the thin pieces of wood. "What'd Reverend Boggs have to say?"

"He counseled me in certain matters," Ma said, still examining the pistol. "Left me with much to think on. He wants you to stop by tomorrow—said you should take some of his corn. He's got more than he needs. You did a fine job plantin'."

The kindling ignited. Ephraim deftly stacked the logs around it and rose, dusting wood chips from the front of his brown wool shirt. "Well, that's mighty kind of him, seeing as how he already paid me to plant it."

Ma rocked the chair in a creaking rhythm.

The fire popped and crackled as it grew, filling the room with flickering light and shadow. Ephraim returned to the table, pulled his knife from its sheath, and began cutting the legs off the coon. Ma was silent as he worked—she often was. She had once been a robust woman, but he could hardly remember her that way now. Her flesh had sunk into her frame, creating hollows in her cheeks and neck where shadows pooled. And ever since the war had claimed Pa's life, she'd taken to staying indoors, especially during cold weather.

Ephraim peeled the backstraps off the coon. He sliced the meat into chunks and prepared a roux of flour and butter into which he chopped carrots, onion, potatoes, and cabbage. He put the meat in, hung the pot on the fireplace crane, and swung it over the flames.

The fire soon turned to coals. When the stew bubbled in the pot, Ephraim opened the lid and stirred it. The dark stew filled the air with a savory aroma.

He pulled a chair from the table to sit by Ma. She had drifted off to sleep in her chair, the pistol still resting in her lap. When he took it from her, the walnut grip of the Colt's Army Model felt smooth in his hand. Toward the top and bottom he could still feel checkering that hadn't worn away. He opened the cylinder, shut it again, and gave it a spin. He tried to picture his father carrying the gun, but only managed to summon the vague image of a soldier dressed in gray.

After a while, Ephraim tasted the stew. Satisfied, he ladled some into a clay bowl, stuck a wooden spoon in it, stooped, and cupped his mother's shoulder in his hand. "Ma," he said. "Dinner's ready."

They ate in silence. Ma drifted back to sleep with her bowl still half full. Ephraim removed it from her grasp and covered her with a quilt.

An assortment of carved spoons and roosters whittled from sticks lined the mantel above the fireplace. The roosters' tails, made from curled shavings left delicately attached at their bases, cast spiraled shadows on the wall. Seeing that one of the roosters had an unfinished tail, Ephraim pulled it from the mantel. He'd work on it, then go to bed.

He pulled his knife from its sheath and set its edge to the wood.

3

BAREFOOT NANCY

The morning came up sunny and clear, the autumn sky an uninterrupted shade of blue. Ephraim rose, made a breakfast of cold stew, then went about his chores, chopping wood and splitting kindling for the day. When he finished, he gathered several tow sacks, saddled Molly, and set off for town.

Ballard Road ran down the slope from the Cutlers' home to the settlement on Sixmile Creek. Ephraim kept Molly in the middle of the road, between the ruts cut by narrow wagon wheels. The mare's hooves clopped in the red dirt, and Ephraim bounced in the saddle. Goldenrod and joe-pye weeds bloomed yellow and purple alongside the dry pods of milkweed in the ditches.

The settlement was a simple affair. At one end stood Coleman's Dry Goods, Manson Owens's forge, and a livery. On the other end, a single-room schoolhouse neighbored a large white church crowned with a wooden cross. Reverend Boggs lived in a slope-off house behind the church. Below it, on flatter ground, his fenced-in garden filled in the space between the churchyard and the cemetery.

Ephraim made his way around the church, tied Molly to a hitching post, climbed the stone stairs to the reverend's cottage, and knocked on the door. After a few moments, Reverend Boggs opened it.

"Ah, good morning, Ephraim." The reverend slipped his white shirt sleeve through the arm of a long-tailed black suit coat. "I just finished my breakfast, and here you are, half your day's work already finished, no doubt." He straightened his black cravat at the stand-up collar.

"Yessir," Ephraim said.

The reverend laughed and clapped a fatherly hand on Ephraim's back. "I would expect nothing less. Come, let's see the fruits of your labor."

Together they walked to the split-rail fence that surrounded Reverend Boggs's garden.

"Did you know the apostle Paul was a tentmaker?" the reverend asked, leaning on the top rail.

"No," Ephraim said.

"He lived by the sweat of his brow. Just like the Lord commanded Adam. That's why I never take up a collection after my sermons. To do so would be priestcraft, a grievous sin." He pointed to the garden and smiled. "And that's why I'm blessed to know you, Ephraim. I never could've produced anything like this by myself."

Ephraim had planted the corn in the spring when the hickory buds were the size of squirrels' ears. Now, inside the fence, the leaves on the cornstalks were turning brown. The ears inside would be dry, perfect for shell corn. Pumpkins and winter squash lay on the ground between the corn rows, and blackberry canes stood with thinning maroon leaves along the fence rails. The fertile, black soil here was a far cry from Ephraim's meager scrap of dry dirt on Laurel Knob. In tending the reverend's crops and his own garden patch, Ephraim had become painfully aware of the difference in crops produced by a barren slope and rich bottomland.

Ephraim hopped over the fence and began loading his sacks with corn. A short while later, he had two bulging totes.

"You'll have to come back for some onions and carrots," the reverend said. "There's no way I can use them all. And did you see the pumpkins?" He pointed to where the large squash ripened in the sun.

Ephraim had carefully positioned each pumpkin bottom down when they were only the size of his fist. Each of them had grown well-formed and round, and now they were turning orange evenly on all sides. They were pumpkins to be proud of. "In a few weeks I'll come plow the garden under for next year," he said.

The clatter of a passing cart approached, and they both turned. A russet-colored billy goat was pulling a small, creaky wagon, and a wrinkled old woman walked alongside it, smoking a clay pipe. Her bare feet, covered in red dust, were visible beneath the hem of her patchwork dress.

Reverend Boggs groaned and stepped in front of Ephraim.

"Good mornin' to ye, Reverend," the old woman said around the stem of her pipe. She had a swarthy complexion and pale hazel eyes. Her dark hair, streaked with gray, fell across her shoulders in two long braids.

"Good morning, Nancy," Boggs said with a frown.

The old lady eyed the corn peeking out of Ephraim's sack. "That's some mighty fine corn ye got there. It'll make a fine corn dodger."

"It will," the reverend said. "What brings you to town?"

The old woman reached down and scratched her goat behind the horns. "I've just been a-doctorin' Mrs. Lemons. She burned her hand somethin' fierce."

Boggs's face stiffened.

"They didn't have much to pay me with. All they could give

me were them there shucky beans." She pointed to her cart. Inside, among dried leaves of various herbs and bottled tinctures, lay a single string of dried beans. "You wouldn't be willin' to part with some of that corn, would ye, Reverend?"

"You know how I feel about your doctoring."

Nancy narrowed her eyes. Her lips formed a hard smile. "I know, I know. But I figured it wouldn't hurt to ask. Sharin' with an old woman just seemed like the sort of Christian thing I've known ye to do."

Boggs folded his arms. "I'm afraid I can't give support in any way to a practice that isn't in harmony with the will of God."

"Yeah. Well, me 'n' you don't see eye to eye on the 'will of God,' Reverend." Nancy pulled out her pipe and spat in the dirt. "S'pose I'd best be movin' on. Good day to ye."

She carried on, her goat trotting along beside.

"Why don't you like old Barefoot Nancy?" Ephraim asked.

"It's not her I don't like, Ephraim. She's a child of God just like you and me. What I don't like is her witchcraft."

Ephraim's brow furrowed. "But a witch ain't the same thing as a granny doctor."

Reverend Boggs shook his head. "In the eyes of the Lord, it's all the same. Meddling with life and death, sickness and health, through the use of strange herbs and unholy charms—it's all interfering with the will of the Lord."

Ephraim shrugged and shouldered the sacks of corn. He walked to where Molly stood, tied the sacks shut, and threw them over the saddle.

"You'd do best to stay away from her," Boggs said. "A boy like you ought to pursue a life in the ministry. Have you ever thought about it?"

Ephraim shook his head. "No, not really." He didn't think about much besides taking care of Ma.

"Think on it," Boggs said. "I have a few ideas I'd like to share with you—opportunities for your future. But you think on it first."

"I will. Thank you, Reverend."

As the reverend returned inside, Ephraim examined Molly's hooves. "Looks like you threw a shoe," he said, lifting a bare hoof from the ground. He pulled the reins over her head and led her out into the road. "We'll have to stop at Manson's and get a new shoe put on," he said, patting the mare's flank.

BAREFOOT NANCY STOOD outside Manson Owens's empty forge, waiting for the blacksmith to return.

"You're Lucretia Cutler's boy, ain't ye?" she said as Ephraim led Molly to the forge's hitching post.

"Yes, ma'am," Ephraim said.

Nancy pulled the pipe from her lips and studied his face. Ephraim smelled the sweet scent of tobacco on her breath. "I'd recognize them blue eyes anywhere. Look just like your daddy's did. There wasn't a girl in this county that didn't straighten her skirts when he'd walk by. I was already an old woman when I come to these parts, but if I weren't, I'd've been right there with 'em, battin' my eyelashes."

Ephraim's face grew hot.

"How old are ye?"

"I'm sixteen, ma'am."

Nancy nodded. "I reckoned that was 'bout right. He was a good man, your daddy. Shame he didn't make it home from the war to raise ye." Nancy reached down and scratched her goat behind the ears. "He gave me Earl here in exchange for doctorin' that horse of your'n. She was just a filly then."

She frowned, and her eyes grew distant. "That was back afore the preacher started accusin' me of witchery." She snorted. "He don't know witchery from a hole in the ground. I'd like to see where in the Good Book he come up with the notion that doctorin' is wickedness. Cite me a verse!" She raised her finger in the air. "Quote me scripture on it! My pappy was a man of the cloth, and he healed and cured ten times the folks I have, least that's what Mammy told me. That preacher is so contrary, if ye threw him in a river, he'd float upstream."

Nancy scratched Earl's head. The goat pushed its head against her hand, willing her to continue.

"Used to be that folks called me to take care of everythin' from colicky babes to cows with the milk fever. Now they'd just as soon run me off as look at me. The reverend's got 'em all afeared of my doctorin'." Nancy winked at Ephraim. "It's the least I can do to stop in and needle him from time to time. Got him good and riled this mornin', didn't I?" She wrinkled her nose in a smile.

"He sure don't like your doctorin'."

Nancy glanced down at her goat. "We was as plump as grain-fed hens afore that preacher come to town, weren't we, Earl?" She sighed. "I guess there ain't a solitary soul in this world who don't fall on hard times some time or another. Earl and me has had our turn at 'em for a while now. But we keep hangin' on, just like a hair in a biscuit, don't we?"

She looked back at Ephraim. "Ain't nothin' can be done 'bout it 'cept to wait for the hard times to leave and go lookin' for some-body else. Could be Reverend Boggs they grab hold of next." She grinned and shook her head. "There I go, sayin' un-Christian things. I'd be lyin' if I said I don't think it though."

Ephraim had never spoken directly with the granny woman before. Her eyes twinkled kindly as she spoke, and he found himself smiling. He glanced at the lone strand of dry beans in her cart and felt a kinship with the old woman; he and Ma had known the groaning of empty bellies from time to time.

He hefted one sack of corn off Molly's saddle and placed it in Nancy's cart. "You can have that," he said.

Nancy stepped forward and took his right hand in both of hers. Her skin felt thin and callused.

"Thank ye." Her hazel eyes disappeared in a web of wrinkles as she smiled and patted his hand. "You're a good man, a Good Samaritan, just like your daddy."

Manson Owens walked in through the back door of the forge. "Mornin', Nancy. Ephraim."

"Mornin', Manson," Nancy said. "How are ye?"

The blacksmith's cheeks bulged as he shook his head and blew out a breath. "A bear got into my bee gums sometime last night while I was out coon huntin'. Left 'em lookin' like the hindquarters of hard luck. There wasn't much left worth savin'."

Nancy clucked her tongue. "Them bears is ornery critters."

Manson nodded. "From the look of the tracks, this is an old'n. He's got one hind paw turned inwards."

Nancy raised an eyebrow. "Sounds like Ol' Reelfoot. Last I heard tell, he killed two of Franz Akers's hogs."

Manson nodded. "I figure it's him all right." He pointed to a large wrought-iron trap hanging on a peg. "We may not be eatin' much honey this winter, but I assure you we'll be fat on bear meat."

Nancy laughed. "Best of luck to ye. Reelfoot's a clever one. I've heard a few folks say they was goin' to get him, but no one has yet."

Manson smiled. "I built that trap special for him." He shook his head. "But that's enough about my bear troubles. What brings you by?"

"I just stopped in to see if'n ye could trim Earl's hooves. We're headin' to Pendleton County, and I cain't have him go lame on the trail."

"Sure thing, Nancy."

Manson unhitched the goat from the cart and walked it into the smithy. A small stanchion sat in one corner of the shop. Manson guided Earl up the ramp and fastened him to a crossbar.

"Ephraim, would you get a little feed from that sack over there and put it in the basket for the goat?" Manson pointed to the feed basket on the stanchion.

"Yessir." Ephraim put down his sack of corn and fetched the feed.

Manson rummaged around in a wooden crate for a pair of nippers. He returned to the stanchion and lifted Earl's muddy hoof in one hand. "If I don't catch this bear in my trap, I may have need of your trackin' ability, son."

Ephraim laughed. "Aw, I ain't nothin' special. I just get lucky, that's all."

"You must get lucky every time I go huntin' with you, then."

Ephraim felt himself turn red.

"Don't be shy, boy. When you're good, you're good!" Manson bent over to grab the goat's foot, groaning as he did.

"Let me get that for you, Mr. Owens." Ephraim rolled up his sleeves and lifted Earl's hoof.

"Much appreciated," Manson said. "All these years of smithin' ain't been easy on my back."

Across the street from the forge, a group of giggling girls sat on the porch of Coleman's Dry Goods. Ephraim glanced over at them, and several looked away, giggling even louder.

The door to the store opened, and Isabel Coleman stepped out. When she looked across the street, her eyes widened. "Ephraim!" She ran down the stairs and over the road, dark braids slapping her back. She entered the forge and wrapped him in a hug. Isabel and Ephraim had sat beside each other at the common school, and they had been friends ever since.

"Good morning, Nancy. Good morning, Manson," the girl said, curtseying to each of them in turn.

Nancy smiled at the girl. "Well, ain't ye as pretty as a speckled pup!"

Ephraim couldn't help but smile. "How was Charleston, Isabel?"

"I just got back last night," Isabel said. "I still wish you'd have come with us."

Ephraim looked at his feet. "I wish I could have, but you know how Ma is. Got to look after her."

Isabel nodded. "Well, when your ma gets better, you'll both have to come. Aunt Eliza told me again that I can bring anyone I like. She lives by herself and has three spare rooms."

Ephraim felt a lump in his throat. *When your ma gets better.* Sweet Isabel, always on the sunny side. He felt no such hope.

"You really have to see Charleston for yourself," Isabel continued. "They have iced cream, buildings bigger than anything around here, and the city folk stay out late every night. The streets are lit by gaslights. You should see the clothes they wear!" Isabel's eyes were bright, the way they always were when she got excited.

Isabel's aunt in Charleston sent for her once a year, and every time, Isabel came back to Sixmile Creek sporting fancy dresses, new dance steps, and foreign ways of saying things. She was turning into a lady.

But meanwhile, Ma's failing health was turning Ephraim into a caretaker. He didn't expect Isabel to understand the gap that had opened between them or the pang he felt every time he saw her.

Isabel clapped her hands together, her eyes twinkling. "Ooh! I almost forgot. Tonight is the stir-off at the Ewings' place, isn't it!"

"It is," Ephraim said. "Peyton mentioned it to me."

Isabel clasped her hands together. "Will you come? There's going to be a dance."

Ephraim shifted from one foot to the other. "I don't know." He knew Ma would forbid it if he asked. He'd made the mistake of talking about Isabel for too long a few months ago. His mother, sensing her son's heart wandering far from the cabin, had erupted into a fit of jealous rage.

"Please come," Isabel said. "I brought you a present from Charleston. I want to give it to you there."

A warm bubble rose in Ephraim's chest. Isabel had been thinking about him while she was gone. "I'll try," he said quickly.

"Good! It will be a fine time," Isabel said. "I've got to head home now. Ma's making stack cakes for the stir-off, and she told me to get a bushel of apples over at the Millers' orchard." She waved goodbye and ran back across the street.

At the stanchion, Manson chuckled and raised his eyebrows. "She sure was glad to see you, Ephraim."

Nancy nodded. "I believe she's sweet on you."

Ephraim pulled at the collar of his shirt. "She ain't sweet on me."

Nancy laughed. "Don't you disappoint her, now. You best be at that stir-off tonight."

"Yes, ma'am," Ephraim said, scuffing the toe of his boot on the floor. His face felt hot again.

"That ought to do it," Manson said, laying down the nippers and unhooking Earl from the stanchion. He stood up, wiped his hands on his apron, led the goat down the ramp, and hitched it back to Nancy's wagon.

"What do I owe ye?" Nancy asked.

Manson shook his head. "Nothin'. You've done plenty for me and my family over the years. Trimmin' your goat's hooves is the least I can do."

"I've been done two good turns in one day," Nancy said. Her voice sounded choked. She turned away from the blacksmith, blinking rapidly. "Thank ye both." She led the goat out to the road and strode away, the wagon trundling along beside her.

"Now, what can I do for you, young man?" Manson said, turning to Ephraim.

"Molly's lost a shoe."

"Well, bring her on in, and we'll fix that."

Ephraim led the mare in and passed the reins to Manson. The blacksmith stooped and inspected the shoeless hoof.

Ephraim glanced back at the road after Nancy. "I don't understand it," he said. "How could anyone not like Nancy?"

"You're talkin' 'bout Reverend Boggs, I presume," Manson said. His voice sounded strained from being bent over. He put Molly's leg down and straightened, one hand clamped on his lower back.

Ephraim nodded. "Him for sure. But the way Nancy talks, most people around here don't like her like they used to. Did she really make a scene in church?"

Manson raised an eyebrow. "She sure did. I was there." He selected a few tools from his bench and placed them in the pockets of his leather apron.

"I heard folks say that," Ephraim said, "but I wasn't there." The Cutler family's church attendance had been spotty when he was a child. It had taken several years of visits from Reverend Boggs before Ma had seen the value in Sunday worship.

Manson pulled Molly's foot up between his knees and began scraping dirt out of the sole with a knife. "Well, it weren't too long after Reverend Boggs came to Sixmile Creek that it happened. Come to think of it, it was around the same time they hung Wes Sherman—'bout a year after the war. Everyone pitched in to build the church and Boggs's house. I'm ashamed to say I don't recall what the good reverend was sermonizin' on that day, but he started preachin' against doctorin', said such things were a sin and them that did it were witches. 'Bout that time, Nancy stood up—she went to church in them days—and let me tell you, boy," Manson glanced at Ephraim, "she weren't a-standin' up to say amen. She marched straight to the podium and slammed her fist down smack in the middle of the reverend's Bible. The whole chapel went quiet as a graveyard. Every soul in the congregation had their eyes on Nancy." Manson shook his head. "Even old Hebe Washburne woke up to see what was goin' to happen, and knowin' him, he was probably sleeping off three quarts of red-eye liquor." He pulled out a pair of nippers and started trimming the hoof.

"What'd Reverend Boggs do?"

"Nothin' at first. Nancy leaned over that podium and said, 'Listen here. The good Lord made every herb in these hills, and you mean to tell me that if I use 'em to help folks, He's goin' to send me to Hell?'

"Well, you could just see the color risin' in the reverend's face. After she finished, he walked out in front of her and told the congregation that interfering in matters of life and death was contrary to the will of God."

Ephraim shook his head. "That's what he told me this morning."

Manson held a shoe up to Molly's foot, then moved to an anvil and sized it with a few blows from a hammer. "I think he could've stopped there and folks would've disremembered the whole thing, but he went on and accused Nancy directly. He said he had been out for a walk in the woods the night before—said he often took to the woods at night, because that was where he prepared his sermons. While he was out a-walkin', he said he run across Nancy holdin' concert with a demon. He claimed she was a witch and that her goat wasn't no animal, it was her familiar. Then, he held his Bible up in the air and declared that anyone who sought the services of this witch was worthy of hellfire. He told Nancy to get out of his church, and when no one stepped up to defend her, she did."

"So which one of them do you reckon is right?" Ephraim asked.

The blacksmith grunted as he drove nails through the shoe into the hoof. "I can't rightly say. They've both done a lot of good for folks. But they get along like a drunkard and a temperance society. It's a queer thing."

~

EPHRAIM DEPOSITED the sack of corn in the smokehouse and returned to the cabin. Ma sat wrapped in a quilt, slumbering in her rocking chair.

He stood in front of the fireplace, studying his carvings along the mantel. He wanted to prepare a gift for Isabel. He still couldn't believe that she had brought him something from Charleston! In a city far from Sixmile Creek, a place full of gaslights, fancy clothes, and who knew what other distractions, Isabel had thought of *him*. His heart swelled.

He selected a rooster carving with a tail of shavings that arched higher than its head, pulled out his knife, flipped the carving over, and began notching letters into its base.

TO ISA—

"You're mighty quiet, son."

Ephraim hadn't noticed Ma wake up. "There's a stir-off tonight at the Ewings'," he said. "Thought I might go." He folded his knife and slipped the rooster into his pocket.

Ma coughed. "Wish I could come with you, but I'm feelin' poorly today. I reckon I caught my death last night waitin' for you to come home and get another fire goin'." She pulled the quilt tighter around her.

"Ma, I'm sorry. I forgot to fill the wood box. I had wood split out in the yard, I just—"

"I know how much you like huntin', Ephraim."

"No, I mean, I do like huntin', but I was out there trying to get us some meat."

Ma coughed again and closed her eyes.

Ephraim glanced at the cooking pot. He'd been planning on telling Ma she could have the leftovers from last night's stew for supper, but if she wasn't feeling well, maybe she needed something thinner. "I won't go to the stir-off tonight, Ma. I'll stay here and make you some soup."

"You're gettin' older, Ephraim. Folks your age like to stay out late, go dancin', go huntin', drink moonshine. I won't have you missin' none of that on my account. You go ahead and go on over to the Ewings'. I ain't that hungry. I can manage on my own tonight. Once a widow woman's raised her son, she best get used to sitting in a cabin all alone."

Ephraim pulled a chair out from the table and slumped into it. "It ain't goin' to be like that, Ma. I'm goin' to take care of you just like I always do."

"I hate to be a burden."

"Ma, don't say that. You ain't a burden." Ephraim sighed and hunched over the table, tracing the grain of the wood with his finger.

"Your pa used to do that very same thing when I'd vexed him."

Ephraim looked up. "Do what?"

"Sit there and stare at the table like that. I wonder what it is you two see in that hunk of wood."

Ephraim shrugged.

"You remember when we buried your pa?"

"Sort of. Bits and pieces."

"You were so little then, but you were always a strong boy. I cried my heart out washin' your pa's body and gettin' him dressed for buryin'. But you didn't cry. You just squeezed my hand. You knowed you had to be strong for me, didn't you?"

Ephraim nodded. Ma usually grieved in silence. He'd seen her cry plenty of times before when she thought he wasn't look-ing. Why was she talking about it now?

"He was a handsome man, my Josiah. Hair blond as corn silk and the bluest eyes... You look just like him. I still don't know how I ever managed to win his affection." Ma coughed and pointed across the room. "I have somethin' for you. Go look under the foot of my bed."

Surprised, Ephraim went to the foot of her bed and lifted the draping end of the quilt. Underneath it was a pair of stout leather boots.

"Those were your pa's. Try 'em on."

Ephraim removed his worn brogans, let them fall with a thud, and slipped on his father's boots.

Ma smiled and clasped her hands. "Look. They fit you so well. Keep 'em. You know, Ephraim, lot of folks 'round here act like the war never happened." She coughed again. "They've forgotten what the Yankees did to us. But I haven't."

"You talkin' 'bout the Yankees that killed Pa?"

"That's right." Ma lifted her head, and anger flashed in her eyes. "Did you know that Silas Henson fought with the Yankees?"

"Yes, ma'am." Ephraim recalled Peyton showing him the Yankee rifle.

"Think about that for a minute, Ephraim. Silas Henson fought with the men that cut your pa down." Ma punctuated every word with a jab of her finger. "For all we know, it might've been him that done it."

"I guess so. But there was so many folks that died in the war, there'd be no way to know."

Ma shrugged. "The way I see it, shootin' your pa and fightin' with the Yanks are the same thing. Even if it wasn't him, he would've done it if he'd had the chance. Tell me that ain't true."

Ephraim didn't know what to say.

"I hear that Silas can dance a reel better than any man in the county. Think he'll be at that stir-off tonight?" Ma asked.

"I reckon," Ephraim said. "Peyton told me he's goin'."

Ma stood, lifted the revolver from its place on the mantel, and sat back in the rocker. "Wouldn't it be somethin' if he was cut down right there in front of everyone while he was dancin'?"

Ephraim snorted. "Ma, you're talkin' out of your head."

"I've kept the lead that was in this revolver the day they brought your pa home. I've got it loaded right now." She nodded toward the table, and Ephraim noticed, for the first time, the powder flask lying there. "Take it, Ephraim." She lifted the gun by its barrel and offered him the grip.

Ephraim turned away.

"Come on now. Let me see you holdin' your pa's gun. You already got his boots on."

Ephraim sighed and took the pistol.

Ma's eyes shone with tears. "I wish your pa was here. He'd be proud of the strong son I've raised. He'd be proud of how well you track and shoot. Ephraim, you are an honor to the Cutler name." She reached out and grabbed his hand. "The lead in that pistol has been a-growin' nigh on seven years, and tonight it's ready to be planted in a Yankee's heart. Your pa would be awful proud. If Silas Henson was cut down tonight, I'd wager there'll be daisies sproutin' through the frost on your pa's grave tomorrow mornin'."

Ephraim looked away. "You need to get out of this cabin, Ma. The war's over."

"If I could do it myself, I surely would. But I am a sick woman. I don't have long before I'll lay down next to Pa. It wouldn't be right if I didn't see justice served afore I do. You can cut down the coward that killed your pa. Will you do it for us, Ephraim?"

Ephraim laid the pistol on the table. "I ain't killin' Silas Henson. Or anybody else."

Ma's eyes flashed, and she rose to her feet. "Son, if you don't do this, you will live to regret it!"

She spoke with a ferocity Ephraim had never felt from her. He stepped backward, shaking his head.

"It ain't right to murder a man, Ma. You know that."

Ma's shoulders slouched, and she sat back heavily into the rocking chair.

Ephraim moved to the door. He needed to get away from this crazy talk. Ma would be all right if he left for a while—it wasn't like he left her alone every night.

He picked up his hat and rifle. "I'm goin' to check my

trapline," he said. "And then I'm goin' to the stir-off. I won't be home until late tonight." Ma wasn't looking at him. "There's cornbread in the skillet and some stew left in the pot. Don't wait up for me."

The door creaked as he opened it. He stepped outside and shut it behind him; the clap of it closing echoed across the hillside.

Ephraim peered at the sky and took a deep breath, then shouldered his rifle and set off for the woods, eager to put distance between himself and his wild-eyed mother.

4

MOLASSES AND MOONSHINE

Ephraim owned three steel traps that Manson Owens had made for him in exchange for some work around the smithy. He'd set them along a spring-fed stream that trickled through the woods on the far side of Laurel Knob. He found the first trap on a stretch of sandy soil along the stream's bank. Coon tracks went up to the edge of the water, but the trap was empty. He had similar luck with the other two traps.

As Ephraim stood by the last trap, listening to the musical rushing of the stream, the wind blew gently, setting the shadows of branches wavering on the ground. A rustling came from the underbrush. He closed his eyes, sorting through the sounds. A small bird flitted through the growth in little bursts of movement; squirrels hopped in the dry leaves; an Indian hen woodpecker rattled on a hollow trunk somewhere downstream.

Ephraim opened his eyes. A hollow tree was likely to be a coon den; he'd move a trap near it.

He poked a stick through the trap's chain and lifted it, careful not to touch the metal and taint it with his scent. Following the sound of the Indian hen, Ephraim made his way to the hollow tree. It was a poplar with a hole the size of a pot lid near its base. Ephraim set the trap on the bank in front of it.

He looked up at the sky; the stir-off would be starting soon. Removing his hat, he studied his reflection in the water. His blond hair stuck up in a rooster tail. He wet his hand in the stream and pawed at it, smoothing it down.

A scar split his left eyebrow in two, a mark he'd received from the cloven hoof of Erma Jean, the family milk cow, when he was five years old. Ma had sold the cantankerous animal the day after it'd kicked him. Ephraim licked his thumb and tried to straighten the disorderly hairs that grew on either side of the scar. Finally, he scrubbed his face, straightened his brown wool shirt, and shouldered his rifle.

Lester Ewing's house sat a stone's throw from the base of Laurel Knob. As Ephraim exited the woods, he saw a sorghum gin under a hickory tree in the yard. Lester and several other men were working around it, feeding in stalks of sorghum cane to be ground. A mule, hitched to the machine, provided the power for grinding.

Ephraim felt a lightness in his chest. As Ma had grown more ill, they'd come to gatherings like this less and less frequently. The realization that tonight was his first night attending a stir-off without her filled him with a thrill of independence.

He searched the yard, looking for Isabel.

She stood by a large cast-iron kettle. Her dark braids were tied with yellow ribbons, and she wore a cornflower-blue dress.

The kettle emitted a cloud of pale vapor in the cool evening air. A field hand skimmed the surface of the boiling liquid and poured the green goop he removed into a hole dug beside the pot. As Ephraim approached, Polly Ewing stopped by the kettle and peered into it.

"Mind not to over-boil it, Isabel. We're making syrup tonight, not pull-candy."

"Yes, ma'am," Isabel said.

"Where'd Rindy Sue get to?" Polly asked. "She's supposed to be helping you, but I ain't seen her since the Fletcher boys showed up."

"Last I saw, Jake and her were taking a walk through the orchard."

Polly's nostrils flared. "If Lester comes looking for me, tell him I'm out in the orchard tanning his fool daughter's hide." She rolled up her sleeves and stalked toward the orchard muttering something about her empty-headed Rindy falling for a "whiskey-makin' no-account."

Isabel turned to Ephraim and burst into laughter. "That romantic walk isn't going to last very long." She gave Ephraim a warm smile. "I was hoping you'd come."

Ephraim grinned. "Well, I'm here."

Isabel straightened up from the kettle and clapped her free hand to her forehead. "Oh, no!" she said. "I carried the stack cake here, and I forgot to bring your present."

"That's all right," Ephraim said. He leaned over the pot and inhaled the heavy sweetness of the hot molasses. His mouth watered. "When will this be ready?"

"Not for a few more hours. Don't steal any—you already saw the mood Polly's in."

A few yards away, on the back porch of the house, a crowd of youngsters had gathered around Manson Owens's feet.

"Tell us 'bout Barefoot Nancy and the Skinner witch," one of the children said.

Ephraim looked up from the molasses. He'd heard it mentioned that Barefoot Nancy had banished a witch from Sixmile Creek, but he'd never heard the story.

Manson rocked his chair back a little and smiled. "Nobody can tell that one like Nancy does herself."

The youngsters groaned in disappointment.

Manson smiled. "But, seein' as she ain't here, I guess I can take a crack at it."

The children cheered.

"It seems when I was 'bout you'uns' age, there weren't too many folks 'round these parts. There was a witch that roamed the hills in them days by the name of Josephine Skinner. She weren't too popular 'round here on account of her devilish ways. Folks said she had the evil eye, and it gave her power to perform all kinds of curses. She could cause a cow to give bloody milk, stop hens from layin', and turn the purest spring water sour. Josephine could also spell your gun so it'd never hit nothin' you aimed at."

A hush fell over the children. They all scooted in closer to Manson's feet.

"And that weren't the worst of it," Manson said, leaning in toward his audience. He squinted his eyes and lowered his voice. "If Josephine took a powerful dislike to you, she'd send a black cat into your home, and it'd steal the breath right out of your babe's mouth. Make it die in its sleep. She could call up awful storms that'd ruin a year's crop." Manson paused and shook his head. "But none of that holds a candle to what she did to little Alice Sherman."

"Liza May Williams!" a woman's voice cut in. "Come over here this instant!"

Ephraim turned and saw Francis Williams with her hands on her hips.

"But Ma," protested Liza from the porch, "Mr. Owens is tellin' us 'bout Barefoot Nancy and the witch."

"Liza, you go on home right now, and you might as well find a switch along the way. We do not listen to stories of witches. Such talk ain't Christian."

Manson raised an eyebrow. "Not Christian? Francis, you see me in church every Sunday. I'm just tellin' the young'uns a little local history, that's all."

"Well I don't approve," Francis said. "And neither does Reverend Boggs." She walked to the porch, snatched Liza by the arm, and marched her off.

"Mr. Owens, what'd Josephine Skinner do to Alice Sherman?" a towheaded boy asked in a shrill voice.

Manson shifted in his chair and resumed his tale. "Well, Alice's daddy, Wes, was one of the meanest men what ever lived. He lived up at the head of Butcher Holler—I was just up there myself last night and saw his cabin. He wouldn't let no one set foot in the wood 'round his place without his permission. He claimed all that land for hisself. One night, he saw Josephine Skinner out a-prowlin' in the woods, and he lit up her backside with a load of bird shot. The witch shrieked and run off a-howlin' to beat the band! Wes thought he was really somethin'. He told everyone what he'd done, and said anyone who was afeared of old Josephine was a fool—said she weren't no more than a crazy old bat.

"Couple nights later, Wes sent Alice out to fetch a pail of water from the spring." Manson paused and shook his head gravely. "And the girl never come back."

The children gasped. "Where'd she go?" asked the towheaded boy.

"Weeks passed with nary a sign of the girl," Manson said. "Then one night, Wes was a-cookin' hisself some supper when he heard this scratchin' from up on the roof of his cabin. Well, he lit a lantern and walked outside, thinkin' there was a coon up there or somethin', but when he shone the light up there, it weren't no critter. It was Alice."

"It was Alice!" echoed the children, looking at one another, eyes wide.

"'What're you doin' creepin' atop the roof, Alice?' says Wes. 'You 'bout scared me half to death!'" Manson leaned forward. "Alice jumped down, landed on the ground right in front of him, and Wes saw that it weren't Alice. It was Josephine Skinner, a-wearin' Alice's hide!"

The children huddled in a knot. A few whimpers leaked out.

"But what about Barefoot Nancy?" It was the towheaded boy again.

Isabel elbowed Ephraim in the ribs and giggled. "I know who'll be wetting the bed tonight," she whispered in his ear.

A pleasant fuzziness filled Ephraim's head as he felt her breath on his ear. She kept her face close to his as they listened.

"Well, this is where she comes into the story," Manson said. "See, we didn't have a granny woman 'round here in them days. So someone sent for one when we heard Wes Sherman a-rantin' 'bout what Josephine done to Alice. It weren't too long 'fore Barefoot Nancy showed up." Manson sat back in his chair. "She seemed old to me then, and I'm an old man now. That granny must be as old as the hills." He shook his head slowly. "Anyways, it was her that drove Josephine Skinner away from Sixmile Creek."

"All right, now!" a man's voice called across the yard.

Ephraim and Isabel turned their heads.

Lester Ewing stood on a stump in the middle of the yard, his hat raised in the air. "We're fixin' to have us a turkey shoot! Any of you that wants to shoot come on over here and put your name in my hat!"

Ephraim picked up his rifle.

Isabel looked up from the kettle. "I want to watch, Euly," she said to the field hand skimming the molasses. "Can you take a turn stirring?"

Euly nodded and replaced her at the kettle.

They walked over to where men were writing their names on small scraps of paper and dropping them into Lester's outstretched hat. Ephraim got in line and put his name in, then took his place in a group of contestants bristling with firearms.

Peyton Henson caught his eye and grinned. The older boy had his lever-action slung casually across his shoulders. "I see you brought your relic there, Cutler." The brass gleamed on his rifle as he slid it from his shoulders and patted the breech. "I'm surprised Lester's lettin' me compete with this thing—it practically shoots itself. I won last year at the stir-off."

"Well, you know what they say," Ephraim said. "It ain't the arrow, it's the Indian."

Peyton's brow furrowed. "What're you tryin' to say, Cutler? There ain't no one shootin' arrows here."

Ephraim chuckled and shook his head. "Never mind." What Peyton had in good looks, he lacked in wit.

"You'll shoot in the order you're drawn!" Lester called to the assembled crowd. "Every man can take a rest on this here stump and shoot for that mark!" He pointed across the yard to an "X" marked on a slab of wood. "The man that hits closest to the center gets to take home an apple stack cake made by Miss Coleman, and a willow basket to carry it in!" He bent over and lifted the cake from a basket on a table next to him. It was composed of several dark, gingerbread-colored layers sandwiched together with dried apple filling. Lester sniffed the cake and held it high. "Ain't this a fine-lookin' prize?"

The crowd whistled and applauded.

"Come on up here, young lady!" Lester said, motioning to Isabel.

She stepped forward and curtsied.

The crowd applauded even louder.

Lester turned around and pretended to bury his face in the cake.

Everyone laughed.

The shoot began with Ernest Williams. He went to the stump, knelt down, polished the sight on his rifle with his cuff, then took aim.

Lester shushed the crowd, and they waited in silence for him to shoot.

Ernest took his time, squinting down the length of his barrel. He squeezed the trigger and hit the top left corner of the X. The crowd jeered, and he stepped back, his face turning red.

Old Hebe Washburne was next. He grunted as he knelt by the stump, his massive belly spilling out over his thigh. He rested his elbow on his paunch and sighted his stubby rifle, then turned loose—and missed the slab of wood altogether. The old man broke wind as he struggled back to his feet, sending the crowd into hysterics.

Names were drawn, and men filed forward, peppering the slab with flying lead. Peyton and Ephraim found themselves last.

Lester reached into the hat and pulled out Peyton's name. The older boy went to the stump and fired off a round, striking the X just above the intersection of its two lines. The crowd cheered. Peyton stood, kissed his rifle, and bowed.

Finally, Ephraim took his place on the firing line and fixed his eye on the X. He breathed slowly, letting the bead on his rifle drift into his vision, covering the center of the mark. Then he exhaled and squeezed the trigger.

The rifle barked. He stood and studied the target. A new hole had punched through the X exactly where the two lines crossed.

"We have a winner!" Lester grabbed Ephraim's arm and lifted it high.

Everyone applauded, even Peyton. When Ephraim saw Isabel clapping, his heart swelled.

Lester released his arm. "Young man, the prize is yours. Don't forget to take it on your way home tonight."

The sunlight grew softer, touching the horizon over the ridgetops a faint blue. The whine of a fiddle being tuned carried across the yard.

Isabel's face brightened. "They're going to start the dance! Come on!" Their shadows stretched across the ground as she led Ephraim toward the fiddler. "I'm glad you won the cake," she whispered. "I knew you would."

A giant circle of loose straw in front of the barn marked the dance floor. Dancers stood around in four-couple squares, arm in arm with their partners.

"Come over here," Isabel said. She headed for a group of young folk standing in a circle, then stopped when Ephraim didn't follow. "Aren't you going to dance?"

Ephraim gulped and shook his head. His legs felt shaky at the very thought of joining the dancers. He felt sure such boldness would end in disaster. It'd been a few years since he'd come to a stir-off, and as a child he'd always preferred roughhousing with the other boys to dancing.

"Are you sure?" Isabel asked.

Ephraim shook his head again. "I think I'll just watch."

Isabel sighed. "Suit yourself."

Ephraim sat down on a pile of milled sorghum stalks near the edge of the circle.

Isabel joined the group of dancers. She said something to the people in the group, and they all glanced at him as she spoke. Ephraim felt his face flush. He wished he could burrow into the heap of stalks and watch the dance where they couldn't see him.

In the middle of the ring, the fiddler stepped up onto a wooden crate and drew his bow across the strings. "Square it up!" he said. He smiled at the gathered couples, gave a nod, and pulled down hard on his bow. "Keep your skillet good and greasy all the time, time, time!" he sang.

Ephraim sat back and took it all in. People laughed, twirled, and hollered. The couples moved in synchrony, arm in arm, then passed each other on to other partners as they chained around to meet again.

Silas and Peyton sat down a few feet from Ephraim. He glanced at them, his throat clenching as he remembered Ma's demands. Peyton pointed at Isabel and said something that made Silas laugh.

Others wandered over from the sorghum kettle to enjoy the music. It soon grew dark, and lanterns were lit, illuminating the dancers.

Manson Owens walked over, talking to Lester Ewing.

"—set that trap this mornin' and checked right before I come over here," Manson was saying. He reached into his pocket and showed Lester something in the palm of his hand. "All I got was the ends of the critter's toenails!"

Lester scratched his beard. "If it's the same bear I'm thinking of, he's experienced traps before. His rear paw is twisted because he got it ruined in a trap up at Ellis Frank's place several years ago."

Lester turned toward the barn and narrowed his eyes. Ephraim turned to see what he was looking at.

Clabe and Jake Fletcher, two scruffy young men a few years older than Ephraim, were leading a small group away from the dance floor. They each carried a tow sack. Clabe held the hand of a giggling Rindy Sue Ewing.

Lester sighed. "Excuse me," he said. "It appears my daughter is headed behind the barn with the Fletcher boys." He walked off with a finger leveled in the girl's direction.

5

ACE IN THE HOLE

Sampson dreamed of Wes, his old man. He heard the signature thump of the old-timer's footsteps inside the cabin. One leg was solid and moved with confidence, while the other limped along, its bones remembering a past injury. Sampson knew this because he, too, felt the echoes of old wounds. Sometimes when he awoke in the chill hours of dawn, he could feel the ghosts of a bear's teeth buried in his ear, or the memory of its claws still aching beneath the scars in his hide.

Wes appeared in the doorway holding two wooden bowls. He stumped across the porch and set one bowl in front of Sampson. Sampson sniffed its contents—cornbread and congealed gravy. He lapped the gravy, causing the wooden bowl to rattle on the porch.

With a groan, Wes lowered himself into a rocking chair. He stretched his weak leg out in front of him and positioned his own bowl on his lap. "Just look at us," he said, leaning over to tousle Sampson's ears. "We've both gone gray in the muzzle and stiff with the rheumatiz, ain't we?"

Sampson snatched the hard lump of cornbread from the bowl and settled back on the porch, holding it between his paws while he gnawed on it. The coarse texture was familiar to his tongue; it had been a staple since puppyhood.

The porch boards creaked as Wes rocked in his chair. The creaking grew louder and louder. Dust showered down.

Sampson sneezed and opened his eyes, roused from the dream. Darkness and the dank scent of earth surrounded him. Above him, boards shifted and squeaked as someone stepped onto them.

Disoriented, Sampson tried to rise. But he couldn't; the space around him was too cramped. Muffled voices reached him and Sampson lifted his ears, homing in on the sound.

"Aren't you glad I didn't accept your offer of three and half years, William? You're two weeks shy of the deadline." The man's deep voice came from somewhere off to the side.

"Patience, Scratch," William said. He was standing directly over Sampson's head.

William's voice triggered a flood of disjointed memories in Sampson's brain: the pale orb of a full moon; a man chanting to the dark sky; the flash of a silver blade in the moonlight; pain and paralysis. A slow rage crept through Sampson and his muscles tensed, creaking like the boards above him.

"The boy is unlike any other I've ever persuaded," William said. "By the time all the others have signed your contract, I've been ready to see them go their own ways. I was tired of their presence. But not this one."

"You feel a true bond with Ephraim, do you?" Scratch asked.

"I guess you could put it that way. I'd like to see what we could accomplish together, once he's signed the contract."

Sampson flexed his neck and tried to rise again. His back banged into the roof of the prison. He struggled against it, trying to move the boards, but the weight of the soil above them was too heavy.

"I'll take that into consideration, but the boy needs to be in my hands first. I'm worried, William. You haven't cut it this close in at least sixty years."

"He'll make the deal, Scratch, mark my words. Everything is in place. All that remains is to wait for the inevitable."

Sampson pawed at the floor of his prison. The rage grew hot in his belly, and juices began to pool in the dryness of his mouth. He growled and bucked against the roof.

Scratch sighed. "Yes, well, I just hope you have all contingencies covered. If you fail me, Death is going to be unbearable."

"Ephraim Cutler won't make it out of this valley without signing your deal," William said. "Every good gambler stacks the deck. My ace in the hole is beneath my feet as we speak." He stomped on the ground, showering Sampson in loose soil.

The fury in Sampson's gut reached a fever pitch. He thrashed from side to side, but it was no use. He paused, panting, and the anger bubbled up from his belly and swelled his throat like the pouch of a bullfrog. He opened his mouth and released a gravelly howl. His throat, dry from disuse, couldn't sustain the howl for very long. It faded, leaving the men above silent for a moment.

"Is that what I think it is?" Scratch asked.

"It is."

"Sounds like a real son of a bitch."

"He used to be. I can only imagine what he's like now. He belonged to a man who wasn't too popular around these parts."

"How did you learn the transformation process?"

"I've been studying my almanack."

"I really must take a look at that book sometime."

William laughed. "The Devil needs to consult a book on making hellhounds?"

"It sounds humorous, I know. The term hellhound is actually a misnomer: they aren't my invention. There was a Prussian witch several hundred years ago, a gamekeeper's wife—"

Samson snarled and scrabbled against the floorboards. Splinters flew up between his claws. He lowered his head, seeking purchase on the boards with his teeth.

The roof squeaked as William stepped off. "We best not disturb the beast too much before his time has come."

"Indeed," Scratch said.

"On another note, I'm always impressed by the fineness of your apparel, Scratch. Where did you get those diamond cuff links?"

The men's voices faded as they walked away.

Sampson struggled to free himself. The air inside his prison grew hot with his exertion. But at last he tired, and he lay down in the darkness, his tongue lolling. He thought of the gravy and cornbread in his dream, and his stomach rumbled. He thought of Wes, his old man, and whined.

6

WAYFARING STRANGER

E phraim watched as Silas rose, walked to the middle of
the circle, and hollered, "Play me a reel!"

The dancers all moved aside, giving Silas space, and
formed a circle around him. Ephraim joined them. The fiddler
drew the bow across the strings slowly, producing a long note.
Then he began working his bow furiously. Silas kept time with
his heel and toe, then launched into the reel.

Somebody let out a whoop, and the whole crowd started clapping and stomping in rhythm. The fiddler made his instrument
sing. He played the melody in a loop. And each time he came
around, he upped the tempo.

Silas's feet became a blur beneath him. Ephraim was mesmer-
ized. He felt someone touch his arm and turned to find Isabel
standing next to him.

She smiled. "Do you want to be my partner for the
next set?"

Ephraim's heart gave a hiccupping lurch.

Isabel frowned. "Don't look like I just asked you to hold a
rattlesnake."

"I can't dance," Ephraim confessed. "I never learned."

Isabel sighed. "Ephraim, dancing isn't taught, it's caught. And you can't catch it if you're sitting through the music."

"Oh," Ephraim said, not sure how to respond.

"If you dance with me, I'll help you." Isabel gave him a pleading look.

Ephraim felt giddy. "All right," he said, rubbing the back of his neck. "But don't expect much."

Isabel grabbed his arm and squeezed. "Good! It'll be fun. I promise."

Peyton Henson stood behind them, holding a large board he had fetched from the barn. As soon as Silas finished his reel, Peyton pushed between Ephraim and Isabel, stepping into the ring. He laid the board on the ground, stood on it, and nodded to the fiddler, who responded with an up-tempo jig.

Peyton stood for a moment, his head bobbing to catch the beat, then began to dance. The hard soles of his boots came down on the board, pounding out a rhythm that accompanied the fiddler. The crowd cheered.

Ephraim glanced at Isabel. She was whooping and clapping in time with the music. He studied Peyton's feet. How hard was it to learn to dance like that?

The jig came to an end amid wild applause. Peyton swept off his hat and bowed. The fiddler called for the dancers to "square 'em up" for another set. Isabel seized Ephraim's hand and led him to the group she had danced with before. They took their places in the circle.

The fiddler's voice cut across the crowd. "Ladies and gents, it's time for the Cornshucker's Frolic."

"This one's my favorite!" Isabel said. She bounced from foot to foot.

Ephraim grinned and felt sick. He was going to look like a fool, he just knew it.

The fiddler began to play. Isabel put her arm in Ephraim's and pulled him into a spin. As they rotated, another girl grabbed

Ephraim's left hand, passing him around the square until he came back to Isabel.

At first his feet wouldn't move right. His arms felt jerky and wooden. In spite of this, he couldn't keep his lips from curling into a smile. He stumbled through calls of "Up the river, 'round the bend, grab your partner, we're gone again!" and "Hold her hands, spin her 'round, till the sole of her foot wears a hole in the ground!"

By the third song, Ephraim felt limbered up and was keeping time with the other dancers. Isabel's pale blue dress and dark braids whirled, and she beamed.

After a few songs, the square dancers took a break and the fiddler played another jig. Isabel tapped Ephraim on the arm and pointed across the dance floor to Hebe Washburne. The portly man had left his seat, an expression of inebriated daring in his eyes. He took a pull from his pocket tickler of corn whiskey, and thus fortified, he leaped out onto the floor to whoops of encouragement.

He began with a shuffle step, but upon receiving several whistles from the audience, he quickly expanded his performance. His face glowed from the combination of exertion, cheers, and alcohol. The crowd began to clap in time, and Hebe started stepping so high he put slack in his suspenders. His great rump and belly wobbled back and forth in counterbalanced rhythm.

Hebe jumped into the air, and he would have clicked his heels together had his thighs not touched first. Upon landing, he staggered to one side. Then, giving the crowd an affirmative nod, he did the splits clear down to the ground. His display of flexibility climaxed with a resounding rip as his britches divided along the mid-seam.

Ephraim burst into laughter, and Isabel put a hand over her mouth.

Hebe struggled to his feet, retreated into the darkness, and sought the comfort of his flask.

"Get on up there, Rindy Sue!"

Ephraim turned and saw Lester pushing his daughter toward the fiddler.

"Sing us that song of yours," Lester called, returning to his seat.

Rindy's ears turned red, and she fidgeted with her dress. But the fiddler bent down and whispered something to her, and she nodded.

Everyone on the dance floor sat down where they stood. Isabel leaned toward Ephraim and whispered, "She's really good."

The fiddler put his bow to the strings and drew out a sonorous note. He closed his eyes, filling the air with mellow strains. Rindy Sue clasped her hands in front of her, took a deep breath, and began to sing. Her voice was high and clear, and a hush fell over the crowd.

"As time draws near, my dearest dear, when you and I must part, what little you know of the grace and awe of my poor aching heart. Each night I suffer for your sake, you're the one I love so dear. I wish that I was goin' with you, or you were stayin' here."

She seemed to gain confidence as she sang. The redness left her ears, and she raised her chin, losing herself in the melody.

"I wish my breast was made of glass wherein you might behold." She directed her gaze at Jake Fletcher, who stood, arms folded, next to his brother. *"Oh, there your name lies wrote, my dear, in letters made of gold."*

Ephraim glanced at Isabel, who grinned and shot him a sideways glance. His pulse quickened.

Rindy's voice swirled through the night around them. Isabel shifted slightly, positioning her hand close to Ephraim's. He gazed down at her slender white fingers and was seized by a desire to take them in his own. He'd held her hand plenty when they'd been dancing, but he knew if he took it now, it would be different.

It would mean something. He'd spend the rest of the night and all of tomorrow thinking about it.

Ephraim flexed his fingers and glanced at Isabel. She met his gaze briefly, smiled, and scooted closer, humming along with Rindy.

Ephraim suddenly became aware of Isabel's father, Leroy Coleman, sitting on the periphery of the dance floor. He was a slender man, not quite as tall as Ephraim. Leroy appeared to have taken an intense interest in the state of his daughter's hand. The vision of Lester Ewing marching toward the barn to separate Rindy Sue from Jake Fletcher flashed across Ephraim's mind. He swallowed and leaned away from Isabel, stretching his arm as if afflicted by a sudden cramp. Isabel shot him a hurt look. Ephraim folded his arms and smiled, trying his best to look stupid and good-natured.

Rindy Sue finished her song and curtsied. The crowd applauded while the fiddler struck up a waltz to end the dance. Ephraim wondered if Isabel would teach him how to dance as a couple.

Maybe I should ask her now.

He turned toward Isabel—and found himself facing a pair of boots. The boots belonged to Peyton, who was bent over, extending a hand to Isabel.

"May I?" Peyton asked.

Isabel stood up and placed her hand on Peyton's shoulder. "Of course," she said, glancing back at Ephraim as she moved to the center of the floor.

Peyton shot Ephraim a smug grin, one eyebrow raised. "Better find another place to sit, Cutler. You might get stepped on."

Ephraim's face grew hot. He walked back to his seat on the sorghum stalks in disbelief. Was Isabel upset because he hadn't held her hand? Hadn't she seen her pa watching?

The waltzing couples progressed counterclockwise around

the dance floor. As they swirled, Ephraim saw Peyton's hand on the small of Isabel's back. He felt his stomach twist into a knot.

Then Peyton twirled Isabel, and her dress whirled out about her. She gave a little gasp as she turned. And as she came back around to face Peyton, she smiled.

Ephraim felt betrayed. *I ain't goin' to sit here and play second fiddle to no one,* he thought. *Least of all Peyton.* He stood and wandered past the knot of people gathered around the syrup kettle. Several of them were leaning over it, inhaling the fragrant steam with murmurs of satisfaction. Ephraim continued walking toward the road.

"That was some shootin' you did earlier." Lester Ewing clapped a hand on Ephraim's shoulder and thrust the basket containing the cake into his hands. "I bet your ma will enjoy some of this cake. How's she doin' these days?"

"Fine, I guess," Ephraim lied.

"You tell her I asked 'bout her," Lester said. "And tell her we missed seein' her tonight."

"Yessir."

Lester headed back toward the dancers, and Ephraim turned to leave.

"You sad your girly is dancin' with that Henson boy?"

Ephraim looked back.

Clabe Fletcher stepped away from the kettle and walked in front of Ephraim, licking a piece of sorghum cane he'd dipped in the molasses. His nose had been broken so many times it looked like a staircase.

"You got that same hangdog, lonesome look my brother gets when he ain't seen his Rindy Sue for a couple of days."

Ephraim grunted and tried to sidestep Clabe.

Clabe stepped with Ephraim. He stuck the piece of cane between his teeth and sucked on it. "Them Yankees is all the same. They come down here from Durant County and think they can take what they like—our land, our business, and our women.

Why, the Henson boys hadn't been in Sixmile Creek two months when Silas tried to horn in on Rindy, and I know he seen she belonged to Jake."

He reached into a pocket, pulled out a set of brass knuckles, and offered them to Ephraim. "Why don't you give that Henson boy a taste of these knuckle-dusters when he's finished dancin'? I'll hold that there cake for you."

Ephraim shook his head. "I ain't lookin' for no fight, Clabe."

Clabe laughed. "Ain't you goin' to defend your woman? Boy, if you don't stand up to them Yankees now, who knows what they'll take next?"

"I just want to go on home," Ephraim said, trying to step past Clabe again.

"That so?" Clabe said, still stepping with Ephraim. He pocketed the brass knuckles. "Well, I got just the cure for that. A shot of Clabe Fletcher's liquid courage—that's what you need."

"I don't want none of that."

"What's the matter? You take a temperance pledge or somethin'?"

"No." Ephraim shifted the basket, forced his way past Clabe, and headed toward the road.

"I was just about to cut you a deal," Clabe called after him. "You being a first-time customer and all." He chuckled. "If you're scared it's goin' to burn, I could mix some of this here molassy with it." He erupted into a raucous laugh, and Ephraim heard him slap his knees. "It'll be sweeter than your mama's titty!"

EPHRAIM WALKED down the dark road followed by the scent of wood smoke. The chirping of crickets replaced the fading sounds of the fiddle. Cool night air washed over his face, but the image of Peyton twirling Isabel still burned in his memory. He spat in the dirt and kicked at a stone, sending it careening into the darkness.

Isabel could waltz all the way to Charleston with Peyton, for all he cared.

But seeing those two together on the dance floor had stirred up an eddy of thought that had been lurking in the corner of Ephraim's mind for a while. *What if I'm not good enough for Isabel?* What could he offer her? A drafty log cabin, a few scant acres of mountainside, and a mother-in-law who needed tending every day? Peyton and Silas, on the other hand, were already farming a chunk of the best land in the county.

A figure emerged from the shadows up ahead. Ephraim stopped, and the figure grew closer, passing through a patchwork of darkness and moonlight. The man had a pack on his back; his pants were torn at the knees. On his head was a wide-brimmed hat that looked flimsy from wear, and its brim drooped, obscuring most of his face. Ephraim realized with a start that the man wore the old gray sack coat of a Confederate soldier.

Something white floated in the air just ahead of the stranger. It twirled, the ghost of a falling leaf. It looked like a page torn from a book.

As he neared Ephraim, the man snatched the page out of the air, folded it, and tucked it into his coat. He removed his hat and smiled in greeting, baring rotten teeth. "Excuse me, son, you comin' from that gatherin' over yonder?" His voice rasped like a turning millstone.

Ephraim nodded. "That's Lester Ewing's place." At this proximity, the man's overpowering scent assaulted Ephraim's nose. It was hard to tell if the man had been drinking or if the fermented scent was his own, but in either case, it had clearly been a while since he'd bathed. Ephraim backed up a step.

"You think a traveler could find a meal there?" The man licked his lips.

"I'm sure you could. He's a nice man. They got plenty of food."

The stranger grunted and peered toward the house. His eyes glinted in the moonlight.

A chill ran down Ephraim's spine. "What brings you to Sixmile Creek?" he asked. Any traveler on this road was well off the beaten path.

"Just passin' through," the stranger said, replacing his hat. He made to leave.

A thought occurred to Ephraim. "You want a cake?" He had no appetite after seeing Peyton steal Isabel right in front of him.

The stranger turned around with a greedy look on his face. "Is that what you're carryin' in that basket?"

Ephraim nodded and offered the basket to the man.

The stranger tore it from his hands and flipped open the lid. "Aw, looky here," he said, pulling a knife from his belt. He hacked off an irregular piece of the stack cake and stuffed it into his mouth with filthy hands. He chewed noisily, closing his eyes in ecstasy. "Mmmm, it's been a right long time since I ate somethin' this good."

He opened his eyes and scrutinized Ephraim. "Say, you don't happen to know anyone around these parts by the name of Amos, do you?"

Ephraim thought for a moment. "No, I don't reckon I do."

He's a little older than you, maybe he came to town a few years back, could've just been passin' through, like me. Think about it: you ever meet anyone named Amos travelin' this way?"

Ephraim shook his head. "No, sir."

"Shame," the man said, cramming another handful of cake into his mouth. "I don't reckon you know anyone by the name of Boggs either."

Ephraim watched the man carefully. Could this man be some long-lost relative of the reverend? "Actually," he said, "the preacher here, his name is Boggs."

The stranger stiffened. He wiped his hand on his pants and stepped closer to Ephraim, his eyes narrowing. "Preacher? What's he look like, boy?"

Ephraim nearly choked on the man's stench. His breath was

rancid. "He, uh, well, he dresses like a preacher... 'bout your height, I'd say."

"There more'n one church in this town?"

Ephraim shook his head. "No, sir. Just the one."

The man's eyes grew distant. He fished around his teeth with his tongue, dislodging morsels of cake. "That's gotta be him," he muttered. He tipped his hat and shrugged his pack higher onto his shoulders, then set off down the road without another word.

Ephraim watched him go. As the stranger neared a bend in the road, he stopped, pulled the folded page out of his pocket, and tossed it into the air. The paper unfurled and began darting back and forth in the air, impelled by a nonexistent breeze. It twirled past the stranger's face and came to rest on the ground behind him. He turned and gazed back in Ephraim's direction, his expression grim.

7

FOXGLOVE TEA

Firelight illuminated the top of the Cutlers' chimney. Ma hadn't let the fire die tonight; apparently she'd stoked it to a blaze—heat to match her temper, no doubt. Ephraim steeled himself and opened the door.

Ma stood by the hearth, stirring something in the pot.

"You haven't gone to bed yet, Ma?" Ephraim asked. He hung his hat on the peg and ran a hand through his hair.

Ma peered up from the fire, her eyes alight. "Ephraim, I told you if you weren't willin' to avenge your father, you'd live to regret it."

An ache grew in the back of Ephraim's throat. He swallowed. "Ma, I know you said that, but I ain't killin' nobody."

His mother reached into the pot with a ladle and scooped up a dark liquid, which she poured into an earthen mug. She sat back in her chair and held the mug in both hands. Steam rose from it, and she breathed in deeply. "Yes, you are, Ephraim. You're killin' *me*."

Ephraim's hands began to tremble. He clenched them into fists. "What have you got in that mug, Ma?"

"Foxglove tea."

Foxglove? Ephraim racked his brain. *What is foxglove used for?* A sudden coldness hit him at his core. "That's poison."

"I know it is," his mother said. She rocked the chair slowly, a serene smile on her lips.

Ephraim shook his head. "You ain't goin' to drink that, are you?"

"I will—if you don't shoot Silas Henson."

For a split second, Ephraim imagined shooting not Silas, but Peyton. Gunning down that dandy for stealing the last dance with Isabel. He closed his eyes and shook his head, trying to clear it. "But, Ma... the Bible..."

She held up a hand. "This might be hard for you to accept, Ephraim, but God wants this."

"God wants this? How do you figure?"

Ma rose from the rocking chair. "I just know it." She leaned toward her son and whispered. "In the years of my sorrow, I raised you. You were only a small thing when your pa died. You'd go to school, and I'd go into town to do other folks' washin'. Do you know what folks thought of us? They thought the Cutler name had died with Josiah. They thought we'd never amount to nothin'." She looked down at her mug, careful not to spill any of the tea. "But I told myself: Lucretia, you keep raisin' that boy. Someday he'll do things for you that you never could do for yourself."

"I do," Ephraim said. He gritted his teeth. *I do just about everythin' 'round here.* He pointed to the stew pot. "I put meat in the pot, and corn in the shed." He counted on his fingers. "I chop wood, I hire out to get a little money, I even do the washin'! Ain't all that takin' care of us? Ain't that enough for you?"

His ma sighed. "Ephraim, you do a wonderful job takin' care of me. But you're almost full grown. Pretty soon you'll be married and startin' a family of your own. I need you to do this for me, while you're still mine. My health is poor, I ain't long for this world, and I want to rest easy in my grave."

Somewhere deep inside Ephraim, a dam broke, flooding him with white-hot rage. His ears filled with the pounding of his own heart. "You don't know nothin', Ma! I ain't never getting married! Me and everyone in this town knows I'm goin' to spend my days stuck here in this cabin with your sorry sack of helplessness!"

Ma's eyes narrowed. "Ephraim Cutler! How dare you raise your voice at your mother!"

Ephraim's stomach twisted into a knot. He regretted his outburst instantly. "Ma, I'm sorry. I shouldn't have said that I—"

She turned toward the fire. "If that's truly what you think of me, the woman who brought you into this world, then I'll drink this and rid you of the burden of my presence." She brought the mug to her lips.

Ephraim ran forward. "Ma, wait! Stop! Listen. Put that mug down, and let's talk about this."

She tightened her grip on the mug and stared unflinchingly back at him. "No."

Ephraim put his hands on his mother's shoulders. He tried to force his voice to be calm. "Put it down."

She jerked away. "Don't you place a hand on me!" Her voice rang with the unquestionable authority of a mother. "I know you can take this from me. But if you do, I'll just make more. I'll wait until you're out on one of your precious hunts someday, and do it again!"

Ephraim's hands fell to his sides. The snowflake of a chance he could save this situation melted before his mother's wrath.

"I refuse to walk this earth a day longer with your father's death unavenged, and a son who doesn't love me. If that Yankee ain't dead afore daybreak, I'm goin' to drink this tea, and you'll be left alone in this world."

"Can't we talk about this?"

"I'm through with talkin', Ephraim. Either get that pistol off the mantel or take that shovel by the door and start diggin' my grave next to Pa's."

Ephraim retrieved the pistol. "I'll do it," he said. His thoughts raced. He needed to talk to Reverend Boggs. He'd go wake the preacher and—

Ma set her mug on the mantel and picked up a candle. She walked to the table, picked up a knife, and cut a notch in the candle about an inch from its top. Then she lit it in the fire. "You have until this candle burns to the mark I made to kill the Yankee and return," she said. "If you haven't, I'll drink the tea."

Ephraim was speechless. He stared at the candle. How long did he have? Not long enough to rouse Reverend Boggs and return, he knew that.

A bead of sweat trickled down the side of his face.

Ma stuck the candle in a holder on the mantel, retrieved the mug, and sat down in her rocker. She closed her eyes and began to rock. "Go now," she said. "Let's see how much you really care about your ma."

THE NIGHT WAS cold enough now to elicit a faint vapor from Molly's nostrils. Ephraim held the reins in one hand and the pistol in the other, following the moonlit road north toward the Hensons' farm. Silas would be on his way home by now.

How had this happened? Ephraim stared at the pistol in his right hand. When had Ma decided that this was what she wanted? Was this what she'd been thinking about during all those days and nights at home, pushing her rocking chair back and forth?

He passed the Ewings' place and rode around the bend. A quarter mile later, he made out the sound of two voices singing: Peyton and Silas. He saw the two men strolling in the moonlight. They stopped and turned to face the sound of approaching hoofbeats.

Ephraim's hands began to tremble. He gripped the pistol tighter and pulled on the reins to slow Molly down.

Peyton's gaze traveled from Ephraim to the gun he aimed at Silas. His eyes widened, and he shook his head.

"What're you doin', Ephraim?"

Ephraim breathed heavily, his ears filled with the pounding of his own heart. He drew in a breath and pointed the gun at Silas. "I'm real sorry 'bout this," he said, his voice shaky.

Silas held up his hands and took a step back, his eyes wide. "What's goin' on, Ephraim? I've got no quarrel with you."

Ephraim wiped his eyes with his shirt cuff. "I don't want to do this—it's my ma. She—" He choked on the rest of the words. This just needed to be done.

His thumb felt weak on the hammer; he could hardly pull it back. But he heard the click of the cylinder rotating into place, the click of the hammer seating.

His eyes met Silas's.

Every part of the Colt's firing mechanism quivered in anticipation. Molly raised her head, her nostrils flared, sensing the tension in the air. Ephraim willed his finger to fire the gun. It wouldn't. *I can't do this.* A vision of Ma by the fire, her own death cupped in her hands, clouded his mind.

They stood there for a moment, Ephraim and Silas, locked on the brink of eternity. The very night around them seemed to be holding its breath.

A branch snapped.

Molly lurched.

An explosion split the night. The barrel flashed, and the acrid smell of black powder filled the air. Ephraim's ears rang.

Molly reared up on her hind legs, throwing Ephraim from the saddle. The pistol flew from his hand. He connected with the packed earth of the road and rolled to a stop, lying on his belly.

Silas gave a sharp cry and clutched his chest. His knees buckled, and he fell to the ground in a slack-shouldered heap. A dark stain seeped across his shirt.

Peyton stared down at his brother, eyes bulging. "Silas!" he cried, his voice high and strange. He fell to his knees and cradled his brother's head in his hands.

Silas gasped, a gurgling sound.

Peyton put his hand over the bloody hole in his brother's shirt. "Hold on, Silas! We'll get help!"

Silas's chest rose and fell, rose again—and fell one last time, with a drawn-out sigh.

Ephraim held his breath, hoping that somehow the wound was superficial. Hoping that Silas's chest would rise again.

Peyton shook his brother's shoulders. "Silas? Silas!" He lowered his ear to Silas's lips and listened. Then he looked up at Ephraim, his eyes wide. "He—he's dead." He clenched and unclenched his bloodstained hands, nostrils flaring. "You killed him, Ephraim!"

Something shifted in the leaves at the roadside. Ephraim pushed himself off the ground and stumbled back. The stranger in the Confederate coat stood at the edge of the woods, a broken branch underfoot, staring at Ephraim from beneath the shadow of his hat. He still had the cake basket tucked under one arm and the torn page clutched in his hand. Had he been there before? He seemed to have appeared out of nowhere.

Ephraim turned his back on the scene and ran like he had never run before.

EPHRAIM BURST THROUGH THE DOOR. The fire popped and crackled around a new stack of logs. Ma paced back and forth in the orange light of the blaze. The mug of foxglove tea sat on the table.

"Is he dead?"

"I shot him." Ephraim walked the length of the cabin. Everywhere he looked, he saw Peyton kneeling next to Silas: inside his head, in the crackling flames, and in the face of his mother, who took a deep sigh and shut her eyes, savoring the moment.

She opened her eyes. "You sure he's dead?"

Ephraim didn't respond. He couldn't think straight. *That stain blossoming on Silas's chest—* He looked down at his still shaking hand.

"Where'd you hit him?"

Ephraim placed a hand over his heart.

Ma turned and stared into the flames. "Ephraim, you have done me proud." She whispered. "Justice is served."

"Ma, how am I goin' to take care of you now? Folks'll be—"

She pushed past him and opened the door. "Don't worry about me. You've given me everythin' I could ask from a loyal son. Now go hide. Quickly!" She pointed to the woods.

Without another word, Ephraim ran outside, into the dark trees. He didn't stop until the cabin was out of view behind him. Then he ran his hands through his hair and tried to block the image of Silas falling in the road. Had he meant to pull the trigger? He'd pointed the gun at Silas. Then, the explosion of powder. When had he actually decided to kill the man? Had he really ever decided at all?

He looked from side to side. Where should he go now? If he was caught...

Ephraim closed his eyes. Dark prophecies poured into his skull, darting across his mind like rodents through the underbrush. A torch-bearing group of Silas's kin. Them wrestling him from the cabin. A noose looped over his neck and tightened. His legs, kicking as they left the ground. His face turning blue. Ma rocking in her chair by a stone-cold hearth, her face pale, an empty bowl in her lap.

Ephraim opened his eyes and exhaled a breath he didn't

know he'd been holding. The darkness rushed in on him, pinning him under the weight of what he had done.

He heard voices coming from the direction of the cabin. Ma was there, alone. He couldn't leave her to deal with this by herself.

He retraced his steps until he could see the cabin. Manson Owens stood by the door, lantern in hand. Jubal Early, Franz Akers, and Ernest Williams were with him, each carrying a rifle. Ephraim crouched behind a large tree to watch and listen.

Manson knocked on the cabin door.

"Lucretia, it's me, Manson."

A few moments of silence passed. Manson rapped on the door again.

"Lucretia, open up. We need to talk."

The door creaked open. "What's your business?" Ephraim's mother asked. "Comin' up here in the middle of the night?"

"Your boy just gunned down Silas Henson."

She said nothing.

"You better tell us what this is all about," Manson said. "Peyton Henson just woke me from a dead sleep, demandin' a hangin'. I convinced him to let us come here, while he stays at my place, but I don't reckon he'll stay there very long."

"There'll be no hangin', Manson. Justice ain't a crime," Ma said.

"How in the Sam Hill was killin' Silas justice?"

"Silas was a Yankee. Yankees killed my Josiah. Now I've cut down one of them. An eye for an eye."

"You put Ephraim up to it! Lucretia, it weren't Silas that killed Josiah—you know that."

"One Yank's the same as another to me."

Manson slammed his fist against the door frame. "I fought in the war too, that don't mean I can go around shootin' anyone that was a Yank! The war's over!"

Ma snorted.

Manson blew out a breath. "I hope you're happy, Lucretia. You just bought Ephraim a trip to the gallows. Josiah would never approve of you makin' a killer out of that boy. He ain't even full grown yet!"

"You can't take my son, Manson. Truth be told, I don't even know where he is."

"I don't suppose he's squattin' in that smokehouse yonder?" Ernest Williams said.

"He run off after he killed that Yank." Ma stepped outside, walked to the smokehouse, and opened the door. "Take a look for yourself—he ain't here." She folded her arms. "You can search the cabin, too. He ain't there neither."

Ernest stepped forward. "Listen, Lucretia, we ain't fools. The boy's in the woods somewheres." He turned to Manson. "Let me handle this." Then he jabbed the end of his rifle barrel into the small of Ma's back. "Get them hands up, widow!"

She stiffened and cried out.

"Ernest!" Manson whipped out his revolver and pointed it at the man. "You got no right to do that to the woman!"

"Hold your tongue, Manson," Ernest said, pushing Ephraim's mother toward the woods. "I'm only doin' what needs to be done."

He cleared his throat. "Ephraim!" he bellowed, facing the dark forest. "I know you're out there! I got your ma here. If you don't give yourself up, I'm goin' to throw her in the jail, and I'll make sure she stays there until somebody finds your murderin' hide!"

"He's already gone!" Ma said. "Ain't none of you goin' to catch my boy!" Her skeletal arms shook as she spoke.

Ephraim's mouth went dry. He cursed himself for ever picking up the pistol. Ma was frail; she wouldn't last long in jail.

He made his decision. He stood up and walked from the trees.

Manson shook his head and stepped forward. He grabbed the barrel of Ernest's rifle and wrenched it from his hands. "You've

done enough tonight, Ernest," he said, his eyes flinty. "Go home."
He turned to face Ephraim with a heavy sigh.

Ephraim lowered his head, unable to meet the blacksmith's
gaze.

Manson took a deep breath through his nose. He strode over
and laid a thick-fingered hand on Ephraim's shoulder. "Come on,
Ephraim. We got to get this sorted out."

Jubal and Franz stepped forward. They each took Ephraim by
an arm, and Manson led the party across the yard to the road.

Behind them, Ephraim heard his mother let out a wail.

8

JAILHOUSE

Sixmile Creek's tiny jailhouse had a rough wooden floor, and a single-barred window in the door was the only source of light. Manson made a pallet of flour sacks in one corner for Ephraim, then stepped outside and locked the door. He stood on the porch with Jubal and Franz, and the three of them discussed guard shifts.

When Ephraim heard the men go suddenly silent, he moved to the door and peered through the bars in the window. Peyton Henson was marching toward the jail, pistol in hand.

Manson backed up against the door, his hand resting on the butt of his revolver.

"You promised me justice, Manson! Let me have him!"

"Put that gun down, Peyton," Manson said.

"This ain't none of your affair! He killed my brother!"

Ephraim had never seen Peyton like this. Muscles and veins strained in his face. His hair stuck out at odd angles, held in place by the grease that usually kept it slicked back. A lump rose in Ephraim's throat. *He doesn't deserve this.*

"I'm sorry, son. I truly am," Manson said. "But we're goin' to keep Ephraim till we can get a circuit judge—"

Ephraim took a deep breath. "Manson," he said. "Let me talk to him."

The blacksmith glanced over his shoulder, deliberating. "All right," he said finally, motioning for Peyton to step forward. "I'll be havin' that gun, though. There's been enough murder in this town for one night."

Peyton passed his pistol to Manson with a glare and stepped in front of the jailhouse door. His chin quivered. "You're goin' to hang for this, Cutler!" He spat the words.

Ephraim took a shaky breath. "Peyton, I'm sorry. I—"

Peyton jammed his hand through the bars and seized Ephraim by the throat. "Or maybe I'll just strangle you right now!" His grip tightened, digging into the gristle of Ephraim's windpipe.

Ephraim grabbed Peyton's fingers and tried to pry them free.

Peyton throttled him, bashing his head into the bars.

"Whoa there!" Manson grabbed Peyton by the collar and pulled him back. "None of that now!"

Ephraim stepped back from the door, rubbing his throat.

Peyton's eyes never left Ephraim. His face contorted in hatred. A sick feeling rose in Ephraim's stomach. He closed his eyes, shutting out Peyton's burning gaze.

"You're goin' to rot in hell, Cutler! And when you're dead, I'm goin' to plow your grave under and plant my corn over it!"

"All right, that's enough," Manson said, pushing Peyton away from the door. "There ain't goin' to be no hangin' until we've had a fair trial."

Peyton threw his hands wide. "Squire Barrett isn't due in Sixmile Creek until next month! You expect me to wait that long?"

Manson crossed his arms. "We'll wait until the law arrives, Peyton."

Jubal and Franz stepped forward to stand silently on either side of Manson.

Peyton backed away. "Well, if it's a judge you want, I'll go fetch Squire Barrett myself, and I'm bringin' my kin back with me." He raised his voice. "You hear that, Ephraim? I'm fetchin' the judge tonight!" He spun on his heel and left.

Manson shook his head. "Well, if this ain't the biggest mess I ever seen." Turning to face Jubal and Franz, he sighed. "Jubal, you got first watch?"

"Yep. Ain't no way I'll be sleepin' after all this."

Ephraim lay down on the pallet and stared into the darkness. Anger swept over him in a hot flood. Why had he listened to Ma? Let her back him into a corner like she had? She was crazy, but he wasn't! He should've forced the tea from her hands, thrown her over his shoulder like a sack of corn, and carried her to see Reverend Boggs. Surely the preacher could've talked some sense into her. The events of the night had taken on the disjointed quality of a nightmare. He covered his face with his hands and willed himself to wake up.

9

ISABEL

"Ephraim? Did you say Ephraim Cutler shot Silas Henson last night?"

Isabel couldn't believe what she was hearing. She knew Ephraim had left the dance without saying goodbye. He'd seemed upset, sure, but not murderous. She folded her arms.

"I heard it from Manson," her father said. The small man finished tying the strings of his coffee-sack apron and walked behind the counter to the storeroom door.

Isabel followed him, shaking her head. "How do you know he's telling the truth? I saw the Fletcher boys selling liquor last night. Mr. Owens might've had some."

Her father opened the door to the storage room, releasing the scents of salted meat and water-ground meal into the store. "Isabel, you'd be hard pressed to find a reputation better than Manson's in this town. You know that."

She clenched her fists and stomped her foot on the floor. "He'd never do that. I don't believe it, Pa! I'm going to ask Mr. Owens myself." She ran from the store, letting the door slam behind her.

The midmorning street bustled with wagons, buggies, buckboards, mules, and chickens. Isabel marched straight through them, heedless of those she cut off.

Several horses stood at the hitching rail outside Manson's forge, awaiting new shoes. Isabel shouldered through the animals' owners, who were gathered in a murmuring knot just inside the shop. Manson stood at his bench, sawing a length of board. Isabel felt confused at the sight of the blacksmith engaging in carpentry. She stopped on the other side of his bench, arms crossed.

"Pa says you told him that Ephraim shot Silas last night."

Manson kept his eyes on his work. "He did, Isabel. Silas is dead." He gestured with his chin to a wagon on the far side of the shop. A long object lay inside, covered by a shroud.

"What's that?" Isabel asked, her heart beginning to beat faster.

"Silas. This is his casket I'm makin'."

"No. Ephraim's the nicest boy I know." Isabel marched to the wagon and grabbed the top of the shroud.

A hush grew over the crowd by the door. Isabel felt all eyes on her.

She lifted the shroud and stared down at the pale face of the corpse beneath. Blood stained his chest. Her head swam.

Isabel released the shroud and clutched the edge of the wagon, her knees buckling. "No," she whispered.

Manson stopping sawing. "You all right, Miss Isabel?"

The room lost focus. Isabel felt like she had fallen down a well and was looking out. Her grip on the wagon weakened.

The old blacksmith's bushy eyebrows shot up in alarm. He dropped the saw and ran toward her.

The ground rushed up to meet Isabel, and everything went black.

The next thing she knew, she was staring up into the bearded face of Mr. Owens. He was sitting on the floor, her head cradled in one arm, fanning her with his free hand. "Stand back," he said to the men gathering around, "give the girl some air. She just took a shock is all. She'll come 'round."

Isabel groaned and sat up. Her ears were ringing.

"Steady there, miss. Don't go standin' up too fast, you'll only wind up down here again."

Isabel's face burned with embarrassment. She'd fainted right in front of all these men. She got to her feet, assured Manson that she was all right, and hurried back to her pa's store.

Ignoring her father's questioning glance, she ran upstairs to the living quarters and threw herself on her bed. A lump formed in her throat. She thought of the look on Ephraim's face when Peyton had asked her for the last dance. He'd been jealous. She hadn't thought it'd amount to anything; in the moment, it'd felt kind of nice to know that the two most handsome boys in town were interested in her. Now she felt guilty.

The vision of Ephraim's face, reddening when she'd asked him to dance, filled her mind. Then the cold, lifeless face of Silas replaced it.

Isabel began to cry.

10

THE REVEREND'S COFFEE

A fly buzzed in and out of the slats of early afternoon light that leaked through the cracks in the jailhouse walls. Ephraim heard voices outside; they sounded like Peyton and Manson. He rose from his pallet, moved to the door, and pressed his ear against the metal.

"Squire Barrett didn't come back with you?" Manson asked.

"He didn't," Peyton said, "but he sent this." Paper rustled, and Peyton continued, "Read it, Manson. Read it loud, so that everyone can hear!"

Something pounded on the door of Ephraim's cell, and he pulled back, rubbing his cheek. "Get over here where you can listen to this, Cutler!" Peyton shouted, pounding the door harder. "Your fate's been written!"

Manson began to read. "Go—on—and—hang—him," he said haltingly. "Sanc—sanctioned—by—de... de..."

The paper rustled as if it had been snatched from Manson's hand, and then Peyton's voice sounded loud and clear. "By decree of Judge Sam Barrett," he read. "Look right there, if you don't believe me—that's the judge's seal." He pounded the door again. "Hear that, Cutler? We're goin' to stretch your murderin' neck!"

Ephraim slumped against the wall. Squire Barrett had decided his fate without even bothering to come and ask questions. He was probably doing it as a favor to the Hensons. Ephraim imagined they had considerable political clout in Durant County, and the judge was running for reelection, after all.

Manson cleared his throat. "When do you plan on doin' it?"

"Tomorrow at dawn," Peyton said. "We'll string him from the big oak at my place. My folks are on their way over from Durant County. They'll be arrivin' sometime tonight."

Ephraim slid to the floor. He thought of Ma. His guts ached with something that needed to come up. Saliva flooded his mouth. He gagged, and the bitter taste of bile washed over his tongue.

He wished he could recall the bullet to the gun, wished that someone besides himself had seen Ma sitting there by the fire with a cup full of poison and her mind set on murder.

His thoughts jumped from the sight of her by the fire to the sight of Silas falling in the road. *If Molly hadn't jumped, would I have still pulled the trigger?* He couldn't ignore the feelings of jealousy he'd had watching Peyton waltz Isabel around the dance floor. Had that clouded his thinking?

He put his face in his hands and slid into the swamp of that thought. It didn't matter if his crime was cold-blooded murder or just plain bad luck. Either way, Silas was dead.

Ephraim crossed his arms over his stomach as if compressing an actual cramp. He rocked forward and backward. The more he thought about it, the more comforting the thought of the noose became. He ran a hand across his neck, imagining rough fibers squeezing a raw circle into it—a short, tight end to this torment. *That's the best thing for it. I deserve to die.*

Outside, the men dispersed, and Ephraim heard the jangle of keys as the guard changed.

"You sure you want to take another watch already, Jubal? You were here all last night," Manson said.

"Ain't no problem," Jubal said. "It'll all be over soon enough. Besides, I figure them with wives and children will want to go home and tell 'em 'bout what'll be happenin' tomorrow mornin'."

Ephraim stayed where he sat, listening to the keys clank softly as Jubal shifted in the chair outside. After a minute, all Ephraim could hear was the thudding of his own heart. He wondered: why was it racing? He hadn't exerted himself for hours now. Maybe it knew it didn't have much longer to pulse beneath his ribs and was trying to expend a lifetime's worth of beats before the sun came up tomorrow. He imagined himself being led to the gallows, an old man before his time.

Justice would be served at dawn, and rightfully so. He'd killed an innocent man, plain and simple.

He turned his gaze to the rafters. Why wait?

He stood and walked to the middle of the room. The ceiling in the jail was low and Ephraim put his hand over the rafter from where he stood. He could make amends for his crime right here, right now.

He unbuttoned his brown wool shirt and looped it over the rafter so that the sleeves dangled down on either side. He tied the sleeves together and tugged on them. There wasn't anything in the room to stand on, and even if there was, the ceiling was too low for it to do any good. He'd have to twist the makeshift noose around his neck and try to sit to make it work.

He stuck his head through the sleeves and spun around several times so they crossed behind his neck. At first, a hollow ache filled his chest; he'd only made it to sixteen years old. But then an odd calm came over him. This made sense: a life for a life. Nothing he could ever say or do would bring Silas back or ease Peyton's loss. This was the only way.

He bowed his head and stepped forward, feeling the noose tighten around his throat.

The bump of boots sounded on the wooden porch outside. Ephraim lifted his head.

"Good evening, Jubal." It sounded like Reverend Boggs.

"Evenin', Reverend."

Something heavy hit the porch boards with a thunk.

"I brought you a supper pail," the reverend said. "There's fresh side pork, hot biscuits, and a jug of coffee in there."

"Why thank you, Reverend," Jubal said. "I was gettin' mighty hungry."

"No thanks necessary," Boggs said. He chuckled. "Us bachelors have to look out for each other. A man without a wife often goes too long between hot meals."

"Mmm," Jubal replied, his voice thickened by a mouthful of food. He smacked and swallowed. "It's a cryin' shame. One of these days, I'll find me a woman."

"As you should," Boggs said. "Say, I was wondering if I might ask a favor of you. Being the preacher of this town, I figured I should talk with Ephraim before the execution. Can you let me in?"

Ephraim stepped back. He didn't want the reverend to catch him in the act of dying. He'd envisioned this as a private moment.

"It'd only be right," Jubal agreed through another mouthful. The chair creaked, and the keys jangled as they changed hands. "The middle key opens the lock."

"Thank you."

The hasp of the lock scraped, and the door swung open. Reverend Boggs peered in, squinting in the gloom. When his gaze landed on Ephraim, his eyes widened. He stepped inside and pushed the door shut behind him. "Heavens, Ephraim!" he said in a low whisper. "What're you doing?"

Ephraim turned his face to the wall, eyes burning with guilt. "Figured I'd save the Hensons the trouble."

"This is some good coffee, Reverend!" Jubal called from the porch. Ephraim heard him take a slurp and sigh.

"Get that thing off your neck," Boggs said. "I'm here to collect you."

"What?" Ephraim looked up at Boggs's face.

The reverend gave a curt nod, and his eyes flicked to the door. "I'm going to take you with me, and we'd best be going now while the road is still empty."

"No, Reverend. This is what I deserve."

Boggs folded his arms. "Come now. Any fool can die for his sins. It takes something more than a coward to live with them."

"I killed Silas," Ephraim said. "This is justice."

"Think of your mother, boy."

Ephraim looked up. "She's the one that wanted me to do it. Besides, what good am I to her now? I can't stay in Sixmile Creek."

"I agree. You must leave this town. But you won't be good to anyone, least of all your mother, if you aren't living."

The reverend reached into his coat and produced a tomahawk with a dull iron blade. Ephraim was surprised; he'd never known that the preacher carried a weapon.

Boggs opened the door a crack and peered out, then beckoned to Ephraim. "Come on, we don't have much time."

The reverend's matter-of-fact tone had weakened Ephraim's resolve to take his own life. He turned around until the noose loosened, then he pulled his head out and retrieved his shirt. The sleeves were stretched out, but he put it back on and followed Boggs onto the porch.

Jubal sat sprawled in his chair, his head tilted backward. The overturned jug sat cradled in his lap, a drip hanging from its neck. Spilled coffee pooled around his boots, draining through the porch boards.

"What's the matter with him?" Ephraim asked.

"I drugged the coffee. It'll take him a few hours to sleep it off. Come on now, we need to leave."

"No one knows you're lettin' me out?"

"Not a soul. I heard you were going to be hanged at dawn. As your preacher and friend, I can't abide the thought. Let's go." The reverend laid a hand on Ephraim's shoulder and steered him past the unconscious guard.

As they departed, Boggs laid the keys in Jubal's lap, retrieved the coffee jug and bucket, and refastened the padlock on the door. "Quickly now. Let's get you back to my place. You'll have to stay in the cellar for a few days until we can get you away from Sixmile Creek."

Ephraim paused in the road. "Wait a minute. When Jubal wakes up, won't he realize it was you that let me out?"

Reverend Boggs continued walking. "He might, but he won't speak of it after I tell everyone he was sleeping on the job when I left the jail."

"You think folks will believe you?"

Boggs smiled. "There are advantages to being the only preacher in town."

EPHRAIM AND REVEREND BOGGS took a route through the woods, emerging between the reverend's garden and the church grave-yard. Boggs swept Ephraim inside his home and barred the door behind them, then removed his hat and hung it on a peg by the door.

"Let's get you something to eat, son. Then we'll talk."

"I ain't hungry," Ephraim said.

Boggs cut a few slices of side pork and a wedge from a round of cornbread. He served them, along with a tin cup of spring water, to Ephraim at his bare wooden table, and sat down across from him. "Even a man sentenced to hang gets a last meal. Eat."

Ephraim picked up the cornbread and took a bite.

"So tell me what happened." Boggs's somber gray eyes locked onto Ephraim's.

The lump of cornbread in Ephraim's mouth felt dry. He swallowed, and it scraped painfully downward. "Ma wanted me to shoot Silas. She told me I had to, or she'd kill herself."

Boggs nodded heavily. "I figured it was something like that. I'm certain no one knows your mother and understands your situation like I do."

Ephraim slid forward in his chair. "You knew she wanted me to kill Silas?"

Boggs shook his head. "No. In my visits, she expressed her anger over your father's death, but she never said anything about killing Silas."

"Oh." Ephraim looked down at his plate. "I never even knew she was angry. She held Pa's gun a lot, but she never said anythin' 'bout gettin' revenge until last night." He teased the pork around the plate with a fork. "She was so set on it. She's never demanded somethin' like that out of me. You should've seen her—she had this cup full of foxglove tea and said she was goin' to drink it if I wouldn't shoot Silas. I tried to take it away from her, and she said she'd just make it again, and drink it when I wasn't home. There wasn't no talkin' her out of it."

Boggs sat back and folded his arms. "I hear you, son. There was little I could do for a soul so anguished."

Ephraim nodded. He pushed the plate aside and clasped his hands together on top of the table. "But, I'm the one that pulled the trigger, Reverend. I'm a murderer now, ain't I? Does that mean I'm goin' to Hell?"

Boggs raised his eyebrows. "Well, Ephraim, that's a good question. I can see why you'd ask that." He leaned forward. "There are many ways to damn yourself in this life, but there's also more than one path to redemption."

"So you think there's a way for me to make things right?"

The reverend thumbed his ear. "I didn't say that. Silas is dead, Ephraim. That can't be undone."

"Then what do you mean?"

"All I'm saying is, sometimes you just have to find a new way to approach the issue. A back door, so to speak."

"Heaven's got a back door? That don't sound right."

Boggs frowned. "Do you remember the story of Jonah?"

Ephraim nodded.

"Do you think right after he was swallowed by the whale, that he believed he could make it out alive?"

"No, I don't suppose he did."

Boggs nodded. "That's right. But eventually he decided to barter his way out, didn't he? He told the Lord he would go prophesy in Nineveh. And the fish," Boggs opened his mouth wide and brought his hand to his mouth with spread fingers, "spewed him out." He leaned back in his chair. "Jonah found a way to escape the inescapable."

Ephraim furrowed his brow and stared at the ceiling. "So maybe I can make a deal with God."

Boggs pushed his chair back from the table and stood. "Perhaps. The point I was trying to make is that Jonah didn't give up. He got what he wanted, but there was a price. Everything has a price." He stretched and yawned. "Let's continue this discussion some other time. It's late, and I have a sermon to prepare tomorrow."

Boggs walked to his bed, picked up a folded blanket and quilt, and handed them to Ephraim. "It may not seem hospitable, but I think you'd best sleep in the root cellar. Once people realize you're missing, they'll be searching everywhere." He opened a hatch in the floor immediately in front of the hearth. A ladder provided access to the rock-lined hole.

Ephraim climbed down and arranged the blanket and quilt on the floor.

"All settled?" Boggs asked.

Ephraim nodded. He suddenly remembered the stranger he'd seen the night of the dance. The man had asked about Reverend

Boggs. Ephraim looked up. "Did that man passin' through town find you?"

Boggs looked confused. "What man?"

"I saw him two nights ago before I killed Silas. He asked about you and someone named Amos." Ephraim stopped. "Come to think of it, he saw me shoot Silas too."

Boggs scratched his jaw. "I can't think of who it would be. What did he look like?"

"He was dirty, smelled real bad."

Boggs shook his head. "I haven't the faintest idea. Sounds strange."

"He was."

"Well, we'd best get some sleep," the reverend said. "Good-night, Ephraim." And he shut the hatch, leaving Ephraim in hollow darkness.

11

THE SNAKE AND THE SHOVEL

A dim awareness crept over Jubal. He was being dragged by his ankles. His body cut a furrow through the dry leaves of the forest floor like a plow behind an ox. His mouth felt dry—it reeked of coffee and something else. His stomach curdled at the taste.

Through the trees, he could make out a light shining from the back window of Coleman's Dry Goods store. The light was growing more distant.

Jubal tried to remember leaving his post at the jail, but couldn't. Maybe he'd had a jug of the Fletchers' moonshine? Jubal blinked. He couldn't remember doing that either.

A branch snagged the cuff of one of his sleeves. Whoever had him kept pulling. The dead wood bent and broke with a snap that sounded like a gunshot in the stillness of the night.

A rock beneath the litter scraped up his back. Jubal tried to lift his head, but a hazy weakness saturated his entire body, and the back of his skull jolted over the rock. He moaned deep in his throat.

The memory of a black rat snake he'd found in his chicken coop swam through the fog of his mind. Nearly five feet long, the serpent had gorged itself on an entire clutch of eggs. When Jubal discovered it, the end of one white orb still protruded from its unhinged jaws. He'd seized the snake by the tail and dragged it into the yard like a limp string of sausages. Bulging and too sluggish to resist, the reptile had watched through dull eyes as he'd fetched an ax and cut off its head.

Jubal felt like that snake right now.

Without being able to raise his head, he could only catch occasional glimpses of the figure pulling him. He could see one hand clutching the rope lashed between his ankles, the other hand using a shovel like a cane. Where was this stranger taking him?

He breathed in sharply, summoning as much strength as he could, and tried to kick free. His legs flopped like dead catfish. Jubal cursed himself for being so weak.

The shovel-wielding figure stopped abruptly, dropped Jubal's feet and studied the ground. In the darkness, Jubal could just make out the lines of a man's face shadowed by the brim of a hat. The man stuck the tip of his shovel into the dirt, put his heel on it, and drove the blade into the earth. He dug hastily, hacking at tree roots with the side of the shovel. The metal clanged dully with each impact.

After what seemed like an eternity, the man stopped digging. He stood with one foot on the shovel, leaning forward, looking at Jubal's prostrate form as if gauging its size. He climbed out of the hole, lifted the shovel in both hands and walked to where Jubal lay.

Jubal made the only sound he could: a pitiful, doglike whine. He tried to move again but succeeded only in shrugging his shoulders.

The man placed the back of the shovel blade on Jubal's face. The cold metal pressed against his lips, and he tasted dirt on the end of his tongue. Questions swarmed through Jubal's thoughts. Who? Why?

When the man raised the shovel above Jubal's head as if to strike, Jubal found, in his desperation, the strength to move. He rolled onto his stomach and thrashed in the leaves, trying to wriggle away. He wouldn't die like this, not here in the woods, as helpless as that stupid rat snake!

The man stomped on Jubal's back, driving the air from his lungs. Jubal stopped moving, stunned. The man slid his foot under Jubal's belly and turned him over.

Jubal got one last glimpse of the stranger's shadowed face before the shovel swung down in a single swift motion.

12

WANTED AND UNWANTED

Isabel awoke to the sound of raised voices. She tumbled out of bed and ran downstairs to the dry-goods store, not bothering to change out of her nightgown.

"Now hold on a minute," her father was saying. "Let me light a lantern so we can see each other."

Isabel heard him strike a match. An oil lamp flared to life, illuminating the faces of Manson, Franz, Ernest, Hebe Washburne, and a dozen other men.

"You say he's escaped from the jail?" Isabel's father asked.

"That's what it looks like," the blacksmith answered. "Ralph went down there to take over guard duty at midnight. Jubal wasn't there. The jail was locked and empty."

Isabel's pulse quickened. Ephraim had escaped.

"You think Jubal let him out?" her father asked.

"I can't figure why he'd do a thing like that, but I reckon there ain't no other reason they'd both be missin'," Manson said. "Besides, there ain't no signs of a jailbreak."

A horse snorted in the road outside, and Isabel's father looked out the window. "The Hensons are here," he said.

Peyton's voice came from outside. "Manson, you got Cutler up there?"

Manson stepped out onto the porch. The other men filed out behind him, and Isabel hurried to the window. Peyton was sitting astride his horse outside, and behind him, in a cabriolet, sat a well-dressed couple, their stony faces lit by a lantern.

"No, Peyton, we don't," Manson said. "I'll be straight with you: we just went down to the jail, and both Ephraim and Jubal are gone."

Peyton glanced at the couple, then back to Manson. "When do you reckon this happened?"

"Sometime between when I left Jubal and midnight."

In hushed tones, Peyton conferred with the man in the cabriolet. After a few moments, the man smoothed his mustache and rose from his seat.

"I am Wyatt Henson," he said, "father of Silas and Peyton. Ephraim Cutler murdered my son. And for all I know, one of you may have assisted him in his escape."

"Weren't none of us," Ernest Williams said quickly. "But there's a stranger in town. I saw him at the stir-off a couple of nights ago. Thought he acted funny."

Several other men murmured agreement.

Wyatt raised a hand to silence them. "Let me be clear: I am not accusing anyone. But I cannot rule out the possibility that someone here knows where the Cutler boy is. So I'm going to make this simple. There'll be a bounty: two hundred dollars, from my own purse, to anyone who brings us the Cutler boy alive so that we can watch him hang. One hundred to anyone who can produce his corpse. Spread word of the reward. That is all." He sat down in the cabriolet and grabbed the reins.

Isabel's mouth went dry. Two hundred dollars was an unheard-of sum in Sixmile Creek— enough to overcome any sympathy toward Ephraim.

Mr. Henson drove off, leaving the knot of men standing on the porch of the store.

"Where do you reckon he got to?" Isabel's father asked.

"He ain't run far," Manson said. "That boy wouldn't leave his ma. I bet he's hidin' out in the woods somewhere."

"Two hundred dollars," Ernest said, stroking his beard. "Don't think I've ever had that much money at one time in my life. Boys, I believe I need to go get my dogs!"

Manson spat off the side of the porch. "You men do what you think is best," he said, walking down the steps and toward his forge. "I don't have the heart to hunt Ephraim. Don't matter what the price on his head is."

Isabel's eyes grew hot, and heavy tears began to course down her cheeks. She turned away from the window and ran upstairs to her bedroom.

Peyton returned at noon, a stack of printed bounty notices in hand. Isabel stopped polishing the candy counter as he removed his hat and approached her father.

"Can I post one of these outside your store, sir?" he asked.

Her father glanced at the paper and nodded. "Of course."

Isabel's whole body felt tense. "You're going to let him post a bounty for Ephraim," she snapped, "on *our* store?"

Peyton and her father both turned to face her. Peyton set the bills on the counter, removed his hat, and walked over to her. "Isabel, I'm sorry. I didn't mean to upset you."

Isabel's eyes pricked, hot tears blurring her vision. She slammed her fist down on the counter. "Everyone's in a hurry to hang Ephraim, but he's the nicest boy I know. Anyone that knows him would tell you the same."

Peyton reached across the counter and put his hand on

Isabel's shoulder. His brows knitted together in genuine concern. She hated it.

"I know he was your friend, Isabel. I can't believe he did what he did either. Just a few nights back, I was out huntin' coons with him."

"Well, I don't care what you say. I still don't believe he shot Silas." Isabel felt her face reddening. Deep down she knew the truth, but she dared Peyton to challenge her.

Peyton shrugged. "Good folks go bad sometimes, I guess." He cast about, looking for the right words. "My pa had a dog once, one of the finest foxhounds around. He was an excellent hunter, gentle with us when we were little. One day, he just went mad. Nobody could figure out what was wrong with him. He snapped at anyone that came near him. So Pa had to put him down."

Isabel skewered Peyton with her gaze. "Don't you dare compare Ephraim to some dog."

Peyton retreated. "Isabel, I'm sorry. I was just trying to—"

"Go hang your reward outside, and get out of here," Isabel said, raising her chin.

Peyton bowed his head and left the candy counter. He retrieved the bounty bills and went to the front door, arms hanging loosely by his sides. In the doorway, he turned and regarded Isabel with a heavy expression.

She glared at him, eyes still burning with hate and tears. "What?"

"I enjoyed dancin' with you the other night. You're quite a fine partner."

Isabel didn't know what to say.

"I was goin' to ask if I might walk you to church this Sunday, but I don't suppose you'd want that now. Look, I know you're hurt because you've lost a friend. I've just lost a friend, too, and a brother. If you ever want to talk about it, I'm here."

He tipped his hat and left.

Isabel glared at her father. He glanced from the door to her, his brow furrowed.

She burst into sobs and hunched over the candy counter, burying her face in her arms.

Her father's footsteps came nearer. He cleared his throat and patted her back. "I know you were friends with the Cutler boy, Isabel, but I had no idea you were so attached to him."

Her sobs grew louder.

"I didn't mean that I don't care for the boy, too," her father continued. "What happened is a shame. His life ain't been easy. His ma ain't been well for some time. For all we know, she's been filling his head with all kinds of madness. Even a straight tree will start to bend if the wind don't let up."

Isabel looked up from the counter. Her breath left a cloud on the glass she'd just polished, right over the horehound candy and lemon drops. "So you don't think he's all bad, then?"

"No, I don't." Her father rubbed his chin. His gaze drifted toward the window. "Some folks are the product of their own wicked ways; others are just victims of the times. There's a lot of things around here that ain't been the same since the war."

A fresh flood of tears took Isabel. She walked into her father's arms and buried her face in his shoulder.

"Don't worry," he said. "I think you must have fancied him your beau, and your heart's broken, but that Henson boy is an honorable man. And Isabel, he aims to court you."

ISABEL DIDN'T WAIT to see if Peyton showed up on Sunday. At church, she found a seat in the back, far from him and everyone else.

She'd heard the talk. Every man and boy in town who owned a hunting dog had been combing the woods at all hours of the day and night, searching for Ephraim. And he'd been spotted in countless places: the old Sherman cabin, the Millers' apple orchard, the Ewings' farm. Hebe Washburne swore he'd had the boy on the run until he disappeared down a badger hole. Men had been stampeding from one end of the county to the other, flocking to every rumored sighting like prospectors in a gold rush. Everyone who stopped at the store talked about what they would do with the reward money.

Isabel surveyed the congregation and wished that lightning would strike every one of them. Here they were at church on Sunday morning, like good Christians, yet as soon as the sermon ended, they'd be back out hunting Ephraim. To them, he was no more than a coon with a two-hundred-dollar hide.

Isabel had the backmost pew all to herself. As she sat there, contemplating the hypocrisy of the congregation, the door to the church opened. She looked over her shoulder and saw a piece of paper flutter through the open door. A man entered behind it, snatching the paper out of the air. He ducked his head and took a seat next to Isabel.

The stranger's clothing was practically in rags. He removed his broad-brimmed hat, revealing a head of greasy black hair, and smiled at Isabel, then turned his attention to the front. The warm scent of an unwashed body wafted over to her.

A moment later, Reverend Boggs appeared, Bible in hand, and walked to the pulpit.

The newcomer's eyes narrowed at the sight of the preacher, and he fiddled with the scrap of paper in his hand. Isabel squinted at it. It was covered in a layer of grime, but several rows of tiny, neat handwritten script showed through the dirt.

Reverend Boggs cleared his throat and opened the Bible. "Brothers and sisters," he began, "as you know, a dear member of our congregation has recently passed away."

The man next to Isabel leaned forward, his jaw clenched.

Boggs continued. "I'll save the eulogy for the funeral this afternoon. But suffice it to say that Silas Henson was a devoted servant of the Lord." He laid the Bible on the pulpit and flipped it open. "Let us turn our attention to the Book of Exodus, chapter twenty, verse thirteen. It is from this verse I will be taking my sermon today, as it is a matter that concerns this small town of ours. The sixth commandment tells us, 'Thou shalt not kill.' It literally means, 'Thou shalt not murder.' You see, while all murder is killing, not all killing is murder."

Next to Isabel, the stranger shifted. He leaned over to her and whispered, "This preacher, how long's he been here?"

Isabel leaned away from the man's rank breath. "Um, about seven years, I think."

The man nodded and sat back in his seat.

Reverend Boggs got into the swing of his sermon. "Those who kill in war are not murderers. However, those who engage in brutal crimes are." He paused and held up a finger. "May I pose this question to you? Why is murder a sin against God?" He walked out from behind the pulpit, hands clasped behind his back. "Why do we find this injunction in the Ten Commandments?" He took several paces, frowning. He stopped suddenly and turned to face the audience. "It is because murder intrudes into God's territory."

A few murmured amens came from the front row.

Boggs paused for a moment and studied the congregation, judging the effect of his pronouncement. "Murder intrudes on God's territory, brothers and sisters. God controls man's entrance into life, and he controls man's exit from life as well."

He turned and resumed his pacing. "Many of you have heard me denounce, from time to time, the practice of doctoring, the work of so-called 'granny women.' It is for this selfsame reason that I do so. Doctoring—attempting to prolong life through the works of man—intrudes into God's territory in the same way that murder does."

He turned and stared out over the audience again. Isabel thought she saw a flicker of recognition in the reverend's eyes as they passed over the stranger sitting next to her. The man shifted in his seat, quickly bowing his head and clasping his filthy hands together in mock prayer.

Boggs frowned and shook his head. He appeared to have lost his place. He glanced back at the Bible before resuming. "Brothers and sisters, if there are any of you here today with a murderous spirit in your hearts, I am calling you to repent and forsake your evil ways here and now!"

Someone in the congregation called, "Amen!"

Boggs nodded. "Now, on to the subject of those who have committed this heinous crime. Murder demands justice!"

Isabel heard Peyton say, "Amen."

"When a man commits murder, it is the duty of the law to make every effort to catch and punish the guilty. There is a price for murder—and that price is death!"

A flurry of amens erupted from the pews containing Peyton and his kin.

The stranger leaned toward Isabel again. "He's talkin' 'bout that boy, ain't he?"

"What?"

"The boy, the one who shot that feller the other night."

Isabel nodded. Did the whole world know what Ephraim had done?

"What's his name? The boy's?"

"Ho! In the back there," Boggs said.

Isabel jumped. All the heads in the congregation turned to face her. She folded her hands in her lap and looked away from the stranger.

"Is there something the folks on the backmost pew would like to add to my sermon?" Boggs asked, his eyebrows raised.

The stranger ducked his head, donned his hat, and pulled the brim over his face.

"I don't believe I've met you before, sir," said the reverend.

"What is your name, and what brings you to the church at Sixmile Creek this Sunday morn?"

Without a word, the stranger rose and walked quickly to the door. He opened it, stepped outside, and disappeared.

The buzz of a few whispered conversations arose, but Boggs cleared his throat, and the congregation quieted as everyone turned back to focus on the pulpit.

The reverend picked up the Bible and sauntered in front of the pulpit. "Romans thirteen, verse four," he read. "But if thou do that which is evil, be afraid."

THE SINKHOLE

E phraim felt stir crazy. Five days had passed since Boggs had freed him from the jail, and apart from cautious trips to the privy, he hadn't left the preacher's home at all. After the church service on Sunday, Boggs had tried to talk with Ephraim about leaving Sixmile Creek, but Ephraim wouldn't hear of it. He couldn't leave Ma to fend for herself.

For most of the past few days, the reverend had been out helping with manhunts—to avoid drawing any suspicion to himself. Today, however, the reverend stayed home, sitting at the desk next to his bed. He had several volumes open, and he scratched notes in his book of sermons. Ephraim sat near the hearth and watched quietly.

A knock sounded at the door.

Boggs rose quickly from his chair. He reached into his coat and pulled out his tomahawk. "Hide in the cellar," he whispered.

Ephraim lifted the hatch in the floor, climbed inside, and pulled the hatch shut. But he stayed at the top of the ladder, where he could hear what went on above.

There was the sound of the front door opening, and then a

voice said, "Reverend Boggs, you'd better come quick! Lucretia Cutler has poisoned herself! She's dyin'!"

Coldness struck Ephraim at the core. *No.* He backed down the ladder, putting distance between himself and the grim news. His mouth felt dry.

But... but I shot Silas! Ma said if I killed him, she wouldn't drink the foxglove.

"I'm coming," came Boggs's voice from above. "You run along and tell her I'm on my way."

As soon as the front door shut, Ephraim emerged from the cellar. "I'm comin' too."

Boggs slid into his coat and grabbed his hat from the peg by the door. "I wish you could, Ephraim, but under the circumstances it wouldn't be wise. Let me go and see how she is. I'll come back as soon as I can. We'll find a way for you to see her if things are as dire as Lucy says. But until then, please stay here."

Without waiting to hear the boy's protest, Reverend Boggs stepped out into the yard and shut the door behind him.

Time trickled by. Ephraim sat the table, his head in his hands. Boggs's words about Jonah's bargain surfaced. *Maybe I can bargain for Ma's life.*

He tapped a curled knuckle against his lips. Unable to sit any longer, he rose from his chair and paced the floor.

"Lord," he said, "please take me and spare Ma. She's crazy, and she don't know what she's done. I killed Silas, and I knowed better. Take me and let her live." Ephraim looked at the ceiling, wondering if his prayer had been heard. He couldn't bring himself to speak anymore, so he continued his pleading in silence. *God, please save Ma. I'll do anythin'!*

As he passed the reverend's desk, a book caught his eye: a handsome volume bound in leather the color of black cherry juice. Brass fittings protected its corners, and the cover was adorned with gold leaf in the shapes of stars and a crescent moon. Despite the turmoil of his thoughts, Ephraim felt an inexplicable curiosity.

He opened the cover.

The first page was torn; its right half was missing. Ephraim read the handwritten words that remained:

T HE R ECORD *of Abe*
For the year of Christian Account
Containing a calendar of every season

A SINGLE DRY leaf slid out from between the pages. Ephraim picked it up. It reminded him of the dried herbs Barefoot Nancy carried in her wagon.

Barefoot Nancy.

Ephraim looked up from the book. If anyone could save Ma, the old granny woman could.

I've got to find her.

He placed the leaf back in the book and closed the cover.

"HOW'S MA?" Ephraim asked before the preacher had even finished shutting the door.

Boggs hung his hat on the peg before answering. "She's weak, Ephraim. Only the Lord knows if she will survive this."

"I think Barefoot Nancy could help. I need to find her."

The reverend pulled out a chair and sat down at the table across from Ephraim. "Ephraim, you know what I'm going to say about that."

"You don't like Nancy, I know. But if anyone can draw the poison out of Ma, it's her."

Boggs leaned across the table and fixed Ephraim with a firm

look. "Your ma has tried to take her own life. This is a matter for the Lord, and the Lord alone, to sort out."

Ephraim's chest felt hot. "You told me that for every problem in life there's a way to work around it."

The reverend gave him a sharp look. "There's a difference between working out your own salvation and appealing to the witchery of a godless crone."

"That's easy for you to say—it's not your ma that's dyin'!" Ephraim snapped, slamming his fist on the table. He stood. "I'm goin' to find Nancy."

"Ephraim. I forbid it." The reverend's tone was icy.

"You can't do that."

"Indeed I can. You are a guest, a refugee in my home. I demand that you keep my rules. Barefoot Nancy is a sorceress, a witch. She meddles in matters of eternal consequence, things that should be left to God. You cannot go. She is not your ally. I am."

Ephraim slumped in his chair.

"Besides," Boggs said, folding his arms, "in addition to the whole town hunting for you, I saw the stranger you mentioned the other day."

Ephraim looked up. "The one that asked about you?"

"I believe so. He came into the church today." Boggs's expression grew grave. "I don't have a good feeling about him, Ephraim. And if there's one thing I've learned as a preacher, it's to trust my intuition."

"What do you mean?"

"There's something demonic about that man."

"Demonic? You mean like the Devil?"

Boggs stood. "We should be careful speaking of such things. Evil hears its name called. I'll say this, and no more: it could be that your crime has drawn forces far more sinister than a lynching party to Sixmile Creek."

AFTER A SUPPER EATEN IN SILENCE, Boggs lit a lamp and lay on his bed reading the Bible, while Ephraim lay on a blanket near the hearth, staring into the flames.

Ephraim felt grateful to the reverend for freeing him from the jail. And Boggs was right about the foolishness of leaving the safety of this house: if anyone caught him, he would die. But somehow, this didn't matter that much. Ephraim still hadn't gotten past the idea that death might be exactly what he deserved. And now, with Ma's life hanging in the balance, he felt he had no other choice. Ma was crazy, she was bitter, she had pushed him to do a horrible thing... but she was still his mother. Pa had left him to take care of her, and that duty mattered more to Ephraim than anything else.

Boggs closed his Bible and knelt by his bed, hands clasped in prayer. After a few minutes, the reverend stood and looked at Ephraim.

"Are you going to sleep soon?"

"After a bit. I can let myself into the cellar when I'm ready."

The reverend nodded, blew out the lamp near his bedside, and lay down. Before long his breathing slowed and the tuneless whistle of his snores sawed through the air.

Ephraim waited, counting the preacher's breaths. He eyed the door. If he didn't try to save Ma, he'd have the weight of *two* deaths burdening him for the rest of his days. Whether he got caught or not didn't matter. And as for the strange man, he didn't share the reverend's worry. The stranger had smelled worse than a rotting catfish, but he hadn't seemed devilish.

Slowly, Ephraim made his way across the room on all fours, gently sliding his hands and knees over the floorboards, trying to spread his weight to prevent the wood from creaking.

The reverend continued to breathe evenly.

But then Ephraim's knee hit a loose board, and it squeaked

louder than an ungreased hinge. The reverend snorted and turned in his bed. Ephraim froze, hardly daring to breathe. The reverend tossed again, then resumed his slumber.

Gingerly, Ephraim removed his knee from the offending board and made his way to the door. He slipped on his boots, grabbed his hat, and opened the door just wide enough to squeeze through. Then he quietly pulled it shut behind him.

EPHRAIM TOOK a route through the woods that paralleled Sixmile Creek. Folks said that Nancy lived somewhere on the other side of Flint Ridge, near where the road and creek diverged.

As he came to a tree-fringed bluff that flanked a bend in the road, he heard voices. He quickly dropped into a crouch and crept toward the edge of the bluff.

About a dozen men were gathered around a fire, cleaning rifles and loading pistols. Ephraim could hear the snort of horses tied to trees. Several coon dogs lay by the fire, warming themselves.

"How long you boys figure it'll take afore some of them Yanks from Durant County start tryin' to horn in on our reward?" said a man wearing overalls.

Ernest Williams spat in the fire. "Not long. I figure they heard 'bout it afore we did. The Hensons is from there, you know. But I tell you what, we're goin' to catch that boy and get that bounty, in spite of any meddlin' Durant County Yanks or all the devils in hell."

The men around the fire murmured their approval.

A whistle echoed from around the bend. "Somebody's a-comin'!" a lookout called.

Ernest got to his feet.

The Fletcher brothers and Frank Moats came into view, tow sacks slung over their shoulders and rifles under their arms.

Clabe smiled and waved. "Relax, boys. It's just us!" He walked to the fire and lowered his tow sack to the ground. "I heard you fellers down here, and I says to Jake and Frank, now them boys must be powerful thirsty."

Ernest Williams laughed. "You never miss a chance to sell a few jugs, do you, Clabe?"

"Well, they ain't goin' to sell themselves."

The men settled back by the fire, and Ephraim heard the clink of silver dollars changing hands. The Fletcher boys and Frank unloaded their sacks, tossing clay jugs to men around the ring.

Ernest unstoppered a jug, hooked his thumb in the thumb-hole, and hefted it into the crook of his arm, the cork still dangling from its string. "You boys sure make the best whiskey I ever had," he said, tilting the jug up and taking a swallow. He rested the jug on his knee. "What's your secret?"

Clabe grinned. "I can't go tellin' folks. It'd spoil our business."

Ernest laughed, took another drink, and passed the jug to the man in overalls.

As Ephraim shifted on his perch at the edge of the bluff, a pebble dislodged beneath his boot and tumbled down the slope. It disturbed the dry leaves as it rolled, creating a faint rustle. He gritted his teeth, hoping no one would hear the sound.

Only Clabe Fletcher looked in the direction of the pebble. His gaze traveled up the slope, coming to rest on Ephraim's hiding place. Ephraim held stock still, not daring to breathe. He doubted Clabe could see him in the darkness, but he wasn't taking chances.

Clabe took a few steps toward the edge of the road, then abruptly looked down and cursed. "Whose dog left this mess over here?" he said, wiping his boot on the ground.

Several men by the fire laughed.

Clabe returned to the circle, joining the small talk.

Ephraim breathed a sigh of relief and retreated from the edge of the bluff a little.

The jugs made their way around the fire. Neither of the Fletcher boys drank, but Frank Moats took long pulls of some whiskey he'd kept for himself. Ernest tipped a jug high in the air, draining the last few drops, then let it fall, smacking his lips. "You boys got any more of this?"

Clabe stood. "I'm afraid that's all. We got another batch about ready though. Speaking of which, we'd better get to it." He slapped Jake and Frank on their backs. "In fact, let's take the short way back to the still." They gathered the empty jugs into their sacks, bid the bounty hunters goodnight, and slipped into the forest.

Ernest stood up and clapped his hands together. "Boys, what do you say we take these dogs out and see if we can't scare us up a murderer?"

The man in overalls belched and stretched his arms. "I'll come with you," he said through a yawn.

Ernest laughed. "You sure about that, Toby? He'll be hard to see if your eyes keep fallin' shut."

The men rose to their feet amid snorts of laughter.

Ernest roused the dogs. The hounds didn't need much encouragement, leaping to their feet with barks of excitement, tails wagging. Ephraim shook his head. These dogs weren't used to tracking people; they'd probably pick up the scent of a coon and lead the men on a wild-goose chase. Still, it was time for Ephraim to be moving on.

He stood and looked toward Flint Ridge.

Strong arms encircled him from behind, pinning his arms to his sides. His captor pivoted, pulling Ephraim with him and knocking Ephraim's hat to the ground.

Then Clabe Fletcher stepped into view, holding his empty tow sack, which he slipped over Ephraim's head.

Ephraim left out a muffled yell and twisted his body. He freed his right arm and swung blindly, connecting with what felt like Clabe's face. Clabe swore.

"Shhh!" someone hissed in Ephraim's ear. Judging by the stench of corn whiskey, it was Frank.

"What's goin' on up there?" Ernest called from the road.

Clabe cursed again. "It's just us, Ernest. I lost my footin' in the dark and fell." He clamped his hand over Ephraim's mouth, pressing the rough burlap against his lips. "Listen, Cutler," he whispered. "You got two choices: make a ruckus and wind up with Ernest, or keep quiet and come with us."

Pain shot up Ephraim's arm. When he tried to move his right thumb, he winced. It felt like he'd broken it when he hit Clabe. But he stayed silent, hoping to buy time.

"Jake, make sure he stays quiet while I tie him up," Clabe said.

"He ain't goin' to bite me, is he?" Jake asked.

"Shut up and get your hand over his mouth."

Jake obeyed, and Ephraim felt a rope being wound around his wrists and ankles. The knots were pulled tight, and the excess rope cut off with a knife.

"Well, looky there, we got enough rope left to do this," Clabe said. He wrapped the remainder of the rope around Ephraim's neck, cinching it snug. "That ought to keep your hood on. Come on boys, let's go."

Ephraim was picked up and slung across someone's shoulders—Frank, he decided. His arms and legs were held together like a gutted deer. "Lead the way," Frank said to Clabe, and they set off into the woods.

FRANK CARRIED Ephraim for what seemed like an hour. But finally, Ephraim was set down and the sack was pulled off his head.

They were in a hollow, Ephraim guessed somewhere on the

side of Flint Ridge, sitting by the remains of a campfire and a contraption made of a stone furnace, stove pipes, copper tubing, and two barrels—the Fletchers' still. A mountain spring burbled somewhere nearby.

"Make yourself at home, Ephraim," Jake Fletcher said.

Frank walked over to the still's mash tub and scooped out a gourd dipperful. His Adam's apple pumped up and down as he drained the slop. He dipped a second time, looking at Ephraim, then smiled, revealing black gaps between rotten teeth. "You want a drank?"

Ephraim cradled his injured hand in his lap and shook his head. He felt sick as he watched Frank guzzle the second dipper of sour mash.

"Don't you go drinkin' all the mash before we turn it into whiskey," Clabe said. To Ephraim he added, "Frank likes drinkin' it more'n he likes makin' it."

Frank waved Clabe away as he drained yet another dipper. "It's my corn in the mash. I'll drink it when I want to."

Clabe shook his head and sat down in front of a stump. He threw a few billets of wood onto the embers and teased them with a stick until flames began to lick to life. "Lot of folks lookin' for you," he said.

"Yeah," Ephraim said. *Why are they being nice to me all of a sudden?*

Clabe looked up from the fire and grinned, pointing to a purpling bruise on his forehead. "You got me pretty good."

Ephraim looked at his throbbing thumb. The last knuckle was turned up, like a nail with its head hammered over. He tried to move it and grimaced.

Jake settled down across the fire from his brother. "I still cain't believe you gunned down Silas Henson. Boy, you got some balls! If I remember right, it was his little brother that stole your girl at the dance, though. You get 'em mixed up when you pulled the trigger?"

Ephraim shook his head and looked away.

Jake laughed. "Not that it matters much. A Yank's a Yank."

Clabe threw another log on the fire. "We didn't know you had it in you. Guess a man's backbone don't print through his clothes."

So that was it—they thought he hated Yankees like they did. Maybe this meant they would let him go.

Ephraim held up his hands. "How 'bout I tell you fellers the story? Care to untie me first?" He felt sick, offering to talk about killing Silas like it was some coon-hunting story, but he had to get out of here and find Nancy.

Clabe clasped his hands behind his neck and leaned back against the stump. "Well now, I'd really like to hear that, Ephraim, but me and Jake are in a bit of a bind. See, we got to raise a bundle of cash. We're fixin' to get ourselves out of these mountains and down to Louisville."

Ephraim's heart sank. They wanted the reward.

"We got a cousin down there, works on a barge they take up and down the Ohio," Jake chimed in from across the fire. "He told us we could make a fortune runnin' a saloon for the roustabouts and river men that come through there." He leaned back on both hands and puffed out his chest. "And Rindy Sue said she'd marry me if I take her with me. She wants to live in a big city, she ain't picky 'bout which one—said Louisville would suit her just fine."

Clabe's face broke into a grin. "That what you and her was gigglin' about at the stir-off?"

"Sure was."

"You gonna marry her then?"

"'Course I will. Don't you think she'll make me a fine wife?"

Clabe took a black twist of chaw out of his pocket and gripped one end between his teeth. He pulled out a knife and sawed it off at his lips, then put the remainder back in his pocket. He chewed methodically, considering the question, then said through amber teeth, "I don't care what you do with her, long as she sings in my saloon."

At the mash tub, Frank erupted into snorts of laughter while sucking down another dipper of mash. He coughed, "Clabe sure knows what to do with a woman!"

Clabe grunted, reached over with his knife, and cut through the ropes that bound Ephraim's ankles. He stood, put his hand in the small of his back, and stretched. Then he pointed his rifle to a place outside the light of the fire. "Come on, Cutler. I got somethin' to show you. You'll like this."

I doubt it, Ephraim thought, getting to his feet.

Jake rose and followed them.

A few yards outside the firelight, they came to a sinkhole. The jagged mouth of the pit was darker than the night around it. Clabe pointed down with the barrel of his rifle. "Back in '65, Jake and me was up here buildin' our first still. This Yankee kid came a-runnin' through the woods. He'd deserted his regiment and was tryin' to make it back to Ohio."

Jake interrupted his brother in a mock-weeping voice, "Said he didn't want to fight in the war no more."

Clabe laughed. "I shot him, and we threw him down there in the sink. Couple days later, we come up here, and a hog was down there with him. I think it was one of Franz Akers's shoats. It'd climbed down there with that blue-belly, and was eatin' his head, just like it was a turnip."

The Fletcher boys both burst into laughter.

"I looks at Jake, and I says, well, that proves that only a hog can stomach a Yankee." Clabe wiped tears from his eyes, shoulders shaking with mirth.

Ephraim felt ill. Was he like them? What made one murderer different from another?

Forcing a smile, he looked at the Fletchers. "That's some story you got there. Listen, my ma is powerful sick, and I really need to find Barefoot Nancy. I know you boys want that reward, but I'd sure appreciate your help." He gulped. "Seein' how we got so much in common and all."

The Fletchers grew quiet, the smiles fading from their faces. "Killin' Yanks and lookin' after your mammy," Clabe said. "I got to respect a man like that." He scratched his nose. "Tell you what, Ephraim. I like you so much I'm goin' to give you a choice: you can climb down in that hole and stay there, nice and quiet, while we finish this run of liquor... or I can put you down there myself."

Ephraim threw himself forward, crashing into Clabe. He swung his hands together, landing a blow across Clabe's crooked nose, then rolled to his feet and ran for the cover of darkness. A shot rang out, spraying dirt inches in front of Ephraim's feet. He stumbled to a halt.

"You're still worth a hundred dollars dead, Cutler," Jake Fletcher said. "Don't matter what condition you're in when we take you in, we're goin' to make a profit."

Clabe sat up and wiped a trail of blood from beneath his nose. "That's twice you've hit me tonight," he said, getting to his feet. He strode over to Ephraim, his rifle held at belt level. "The first time I reckoned it was because we scared you, so no harm done. But that last one was just plain meanness. So now it's my turn." He jammed his rifle into Ephraim's ribs and backed him toward the sinkhole.

"Listen, Clabe, I'm sorry, my ma—" Ephraim stammered, stopping as his heels reached the edge.

"I know. I know," Clabe said. He flipped his rifle around and slammed its butt into Ephraim's stomach.

Ephraim gasped and doubled over.

"You're just tryin' to save your ma," Clabe said. He planted the sole of his boot on Ephraim's crown and shoved him into the pit.

Ephraim landed on his back with a thud. The breath was knocked from his lungs.

Clabe leaned over the edge of the hole and spat a giant glob of tobacco juice. It splattered next to Ephraim. "This ain't nothin' personal," he said. "We're just tryin' to make some money. Two hundred dollars is two hundred dollars."

~

EPHRAIM'S STOMACH and back ached, and his hand throbbed. He got to his feet, ankle deep in dry leaves. The remains of a dead possum lay a few feet away, bones jutting from its rotten hide. The sweet smell of ferment drifted down from above.

He walked the circumference of the sink, inspecting the walls. The pit was easily fifteen feet deep, and its sides were steep. A gnarled tree root bulged out of the side farthest from the still.

Ephraim considered. He could maybe use that root to get out if the opportunity presented itself. And he had to try. He needed to find Nancy and make it back to Ma in time. *All I need is for them to get drunk and sleep, or somethin'.*

He heard the murmur of conversation.

"Looks 'bout ready to put the cap on," Clabe said.

A clang sounded, copper on copper.

"Frank! Get out of that slop! You drink any more of that, and you won't make it out of this holler, I guarantee it! You'll be piled up in them weeds over yonder!"

Frank swore.

"Go on now, put the paste around the cap," Clabe said. "We ain't got all night."

Ephraim sat down on the floor of the sinkhole and tried to free his wrists from the rope. It was no use; the knots were too tight. He felt around in the leaves for something to cut the rope with. When his hands settled on something hard, he lifted it from the leaves and studied it in the gloom.

With a cry, he dropped the object. It was a human jawbone, with several teeth still jutting from it.

The Fletchers' story about the Yankee deserter must be true.

Ephraim crawled back away from it and rested his back against the side of the hole, breathing deeply as his heart raced.

~

AS THE NIGHT TRICKLED ON, the sounds of the men's voices grew more infrequent. A few hours before dawn, the conversation by the still lapsed into silence. This was the chance Ephraim had been waiting for.

He moved to where the jawbone lay, sat down, and positioned it between his feet. Pulling the rope that bound his wrists as tight as he could, Ephraim worked it back and forth over the jagged teeth. The rope loosened after a few minutes of sawing. Ephraim stood up, massaging his wrists.

He picked up a loose stone and tossed it out of the hole, then listened as it landed with a dry rustle outside. He waited. There was no sound from the still; no reaction from the Fletchers or Frank.

He moved quietly to the wall farthest from the still, stood on tiptoe, and stretched the fingers of his uninjured hand around the root. He pulled down on it, testing it with his weight. The root shifted a little, showering clods of dirt onto the sinkhole floor, but it held.

Ephraim let go and fetched debris out of his collar. He'd need both hands to pull himself up. Grimacing, he gripped the root with his injured hand, trying to keep his thumb from brushing anything. He pulled himself upward, cheek against the cold soil of the wall, feeling with his good hand until he found another root. He got the toe of his boot onto the first root and stretched, sliding his arms up until his fingers gripped the rim of the hole. He grunted softly and heaved himself upward, arms aquiver. When his chest met the edge of the hole, he began to wriggle forward.

He found himself nose-to-toe with a boot. It smelled strongly of dog droppings.

"I thought I told you to stay put."

Ephraim looked up. Clabe shifted his quid of tobacco around into a brown-toothed sneer. He was holding his rifle with the stock facing Ephraim. Behind him, by the still, Jake and Frank were sleeping.

Clabe gripped the barrel of his rifle in both hands and raised it. "Let's make sure you stay down there this time."

He drove the rifle butt downward with a quick, powerful thrust. The stock connected with Ephraim's skull, and the world exploded in a whirl of lights. Ephraim slid backward into the pit, hitting the bottom like a loose sack of cornmeal, and everything went black.

14

BURNING SCENT

S ampson awoke to the muffled sounds of a spade slicing through the soil above him. Thoughts of Wes, the cabin porch, and cornbread and gravy flashed through his mind in a jumble. He raised his head—and banged it on the roof. His current situation returned to him. He was in prison.

The scraping of earth above him continued. Sampson felt different, though. Even in the complete darkness, he could now see the inside of his prison: rough boards nailed together into a box. His sense of smell felt sharper too. He sniffed the air and smelled a new scent. No, not new—it was the scent from his dreams, a scent he had come to know under the earth. It burned in his nostrils.

The scent reached deep inside Sampson and pulled at his hollow gut. He hungered to follow it. He had to chase, to dig, to attack the source of that scent.

With a thunk, the tip of the shovel struck the wood above him. Sampson raised his ears and listened as the shovel was laid aside. Hands brushed dirt from his prison. Then, with the creak of wood and the squeak of nails, the lid of the box sprang free.

Sampson stood and shook himself from nose to tail. Clods of

soil rained down from his coat. He stared up into the night. Withered tree branches scratched at the moon.

Strength pulsed through his muscles. He flexed his limbs and stepped from the box. He caught a whiff of the burning scent again and wheeled around to face its source.

A man, his face shadowed by a hat, stood by the wooden box, studying him. It was William, the man who'd imprisoned him.

"There you are: my ace in the hole." William set down the pry-bar in his hand and picked up a whip lying curled at his feet. "Your services are needed."

Sampson bared his teeth, snarled. The scent was coming from William, from his hip. There was a bulge there, in William's pocket. Flattening his ears, Sampson began to circle, looking for a place to dart in and attack.

William laughed. "You didn't waste time picking up the trail. That's good. But we can't have you attacking me over it."

He stepped forward suddenly, uncoiled the whip, and swung it through the air in one smooth motion.

Sampson saw the black metal barbs at the ends of the whip's three tails as they sailed over his head. They landed on his back. He yelped in pain as the barbs sank through his fur.

The whip recoiled, then cracked again, and again.

Sampson howled in agony, cowering in the dirt.

"There," William said briskly. "Every hellhound needs taming at first." He walked over to Sampson and looped a cord around his neck.

The burning scent was overpowering at this range. It was all Sampson could do to resist snapping at William's hand. But he didn't want to be whipped again.

"Come." William tugged the cord. "You'll sink your teeth into flesh soon enough."

Obediently, Sampson rose and followed his master.

They walked from the graveyard to the surrounding woods.

William crouched, reached into his pocket, and held something up to Sampson's snout.

The object reeked with fiery vapors, like the fear of a rabbit being chased by a pack of hounds, only deeper, more pungent. Sampson could make out something else too: the scent of metal and wood. A gun. His tongue flicked out and tasted the pistol. Immediately, a ghostly image filled his mind: a boy on horseback, gun in hand. Sampson could smell the boy, the horse, the fear in the air. The horse reared, the gun fired, and the boy tumbled to the ground.

The burning scent blossomed again in his nostrils, mingling with the boy's fear.

"You see him, don't you?" William said. "Find his trail and follow it. Catch him, and bring him to me. Understand?"

Sampson growled.

"Now go," William said, releasing the cord.

15

THE HURRICANE TIMBER

Ephraim awoke with his skull throbbing. He moaned and swallowed. Lifting his bound hands to his head, he gingerly explored the firm lump on his temple where Clabe had hit him.

He sat up slowly, his broken thumb throbbing in time with his head. The pit tilted crazily around him. He closed his eyes and leaned against the side of the hole. Cold clumps of loose soil rained down in his hair. He didn't bother to shake them out.

After a few minutes, the dizziness subsided, and he opened his eyes. He breathed deep, willing himself to master the pain, and stood.

Waning light illuminated the upper half of the hole. *I must've been out most of the day.* His stomach knotted as he thought of Ma. He looked at the sky. *Please, just give me a chance to find Nancy.*

Outside the hole, someone retched.

"I done told you, Frank!" Clabe said. "That mash soured your gut. Now look at you!"

Frank moaned. "I feel sick enough to die."

"Don't think you're gettin' out of helpin' us haul this liquor,"

Clabe said. "I don't care if it takes you all night to tote your load to town."

Frank muttered something unintelligible.

"Say that again, Frank! Go on now, look me square in the eyes and say it again! I swear I'm goin' to whip you till you piss, then whip you for pissin'!"

Sounds like Frank's not much better off than I am, Ephraim thought wryly.

Clabe and Jake appeared at the edge of the sinkhole. Clabe was still clenching his jaw in anger at Frank.

"Well, look who's awake," Clabe said. "That'll make this easier." He trained his rifle on Ephraim while Jake tossed down the end of a rope.

"Grab hold, Cutler," Jake said. "Don't try nothin' funny now."

Ephraim took hold of the rope, favoring his good hand.

Jake walked off with the other end of the rope—probably tying it around a tree. When he returned, he simply nodded. Ephraim tugged at the rope and felt it hold. Gritting his teeth, he climbed out.

The Fletcher brothers had packed the jugs of corn whiskey in their tow sacks. Jake shouldered one, and Frank struggled to do the same. Clabe lifted the third sack and slung it over Ephraim's back. "Better that you're weighted down, not me."

"Ain't nothin' goes together like liquor and a hangin'," Jake said as they set off. "We'll be doing double business tonight!"

The sun sank low as they headed down the slope of Flint Ridge. Fog preceded the darkness, swirling through the trees in thick billows as the temperature dropped. Ephraim struggled to find his footing through the white carpet.

Frank was faring even worse. Still moaning about his aching skull and cramped guts, he stumbled over every rock and branch in his path. He fell several times, and at one point managed to break one of the jugs of whiskey in his sack. That won him a curse from Jake and a kick in the seat from Clabe.

An hour of walking brought them to the Hurricane Timber near the base of the mountain. Years before the settlement of Sixmile Creek, a storm had ripped its way through the mountains, blazing a scar across the flank of Flint Ridge. It had felled many trees, leaving their roots balls twisted together in massive snarls. Others were broken and jagged, jutting from the ground like giant splinters. The party slowed its pace.

A sharp breeze cut across the slope, roiling the mist and chilling Ephraim. Inhaling, he caught a cool tang in the wind. He looked at the sky; a mass of dark clouds teetered on top of the mountain, obscuring the moon. A storm was coming.

He studied the ridge; Barefoot Nancy lived just on the other side. Did it even matter now? It had already been three days since Ma had taken the poison. For all he knew, she might be dead already. And if not, how much time did she have left?

Ephraim had to find a way to escape.

A cold drop of rain hit his cheek. Clabe must've felt one too because he cursed.

"There's a big oak yonder," Jake said. "Let's hunker down under it and wait this out."

Ephraim could see the tree ahead of them, spreading its thick limbs in a shadowy promise of shelter. It stood in the middle of the clear-cut, the lone survivor of the long-ago storm. They ran to it. Frank brought up the rear, stumbling and moaning.

On the lee side of the oak, Clabe dropped to his knees and began gathering twigs. He assembled them into a small tepee. Jake produced a flint and tinder, which he handed to his brother.

The wind picked up, and the dark clouds edged forward. The storm came tumbling down the mountainside, spitting rain.

Clabe shivered and struck the flint, spraying sparks. They dove into the curled strands of tinder and smoked promisingly. Clabe cupped his hands around the tinder and blew gently. When the wood sent up fingers of flame, Clabe snapped a bundle of twigs into pieces and piled them around the smoldering tinder. They all drew near, anticipating the heat.

A howl cut through the night.

At first, it was indistinguishable from the rising wind, but gradually it rose in pitch and volume until Ephraim could tell the two apart.

Ephraim stood and peered into the darkness. What had made that howl? A coonhound? Who'd be hunting on a night like this?

Lightning flashed, revealing a figure standing on a rocky outcrop above them. Ephraim saw him for only an instant, but he harbored no doubt about who it was. It was the stranger from the other night.

He glanced at the other men, who were huddled around the guttering fire, protecting it from the wind. Tickles of fear scuttled up his body like granddaddy longlegs.

The stranger had been standing in the woods the night Ephraim had shot Silas. It was his boot that had broken the branch that spooked Molly—Ephraim felt sure of it. There was something sinister about that man.

"Hey, Cutler," Clabe said. "Sit down here where we can see you. You try to run off and I'll—"

The howl echoed across the slope again. It sounded closer this time—a lot closer. And it wasn't no hound. Ephraim was sure of that. It lacked the excited quality of a coondog on a trail. This was a hollow wail, a funeral dirge.

Lightning flickered across the sky again. The stranger had vanished from the outcrop.

Jake and Clabe were standing now too.

Frank looked up from the fire. "What're y'all doin'?"

"Shhh." Clabe held a finger to his lips. He looked at Jake, and they both raised their rifles.

"Cutler, you're a good shot, ain't you?" Clabe asked.

Ephraim nodded.

Clabe fished out his knife and cut the rope binding Ephraim's wrists. "Frank, pass your rifle to him," he said. "You'll do no good with it as you are."

"You gonna give him my gun? That's stupid," Frank said.

"Shut up and hand it over or I'll knock the rest of your teeth out!" Clabe snapped, peering out into the gloom.

Frank shoved the rifle across the ground.

Ephraim picked it up, looked at it, and snorted. The barrel was plugged with mud. Frank must've stuck it in the ground when he tripped. Ephraim picked up a stick and rammed it into the clogged barrel.

A few minutes passed without incident. Finally, Clabe shrugged and lowered his gun. "Somebody's dog probably got loose."

Frank belched loudly from the fire. Ephraim looked over and saw the man taking a long swig from a jug of whiskey.

"What are you doin', fool?" Clabe strode over and knocked the jug from Frank's hand with the butt of his rifle. The remaining liquor spilled into the fire, causing it to flare higher.

Jake swore.

"I had to drink somethin' for this headache," Frank said. He stared glumly at the jug among the ashes. "You can take that one out of my share of the sale."

"That one, *and* the one you broke earlier," Clabe said. "It was drinkin' what caused your headache in the first place! It's a fool notion to think it'll fix it!"

Frank shrugged.

Ephraim felt amused in spite of his throbbing skull and hand. But as he looked out across the Hurricane Timber, his heart slammed into his ribs. A hulking shadow crouched on a log just yards from the oak.

Without pausing to alert the others, Ephraim raised the rifle to his cheek, his broken thumb jutting off the side like a bizarre sighting mechanism, and squeezed off a round. The rifle barked in his hands. On the log, the shadow tightened and sprang forward, emitting a short howl that decayed into a rattling snarl.

Clabe and Jake snapped off shots at the beast as it drew close. The creature kept coming, making straight for Ephraim, gaining speed. Ephraim glimpsed luminous red eyes and slavering jaws.

Ephraim's fear of the beast vanished with a sudden realization. *This is my chance to escape.*

Dropping the rifle, he launched himself into the air a split second before the beast reached him. He caught a low-hanging bough, crying out as he jarred his broken thumb, swung forward, and propelled himself in an arc that took him over the creature's back. He landed behind it in a crouch, right hand clutched to his belly, left hand on the ground for stability. Bits of rock cut into his palm. Without pausing, he raced out into the darkness, darting through the wasteland of fallen timber. Behind him, he heard shouts. At least two of the others were running, too.

He leaped onto a tall boulder, scrabbled his way to the top, then looked behind him. The moon shone through a gap in the clouds, revealing Frank, standing with his back to the tree trunk, sweeping a branch back and forth in front of the dark beast. Clabe and Jake were nowhere to be seen.

"I ain't got my gun! Somebody help!" Frank bellowed like a lost calf.

The beast growled and flung itself onto Frank, knocking the branch from his hand. It planted its paws on Frank's chest, pinning him against the oak, then took the tender part of his neck in its jaws, and shook savagely.

Frank let loose a gurgling scream.

The creature dragged him to the ground, thrashing its head back and forth. Frank's body whipped from side to side like a windblown rag. The beast twisted and released Frank, sending his lifeless form tumbling. It landed with a whump and lay still.

A violent shudder chattered down Ephraim's spine.

The beast turned toward the boulder where Ephraim stood,

its eyes glowing in the night. It lowered its muzzle to the ground and huffed about.

Ephraim had seen coyotes and the occasional wolf, but this wasn't either. The canine had tattered, hanging ears and mournful jowls. Ribs and the craggy knobs of its spine jutted from its patchy hide like poles beneath a sagging tent. It was a bear hound on the wrong side of death's door. But unlike any hound Ephraim had ever seen, this beast had oversized red eyes. Black drool strung from its jaws, almost touching the ground. And despite its ragged appearance, the hound moved with the confidence of a master predator.

It's a huntin' dog, Ephraim thought. *It's lookin' for a trail.* Blood thundered in his head.

A scuffling came from below him, and he looked down.

Clabe was perched on top of a fallen tree, standing just above the fog. He took aim with his rifle as the creature bounded toward him. The dog-thing bunched up its rear legs and sprang, flying toward Clabe at chest level. Clabe waited until its bulk almost touched the end of his rifle barrel before squeezing the trigger. The gun discharged with a clapping report.

The creature collided with Clabe in a fury of snapping jaws. They tumbled backward off the log, disappearing beneath the carpet of white. The rifle pinwheeled into the darkness.

Clabe yelled and emerged from the fog, running for his life. To Ephraim's surprise, the hound emerged from the fog as well, loping after him.

How did it survive the bullet at that range? Nothing about this creature was natural.

The hound stopped suddenly, raised its nose, and tasted the air. It turned slowly... and sighted Ephraim.

Ephraim wanted to yell, but terror had sewn his lips shut.

The hound bared its fangs and started toward Ephraim.

Ephraim stepped backward.

The hound's body tensed to spring.

Ephraim threw himself off the boulder and ran upslope. He heard the beast gaining on him and risked a glance back over his shoulder. The Hurricane Timber was tough going, but the hound was bounding through it like it was born and bred for this terrain.

A jagged stump rose out of the darkness in front of Ephraim. He dodged it—and nearly fell down a steep slope on the other side. He had come to the edge of the clear-cut, to the mountain stream. He sprinted down the slope into its shallow waters.

Half stumbling, half crawling through the smooth stones of the creek bed, he made for the far bank. He heard the panting of the hound behind him. He pulled himself out of the water. The slope on the other side of the stream was too steep to climb. He had no choice but to run alongside the stream, following the trench it had cut through the earth.

The hound did not cross the stream, but it kept pace with him on the opposite bank. Was it unwilling to cross the water?

Suddenly it gave a low growl and darted ahead, disappearing around a bend.

Ephraim slowed to a walk. When he reached the bend, he came to a stop, searching for any movement in the darkness on the far bank. The creature was nowhere in sight.

A wind-felled tree bridged the stream up ahead. Ephraim froze. Had the beast come across?

He bent down and picked a rock out of the streambed with his left hand. The wet stone chilled his fingers.

Leaves rustled behind him. Ephraim spun around.

The hound was crouched not five yards away, teeth bared.

Ephraim hurled the rock into the beast's face. It connected with a thunk, and as the hound blinked and snarled, Ephraim threw himself into the water.

The creature hurtled forward but halted abruptly at the water's edge. It lifted one foot, raw from running over rough terrain, tested the water, and pulled back.

Despite the panic surging through him, Ephraim recognized

that, twice now, the water had saved his life. He splashed water at the dog. It recoiled from the spray.

Ephraim looked down at the rushing stream. If this creature feared water, his course of action was obvious: he needed to stay in it. But even as he thought this, he felt his feet growing numb in his sodden boots. How much farther was Barefoot Nancy's place?

He turned and sloshed his way upstream.

From the bank, the hound watched him, but to Ephraim's relief, it did not follow alongside. A few moments later, when Ephraim looked over his shoulder, the beast was gone.

THE BETTER PART of an hour passed without a sign of the beast. The rain fell thinly now, but a steady breeze still gusted down the mountain, and Ephraim shivered. His head throbbed so hard it felt like a woodpecker was hammering on the inside of his skull.

He rounded a bend in the creek and saw that it curved away from Flint Ridge. To get around to the back side of the mountain and find Nancy, he'd have to leave the safety of the water.

Ephraim halted mid-creek and listened to the dark woods. It was difficult to hear over the pounding in his head and the chattering of his teeth. He peered into the shadows between the trees, searching for any sign of those red eyes watching from the gloom.

Something crashed through the brush on the bank behind him. Ephraim spun around, a fresh wave of panic surging through his veins. A startled deer bounded into the creek several yards upstream, propelling itself into the forest on the other side. Ephraim eyed the place where the deer had first appeared. Had he spooked the deer, or had it sensed the hound nearby?

It was strange how the hound had chased him with such intensity, then disappeared. He'd seen predatory intelligence in those red eyes. As a hunter himself, Ephraim suspected the beast had changed tactics.

He thought of Boggs's warning that his crime had brought something demonic to Sixmile Creek. He should have listened to the reverend.

He rubbed his hands together; his fingers were ice cold. He'd freeze if he waited here in the water until dawn. He scanned the dark trees again, wishing he knew how far Nancy's home was from here. This creature had the nose of a bloodhound; there was no way it'd lost his trail.

If I can't run, I'll have to fight it, he thought. *It's a gamble, but it's my only chance.*

He slogged over to the bank, casting about until his gaze landed on a fallen sapling lying near the water. He fetched it and returned to the water to examine the wood. It was about seven feet long. Ephraim placed his boot about a foot from the end and stomped down, breaking the wood. He ran his thumb over the jagged place where the sapling had broken. *Sharp, but not sharp enough.* He bent over and plunged his hand into the water, feeling around on the creek bottom. A large stone met his groping fingers, and he pulled it out of the creek bed. Gripping the end of the sapling in one hand, he filed its broken end with the stone, testing it with his thumb. When he had a good point, he threw the stone away and turned toward the dark forest. Now he just had to find the right place to take his stand.

Ephraim hit the trees at a run, the makeshift spear over his shoulder. His boots squelched, water spraying from them with every step. *Too much noise.* He slowed, kicked off the boots, and resumed running in his bare feet. The forest grew thicker. He passed through a deep swath of darkness untouched by the light of the moon.

That's when he heard what he'd been expecting: the creature was behind him, its paws pounding the forest floor, panting.

Ephraim put on a burst of speed.

Up ahead, he spied a gully where rainwater washed down the mountainside into the stream. He sucked in a deep breath and sprinted for it. As he reached the lip of it, he slowed a bit, so he didn't tumble down the embankment. At the bottom, he stood in the water and aimed the tip of the spear behind him, toward the top of the slope. He spread his feet wide, bracing the spear's butt against the gully's sandy soil. His thoughts formed themselves into a wordless prayer.

God, please. Deliver me.

He held the spear firm, muscles taut with anticipation.

A second later the monster appeared at the edge of the gully. Ephraim saw the flash of its eyes, red as the setting sun, as it leaped down at him.

The creature gave a yelp as the point of the spear penetrated its belly. The shaft of the spear splintered, and the beast tumbled to the ground, its emaciated body skewered by the stake like a worm on a hook.

Ephraim retreated a few steps, still clutching a short length of broken sapling. On the ground, the creature writhed. Ephraim watched, his chest heaving, as the creature's movements slowed. Finally, it shivered and fell still.

He dropped the length of wood, wiped his forehead with a shaking hand, and turned to climb out of the gully.

Behind him, he heard a low growl.

He spun around. The beast still lay on its side, but its front leg moved, pawing at the ground. It raised its head and rolled onto its belly, pushing the end of the stake up through its back. It climbed to its feet and bared its teeth.

Panic flared in Ephraim's gut like an ember in the wind. He turned and raced blindly up the gully. At its mouth, his foot caught a tree root, and he crashed to the ground, sprawling in the wet leaves.

A second later the beast was on him. Ephraim fought against a mass of matted black fur, quivering muscle, and snapping jaws. The creature's breath was hot, and its body reeked with the scent of wet dog. Ephraim pushed his hands up under the creature's neck, holding its fangs away from his face by a hair's breadth. The hound's saliva, thick and dark, like blood gone rancid, dripped onto his face.

The canine thrashed, and the two of them rolled across the forest floor. As they came around again, the dog's snapping mouth plunged toward Ephraim. He blocked the attack with a bent right arm, but the dog's fangs sank into his flesh below his elbow. Ephraim screamed and thrust his knee hard into the beast's wounded belly. Its jaws loosened their grip, and Ephraim was somehow able to toss it aside. He sprang to his feet, clutching his arm. Black drool clung to the skin around his wound.

The hound darted in front of Ephraim, head held low.

Behind it, Ephraim caught a glimpse of light shining through the trees.

Nancy.

His body reacted to the thought, pouring its final reserves of energy into his cramping muscles. A primal yell erupted from deep within Ephraim, and he dashed past the red-eyed hound. Branches slapped his face as he plowed through the forest toward the light. To his surprise, it came from a hole in a giant tree.

Ephraim sucked air into his aching lungs. "Help!"

A door swung open in the tree trunk, and a woman appeared, holding a long-barreled gun, silhouetted against the light spilling out. "What in tarnation?"

"Nancy!" shouted Ephraim, putting on his last burst of speed.

A howl sounded behind him. The hellish animal was at his heels. He wasn't going to make it.

Nancy raised the gun and took aim. A boom echoed through the forest, and fire flashed from the barrel.

The hound kept coming.

Nancy threw the gun aside, reached into her skirts, and threw a handful of powder in the air. "Banished be all evil! I drive ye before me, foulness!" she chanted. Then she pointed at Ephraim. The cloud of powder rushed toward him, passing him. It felt like a gust of warm air, leaving a pungent aroma in its wake. Behind him, the hound let out a startled yelp.

Ephraim kept running until he reached Nancy, who was standing resolutely with her hand outstretched. He turned and saw the dog prowling back and forth behind a cloud of powder, the stake still protruding from its back.

"You stopped it," said Ephraim between great gulps of air. The forest began to tilt and spin around him.

Nancy walked toward the animal, hand still outstretched.

The dog's ears pricked. It cocked its head at the old woman, blinking its red eyes.

"Begone, dark one."

The dog tucked its tail and disappeared into the night.

A throbbing pulse filled Ephraim's head. He looked down and saw blood leaking out of the puncture wounds on his arm, mingling with the darker saliva. His mind felt fuzzy.

Nancy's fingers closed around his wounded arm. She held it up, examining the bite wound. Then her gaze fell on his thumb; she took it in her free hand. "Ready yourself," she said. Her voice sounded strange, like Ephraim's ears were full of water.

"For what?" Ephraim asked.

"For this," Nancy said.

She yanked sharply on his thumb.

Ephraim screamed. His knees gave way, and the world around him faded.

16

HUNGER

Sampson returned to the creek bank, lay down, and licked his belly. He felt no pain, but the instinct to lick his wounds was strong. He stretched his neck as far as he could and set to work removing the sharpened sapling from his body. When he'd finished with that, he stood and sniffed, following traces of the boy's scent. He came upon a leather boot. He gripped the prize in his teeth and limped back to the graveyard.

The sun was cresting the mountaintops when he returned. Drool coated the boot, making it slick in his mouth. The taste of the leather tempted his empty belly.

William waited by the unearthed grave—Sampson's old prison.

A whiff of the burning scent wafted out of the hole. Sampson turned his nose away from it and laid the boot at William's feet. His stomach gurgled, and he whined. Since emerging from the ground, his hunger had grown at an alarming rate.

"I told you to bring the boy to me." William pulled the whip out from behind his back. He snapped it through the air, burying the barbs in Sampson's back.

Sampson cowered and yelped.

William jerked the whip, ripping the metal barbs free from Sampson's hide. "Don't like the taste of iron, do you?"

Sampson answered with a high-pitched bark. He flattened his ears, arched his back, and pulled his lips back to reveal his fangs.

William raised the whip again.

Sampson sprang, hitting William square in the chest. They tumbled to the ground together. Sampson leaped off the man and landed a body's length behind him.

William rolled over and pushed himself up, grabbing the fallen whip.

"Fool hound!"

Sampson bounded away, returning to the woods. He felt blood running through the fur of his back. The whip's barbs hurt worse than any bear's claws ever had. He longed to return to Wes's porch and eat a bowl of cornbread and gravy. His new master had yet to learn that the only difference between a hunting hound and a mountain wolf was a full belly.

17

OMEN IN THE SUDS

Ephraim awoke in a circular room, its walls tapering and disappearing as they ascended into darkness. It was like gazing up a chimney. The upper reaches of the walls were hung with bunches of drying herbs, braids of onions, and strings of dry beans.

Ephraim sat up. The room spun around him, and when he raised his arm to steady himself against the wall, he winced. *Not that arm.* He lowered it, noticing it was now swathed in bandages that gave off a pungent smell—like onions, garlic, maybe both. He shifted and placed his other hand against the wall. It felt rough and dry.

The room was large, about twenty paces across. Ephraim's small bunk sat across from a table with two chairs and a tiny stove vented to the outside through a stovepipe. A ladder rested against the wall near his bunk. Light came through a door, cracked open. Ephraim realized with a start that it was daylight outside. *How long have I been here?*

He slid his feet off the bunk onto the packed earth floor, then stood, slowly and carefully, and walked to the doorway. The door frame was ornamented with relief carvings: birds, tulips, hearts, curly trees. Ephraim pushed the door open and stepped outside.

He found himself beneath the soaring branches of the biggest sycamore he'd ever seen. Ephraim glanced back at the door in disbelief that he'd just been inside this forest giant. The outside of the door held another surprise for him. It was painted with a garish geometric pattern that reminded Ephraim of a quilt. A horseshoe was pinned to the trunk above the door by an iron spike.

Ephraim took a few steps away from the tree and began walking around it.

On the other side, Nancy was hanging clothes on a line tied between two smaller trees. Earl was browsing nearby, and Nancy's wagon was sheltered by a lean-to.

Ephraim walked over to Nancy, stopping by her washtub just as she finished hanging a tattered, cream-colored shirt on the line.

"Nancy, thank you. I—"

The old woman held a finger to her lips.

Ephraim quit talking, suddenly aware of the focused look of reverence on the old woman's face.

Nancy knelt down in front of the dangling shirt.

Ephraim rubbed the back of his neck and stepped back. What was the granny woman doing?

"What do ye know of this?" Nancy asked, her eyes locked on the shirt.

Ephraim didn't understand. What was she asking him?

A gentle breeze blew through the trees, sending dry leaves twirling through the air. The clothing on the line fluttered.

Nancy studied the shirt as it billowed. "Blood in the snow and death laid low? What in tarnation is that supposed to mean?"

Ephraim followed her gaze, watching the shirt. Its sleeves bounced and waved like all the other clothing, but its movements seemed exaggerated.

Nancy put her hands on her hips. "Well, it ain't my fault ye decided to blow off the clothesline and get yourself tangled in the blackberry patch, now is it?"

The sleeves flapped and went limp.

Nancy nodded. "All right. I just wanted to be sure ye weren't blamin' me."

A gust pushed through the forest, and the shirt flared out from the line, the sleeves weaving in complex patterns. Nancy's eyes followed their movements. She muttered under her breath. "Evil comes forth from dark places... now is found in friendly faces."

The wind died, and the shirt went slack. It looked as lifeless as all the other clothing.

Nancy sighed and got to her feet. "Dang shirt. It's as hard to understand as it is scratchy." She turned to Ephraim and smiled as if just now noticing him. "Do ye know how long it's been since I had a good-lookin' man a-runnin' toward me and a-hollerin' my name?"

Ephraim opened his mouth, but nothing came out. He felt his face redden.

"What do ye think of the Laura?" Nancy asked.

"The what?"

"The Laura." Nancy pointed to the sycamore.

Ephraim shaded his eyes with his hand and looked up to where the hoary branches speared the blue sky like giant antlers. In the presence of something so ancient he felt humbled. "I've never seen anythin' like it," he said quietly.

"It's been quite some time since she's seen anyone besides me and Earl," Nancy said. "We're pleased to have ye, but I 'spect you ain't stoppin' by just to be sociable." She squinted at Ephraim. "What with that critter chasin' ye up here last night and all."

Last night. Ephraim breathed a sigh. "I'm glad to hear that I ain't been out long. We got to get back to Sixmile Creek quick, Nancy. My ma needs your help."

Nancy nodded. "I can do that."

Earl had wandered over during their conversation. The goat now nosed the bandage on Ephraim's arm.

"Careful, he'll eat anythin'," Nancy said. "But he just reminded me to take a look at that arm of yours."

Ephraim held out his arm. "What was that thing that chased me up here?"

"Near as I can figure, it was a hellhound." Nancy nodded her head toward a battered, ancient-looking musket propped against a tree. "Ol' Ruination sure didn't do no good against it."

Ephraim looked past Nancy to the last place he'd seen the creature. "What's a hellhound?"

"Truth be told, I don't know much 'bout 'em. I never crossed paths with one." Nancy pulled apart the knotted ends of the bandage and began to unwind it. "I used to handle witches in my younger days, but never a hellhound. I did hear an old-timer tell of one once though, and it sure sounded like that critter I seen last night. It gave ye quite a nasty bite!"

Under the dressing, Ephraim's forearm was covered in a foul-smelling concoction of mashed leaves and onion-like roots. Bits of the poultice fell off as Nancy unwound the bandage. Earl rushed over and gobbled them up.

Ephraim swallowed. "Ain't that bad for him?"

Nancy balled up the bandage and wiped Ephraim's arm clean. "I used to worry 'bout him, but I've learned over the years that a goat's belly must be made of cast iron."

Ephraim examined his arm. The hellhound's fangs had left ragged holes in his flesh, and each puncture wound was ringed by blackened skin. There wasn't any scab or clotted blood; the flesh around the wound looked dead. Ephraim felt dizzy at the sight.

Nancy clucked her tongue. "'Tain't a shade better than it looked last night. A poultice of ramps usually heals ye right up."

She grabbed the musket and walked toward the Laura. "Come on, let's try somethin' else on it."

Ephraim followed the old woman back into the tree. He stood by the door and watched as she rummaged around in some baskets by the stove.

"What was that powder you used to drive the hellhound off?" he asked.

"That's somethin' I come up with myself. I calls it phidity. I always keep some on hand."

"What is it?"

Nancy pulled a handful of dry leaves from one basket, shook her head, put the leaves back in, and moved to another basket. "Powdered yarbs and a few other things," she said. "It's about as reliable as anythin' when it comes to runnin' off evil. Things tainted with witchery cain't stand the stink of it."

"Where do you reckon that hellhound came from?" Ephraim asked.

"That's what's got me a-scratchin' my head," Nancy said. "Used to be that most wicked folk knew how to make a hellhound. There was old almanacks and physick books that told ye how to do such things." She pulled a handful of tiny dry leaves and flowers from a basket and moved to the table, where she unstoppered a jug of molasses. "Way I understand it, ye got to kill a black dog, then bury it in the grave of a murderer." She crushed the leaves in her hand and dropped the powder into a bowl, then tipped the molasses jug over it. "There's more to it than that, I'm sure. Witchery always calls for locust wood, the fat of a stillborn lamb, moonlight, and such-like. The old almanacks would've told the particulars, but they all were burned in the Old Country, well before my time. The ones that made it here eventually fell into the hands of men who destroyed 'em, on account of the powerful evil witches could do if'n they learned to reckon by the stars and the signs."

She shook her head. "What I can tell ye is, the dog soaks in the grave for a good long while. While he's down there, he learns the scent of a guilty soul, and at the same time he's changin', turnin' into a critter, like the one that latched ahold of your arm." She shook the molasses jug and slapped it on the bottom. "I might have to sit this out in the sun afore any will come out. Anyway, after the hound is dug up, it can be used to hunt down folks who've done grievous wrongs. It smells their guilt and trails 'em, same as any huntin' dog after a rabbit."

A dark glob of molasses worked its way down to the mouth of the jug. Nancy stuck her finger inside and scooped it into the bowl. She licked the black residue from her finger, smacked her lips, and eyed Ephraim. "Which means ye done got yourself into a mess of trouble since I last saw ye."

Ephraim took a deep breath and closed his eyes. He wasn't prepared to talk about this. "You're right, Nancy. I did somethin' terrible. But that ain't why I'm here. My ma, she's taken foxglove, and she's dyin'. I need you to help her. Whatever happens to me don't matter."

Nancy motioned for Ephraim to lay his arm on the table. "Well, I'm goin' to try this remedy on ye, no matter what ye did. There's no sense in saving ye in the middle of the night just to let ye die of the hydrophoby the next day." She used a wooden spoon to mix the molasses with the crushed leaves. "This is chickweed and molasses. I seen it work on mad dog bites, so I reckon it might get ye healed up and haired over. I don't know what you got mixed up in, Ephraim Cutler, but I've had a feelin' of late that somethin' strange is a-brewin' in these parts."

"What makes you say that?"

"I was over in Pendleton County, couple days ago, and heard tell of a mule givin' birth. And only this mornin', when I was doin' my washin', I saw an omen in the suds." She pointed the spoon at Ephraim. "Lye soap don't never lie. Remember that." She tilted the bowl and scraped down the sides with the spoon. "That, and my pappy's old shirt, are all pointin' to somethin'. I seen times like these afore. The whirlwind's a-comin'."

A shiver ran through Ephraim. He sat in silence while Nancy used the spoon to daub the mixture over his wound. He knew the old woman was waiting to hear what had happened, what he had done to draw the hellhound's attention. He didn't know how to begin.

Finally, he took a shaky breath and closed his eyes. "I shot a man," he said. "Silas Henson."

"You kill him?" Nancy asked, still looking at Ephraim's arm.

Ephraim nodded. The words tumbled from his mouth. "I didn't want to do it. Ma—she wanted me to kill a Yankee, said she'd drink poison if I didn't."

"She must've figured they'd caught ye. I reckon that's why she drank it anyway."

"Yeah, well they did, but I got away."

Ephraim paused for a minute. He thought of what Nancy had said about wicked people creating hellhounds in the old days. The image of the stranger in the Confederate coat flashed through his mind, along with the piece of paper that floated ahead of him with a life of its own. He heard the reverend's warning again: *It could be that your crime has drawn forces far more sinister than a lynching party to Sixmile Creek.*

"Nancy," he said. "I don't think I shot Silas on purpose. I think the Devil made me do it."

"I'm sure many a man has told a tale like that at the gallows," Nancy said. She tore a fresh strip of bandage from an old shirt and wound it around Ephraim's arm.

"You don't have to believe me, but I think I saw him."

"Who, the Devil?" Nancy raised an eyebrow.

Ephraim nodded. "I had my pistol pointed at Silas, and I was trying to work up the nerve to pull the trigger. I couldn't bring myself to do it. Then my horse jumped, and the gun went off.

This man, he's a stranger passin' through Sixmile Creek. I saw him in the woods, watchin'."

"Ye think the man is the Devil."

"I didn't before, but what you said 'bout the hellhound makes sense. Somebody had to make that thing and send it after me, right?"

Nancy frowned and looked out the door. "Could be," she said. She pulled out her pipe and filled the bowl. "He's been known to show up every now and again." She walked over to the stove, struck a long match on it, got the tobacco smoldering, and turned around. Smoke framed her face. "And he certainly could conjure up a hellhound, I reckon. If a witch done it they'd have to be mighty powerful; they'd have to know the old ways." She shook her head. "Perish the thought!"

"I've heard folks talk 'bout witches, but I don't reckon I really know what they are," Ephraim said.

Nancy snorted as she walked over to the stove. "Most folks you hear talkin' 'bout 'em don't neither. That don't stop 'em from talkin' though."

She opened a pot and served Ephraim a bowl of cornmeal mush. While he ate, she sorted through bunches of dry herbs, placing some into a pack-basket, muttering to herself.

Ephraim wolfed down the food, watching Nancy.

"Sounds like your mammy needs tendin' to. I best get goin'. I don't figure ye ought to trek back down to town in the shape you're in."

Ephraim jumped to his feet. "No, I'm comin' with you."

"There'll be folks a-huntin' ye."

"I know. I've seen 'em."

Nancy inspected him. "You ain't goin' to slow me down, walkin' on them bare feet, are ye?"

"No, ma'am," Ephraim said. "I'll be just fine."

Nancy slid her arms through the straps of the pack-basket and hiked it onto her shoulders. "All right, then. Let's get goin'."

They stepped outside. Earl raised his head and looked in their direction. Nancy shook her head at him, and he bleated mournfully. "We can't take ye this time, Earl. Got to move quickly." She walked over to the goat and scratched him between the horns. "Stay 'round here till I get back. Ye can find your own food for a few days."

Nancy led the way down a steep path that wound its way in switchbacks down toward Sixmile Creek. Ephraim wished he'd found this path last night; it was much easier than the route he had taken. As they walked, he felt the soreness in his arm subsiding a little. Maybe this new poultice was working. He wondered how many cures the granny woman had stored in her head.

"Nancy, is it true?" he asked. "That story 'bout you driving off the Skinner witch?"

"Ol' Josephine," Nancy said, nodding. "Who told ye 'bout that?"

"I heard Manson tellin' the story."

Nancy smiled. "It's good to know that some folks still remember what I did for Sixmile Creek." She squinted at Ephraim. "He tell you what she did to the Sherman girl?"

Ephraim grimaced. "Yeah."

Nancy pulled her pipe out of her mouth. "When I first came to Sixmile Creek, Josephine Skinner had the run of the place. Did whatever she wanted, whenever she wanted to do it. Nobody put up a fight. Well, besides Wes Sherman pepperin' her hind end with birdshot, and to a witch that ain't nothin'.

"The first thing I did when I arrived was to go around the settlement and make sure that every last family put horseshoes over the doors to their homes and barns."

"Like the one you've got on your tree—er, the Laura?" Ephraim said.

Nancy nodded. "Like that. But most folks in the settlement

took theirs down after hearin' Boggs preach against witches." She snorted.

"What's the horseshoe for?" Ephraim asked.

"Well, anybody who knows anythin' 'bout witches knows they've got the evil eye." Nancy pointed at her eye with the stem of her pipe. "It's as ugly as sin, kind of like a goat's eye." She shook her head. "I still cain't believe that preacher got the whole town to believe I'm a witch. Ye see anythin' strange 'bout my eyes?" She turned to Ephraim and opened her eyes wide.

Ephraim shook his head.

"I'm right purty lookin', ain't I?" Nancy winked. "The other thing anybody who knows anythin' 'bout witches knows is this rhyme: *If a wicked glint ye spy, you're under the gaze of the evil eye. Hang a horseshoe over the door, the eye will close forever more.*" She pointed the pipe stem at Ephraim. "Remember that. I can't rightly say why or how it works, but it does. Now, as I was sayin', the horseshoes was the first thing I done. It made it so Josephine had a hard time preyin' on the common folk 'round here. It put the fight between me and her, cunning-folk against cunning-folk."

"What's cunning-folk?" Ephraim interrupted.

"Cunning-folk are anyone who can charm, cure, or read the signs. We're all the same to begin with, born on Old Christmas Day, seventh sons of seventh sons. I was born with a caul. Anyway, the gift we have is supposed to be used to help folks. But some let their gift go sour. See, the very instant cunning-folk use their power to harm someone, to cast a curse, they lose the power to help and heal, and they get the evil eye. Them that do that are called witches, and there's different names for them accordin' to their talents. Josephine was what most folks call a skin-changer. Those of us who stay clear of cursin' folks are called granny women, conjure men, dowsers..." She waved her hand. "There's all kinds. Ye understand?"

Ephraim nodded.

"Anyway, after I got everyone to put up horseshoes, I just

waited awhile. See, Josephine was feedin' herself by stealin' from folks. If she cursed a cow to give bloody milk, that meant that she was gettin' the good milk somehow. I heard someone swear up and down that they seen her wring two gallons of milk out of a dishrag, just like she was squeezin' a cow's tits! She cursed hens to quit layin', and she had a pack of toads up at her place that'd lay the eggs that was meant for the chickens." Nancy waved her pipe stem at Ephraim. "There ain't nothin' a witch likes more than suckin' raw eggs. But when the horseshoes went up, Josephine got hungry."

Nancy tapped her temple. "That's how ye got to think when you're takin' on a witch. Ye got to back 'em into a corner. So Josephine started spendin' more time a-roamin', swappin' her skin and tryin' to trick folks into givin' her victuals. I kept an eye on her place, and one night I saw her slip out, wearin' the skin of a young woman."

Ephraim swallowed, thinking of Alice Sherman.

"I snuck into her cabin and looked around. She had her own hide all folded up nice and tucked down into a trunk. I opened that trunk, dug it out, and rubbed the inside down with salt. Then I put it back, just like I found it." Nancy smiled. "Lordy, you should've seen Ol' Josephine when she came home and wriggled back into her hide!"

"What happened?" Ephraim asked.

Nancy chuckled. "The salt shrunk it, made it tighter'n a bull's backside in fly season! She came a-runnin' out of that cabin lookin' like somethin' the cat coughed up. She couldn't close her eyes because the lids was all drawed up!" She spread her own eyes wide with her fingers, exposing their whites. "Her mouth was like that too." She hooked her fingers into the corners of her mouth and stretched back her cheeks. "She had a great big split runnin' from the top of her head, down her back, and down the backs of both legs. That was where she'd pull her skin off, see, but with it all drawed up like that, she couldn't make the ends meet."

Nancy erupted into a fit of laughter. She pulled out her pipe and coughed.

Ephraim shuddered, picturing a half-skinned possum of human proportions.

"I never, in all my days, thought I'd see somethin' like I seen that night," Nancy said once she'd caught her breath. "Josephine was caterwaulin', swattin' herself all over, like she'd stepped on a hornet's nest! That salt must've stung somethin' fierce. She saw me and said, 'You done this!' Well I looked right back at her. 'Yes, missy I did,' says I, 'and ye deserve every lick of it!'" Nancy laughed and wiped her streaming eyes. "Then I set fire to her cabin, with all her spare skins inside, and I told her she'd best leave Sixmile Creek or I'd see that she was burned too. That took the starch right out of her. I ain't seen hide nor hair of Ol' Josephine since."

Ephraim's mouth had gone dry. He gave a shaky laugh and let the old woman walk ahead of him. *I'm sure glad Nancy's on my side.*

18

A HATFUL OF REGRET

Isabel's father stood in the doorway of the store, hat in hand. "I'm headed over to the mill to get some corn ground," he said. "Your ma's coming with me. I need you to stay here and run things while I'm gone."

"Yes, Pa," Isabel said, looking up from sweeping the floor.

She watched through the window as her parents drove off in their wagon.

On a shelf behind the sales counter sat a round box tied with a string. Isabel pulled it down. Would she ever get to give Ephraim the gift she'd brought from Charleston? She doubted it. If Ephraim was still alive, he was likely far from Sixmile Creek by now.

She undid the string and lifted the lid. A black hat with a pale blue ribbon band lay inside. She pulled it out and set it on the counter. She'd thought of Ephraim the moment she'd seen the ribbon, blue like his eyes. Aunt Eliza had bought it for her, and giggled like a young girl when Isabel told her about the boy back home she wanted to please.

The bell on the door jingled, and Isabel looked up to see Lester and Polly Ewing entering. Polly walked to the counter.

"How do, Miss Isabel?"

"I'm fine," Isabel said. "Pa's gone to the mill. Is there something I can help you all with?"

"I need to buy a sack of sugar," Polly said, counting coins onto the counter. Her gaze fell on the hat. "That's a handsome hat you've got there. Lester, come over here."

Lester walked over.

"Try this on," Polly said, handing him the hat.

The hat fit Lester perfectly.

"That looks real good on you, honey!" Polly said. She turned to Isabel. "He had a hat just like that when we first started courtin'. Seein' him wearin' it makes me feel young all over again. How much for it?"

Isabel shook her head. "It's not for sale. It's a gift for someone." Even as the words left her mouth, she wondered why she shouldn't sell it, or even *give* it to Polly—just let go of the hat, and Ephraim too. If she didn't, the hat would sit on the shelf, a silent reminder of dreams never realized.

Lester pulled off the hat and laid it on the counter. "Shame. I kind of like that one."

Isabel took a deep breath and pushed the hat back across the counter. "Sorry, I was thinking of a different hat. You can have this one for two dollars."

Lester's eyebrows shot up. He glanced at Polly. "Two dollars? I'd expect to give four for a hat like that!" He looked back at Isabel. "You sure 'bout this, miss? Your pa isn't goin' to hunt me down and accuse me of stealin' from his store while he was gone, is he?"

Isabel nodded. "I'm sure."

The Ewings paid and left with the hat and sugar. Isabel stared at the empty space where the hatbox had sat on the counter. A lump rose in her throat.

Across the street, outside Manson Owens's smithy, a knot of

people had gathered. Isabel could see the Fletcher brothers at its center, wild-eyed, waving their arms as they spoke.

The bell on the door jingled again, and Peyton stepped in. "Isabel, come out here! You got to hear this!" He returned to the porch, listening to the group, arms folded, shaking his head.

Isabel walked out onto the porch next to Peyton.

"I'm tellin' you, this weren't like any critter I ever seen in my life!" Clabe Fletcher was saying. "The thing had eyes like coals, teeth like jackknives! Didn't it, Jake?"

Manson poked his head out of his smithy. "What're you folks carryin' on about out here?"

Rindy Sue, who stood clutching Jake's arm, turned to the blacksmith. "Mr. Owens, Jake and Clabe caught Ephraim Cutler. They had him last night, but a monster attacked 'em and chased 'em off."

Manson shook his head. "This whole town's gone plumb crazy. First I hear Ephraim's hidin' in badger holes, now a monster's chasin' him around the woods."

"I seen what I saw!" Jake Fletcher said. "It killed Frank Moats up in the Hurricane Timber! I swear it! His body's probably still up there."

Clabe nodded. "Yeah, he's up there, along with my gun. I dropped it. I reckon Ephraim's dead up there, too. Last I saw that thing was after him."

Peyton leaned over to Isabel. "I think those boys have been drinkin' their own product a little too much. When they told me, I said—"

Isabel turned and walked back into the store.

Peyton followed her. "I can't stand this, Isabel. Knowin' you're angry with me. I was just tryin' to say somethin' to make you smile."

Isabel folded her arms and didn't turn around.

"Look," Peyton said behind her. "I didn't ask for Ephraim to shoot my brother. You act like this is all my fault. Well, it ain't!"

Isabel covered her face with her hands. *How is some story about Ephraim getting eaten by a monster supposed to make me smile?* Maybe he was still up there in the woods somewhere, cold and hungry. His ma was dying, and here she had practically given away the hat meant for him. How could she call herself his friend? Her eyes prickled with tears. She'd betrayed the boy she loved.

Peyton stepped in front of her. "Isabel, give me a chance. We had a grand time dancing together. I can make you happy like that again, I promise. All you have to do is let me try." He grabbed her hands and gently pulled them down from her face. "Can't you see? I'm sweet on you."

"Let go!" Isabel said through clenched teeth, ripping her wrists from Peyton's grasp.

Peyton stayed where he stood, mouth open, as Isabel stormed out the back door of the store, not bothering to remove her coffee-sack apron. She wiped her eyes on her sleeve and marched into the woods. She needed to be alone.

19

THE CLEARING

Ephraim hid on the outskirts of Sixmile Creek, crouched behind a boulder, watching the back of Coleman's Dry Goods through the trees. Nancy had left an hour ago, promising to do her best for Ma and to return with news. Ephraim had wanted to hide closer to the cabin, but Nancy had told him that would be a poor idea.

"The folks a-huntin' ye will be keepin' a close eye on that cabin. With your ma fixin' to die, they'd be right in thinkin' you'll try to look in on her," she'd said.

Ephraim gnawed on a piece of dried meat that Nancy had given him. His stomach rumbled, and he thought of how little he'd eaten over the past few days. His appetite was returning.

Cold from the rock seeped into his body. He moved away from the boulder, staying low, and sat down in a patch of sunshine. The warmth felt good.

He felt a twinge in his wounded arm and rubbed it. It seemed to throb with a pulse of its own. He laid it in his lap.

As he waited for Nancy to return, his eyes grew heavy. After a few minutes, his chin began to tilt toward his chest, and his arm fell back to his side.

He was awoken by the sound of distant sobbing. His head snapped up, and he scurried back to the shelter of the boulder. Whoever it was, they were downslope from him. He waited, making sure that the person wasn't drawing any closer, then crept out from behind the boulder and picked his way through the trees toward the sound.

In a small meadow he found the source of the sobbing. It was Isabel, in her coffee-sack apron, sitting in the dry grass, her face cradled in her hands.

Without thinking, Ephraim walked toward her. She looked up and started.

"Ephraim! What are you doing here?"

He sat down beside her. "Hidin'. What are you doin'?"

Isabel's mouth became a hard, thin line. "None of your business."

"Oh." Ephraim looked down.

Isabel's face contorted with a strange mixture of anger and relief. "I'm up here because of you! You killed Silas Henson! Why? Didn't you stop to think that you'd wind up being hunted like some stupid coon?" She wiped her reddened eyes. "Didn't you think... that I'd be worried sick about you?"

Ephraim pulled a dry blade of grass from the ground and wound it around his fingers. "I don't know how to explain what happened," he said softly. "Ma... she ain't been well for some time. She's been goin' on and on about Pa. Takin' out his pistol. Talkin' to it." The blade of grass broke, and he picked another. "She wanted me to kill a Yankee for Pa. I told her I wouldn't do it. Told her it was wrong."

Isabel's expression softened.

At the sight of her warm face, a dam broke within Ephraim. The words rushed out of him. He told her everything, absolutely everything, that had happened since he'd left her at the stir-off.

"So a monster really did chase you and the Fletcher boys through the woods?"

"Yeah. Nancy said it was a hellhound." Ephraim held up his arm. "I got the bite marks right here."

"And this stranger you keep seeing—you think he's the Devil?"

Ephraim shrugged. "That's the only thing that makes sense to me."

"I think I saw him too," Isabel said.

"What? Where?"

"At the Ewings' stir-off, after you left. And again at church. He sat next to me, then left when Reverend Boggs asked who he was. It was strange. He smelled really bad." She sat up straight. "Wait a minute—he asked me about you. He asked for your name."

A chill ran over Ephraim. "Why?"

Isabel shook her head. "He didn't say."

Talking to Isabel was comforting. Ephraim felt like he should be more concerned about all that was going on, but somehow, just telling Isabel about it all seemed like a step in the right direction, the seed of a solution. He remembered the last time he saw her, dancing with Peyton. It seemed like years had passed since then.

"I'm sorry I left the stir-off like I did," he said.

"What upset you?" Isabel asked.

"I thought you were vexed because I didn't hold your hand. I was goin' to, but then I saw your pa watchin' me."

Isabel laughed. "He wouldn't have said anything. Why'd you think I was vexed?"

Ephraim stared at the ground, his face turning red. "Because you danced with Peyton instead of me on the last dance."

"Ephraim, I was just being polite. Aunt Eliza told me a lady never turns down a dance." She picked up a corner of her coffee-sack apron. "A lady never does this either," she said with a grin, and blew her nose on the apron.

Ephraim laughed.

Isabel sniffed. "So what happened to Jubal Early?"

"What about him?"

Ephraim looked at the sun. It was sinking in the west. Why hadn't Nancy returned yet? His mind instantly began to play out dreadful scenes: his mother dying, or already dead. *I can't let her die without sayin' goodbye*, he thought. *I'm the only family she's got left.*

"Everyone thinks he's the one that let you out of jail."

"What? No, it wasn't him. It was Reverend Boggs," Ephraim said distractedly. "He gave Jubal some drugged coffee. It put him to sleep."

"Well, where'd Jubal go then? Nobody's seen him since he was guarding the jail."

Ephraim shook his head. "I don't know." An ache radiated from his bandaged arm. It spread through his bones with the intensity of a sore tooth in a winter breeze. He groaned and pulled his arm in tight to his stomach, pressing it there with his uninjured arm.

Isabel's brow furrowed. "What's wrong?"

"It's this hellhound bite. It's really hurtin' all of a sudden." He held it tight until the ache dulled. Then he lowered his arm and got to his feet. "Listen, Isabel. I think I need to go see Ma."

"Are you crazy? Everyone is looking for you!"

"I'm really worried about her. Nancy should've been back by now. Look, it'll be dark soon. I made it out of town without anyone catchin' me; I can sneak back in. Will you wait here for Nancy in case we don't cross paths?"

"Ephraim, the Henson family is all here, and the only business they've got in Sixmile Creek is to find you and hang you."

Ephraim sighed and rubbed his arms. "I know that." He felt himself starting to choke up. "But Isabel, my ma is probably dyin' up at the cabin. I've got to see her. This might be the last time..." He blinked away tears.

Isabel sighed. "I'll pray that no one catches you, and yes, I'll wait for Nancy."

Ephraim grabbed her hands in his. "Thank you. There's only a few folks left in this town I can trust: Nancy, the reverend, and you."

Isabel's cheeks flushed pink. She lowered her eyes. "Just don't do anything stupid, Ephraim. Don't take any risks you don't have to."

"I won't," he said, releasing her hands.

"And if you make it back there, don't forget to get your shoes," Isabel said, pointing at Ephraim's bare feet.

SHALLOW GRAVE

I sabel took a shaky breath and began pacing through the dry grass. This would have to be kept secret. Not even her parents could know that she'd found Ephraim. But it was such a relief to know he was still alive. If only there was a way to get that hat back from Lester Ewing.

She stepped over a patch of disturbed earth. She kicked at it absently, scuffing away a swath of loose soil. Something white poked through, and Isabel knelt to examine it. She took the object between her fingers and pulled, then released it with a gasp.

A human finger protruded from the dirt, stark and pale as a drowned earthworm.

MA

Ephraim skirted the settlement, sticking to game trails, as he made his way toward Laurel Knob. He slowed his pace when he neared his cabin. Nancy's warning echoed in his mind: the Hensons probably expected him to try to visit Ma.

He crept toward the cabin, darting from tree to tree. For caution's sake, he waited just inside the tree line for a few minutes, watching the yard. The yard was empty, and he saw nothing to alarm him, but still he waited.

Finally, he lowered himself onto his belly and slithered through the dry weeds to the smokehouse. As he reached it, his arm suddenly swelled with a throbbing ache, even worse than it had before. He had to press his back against the smokehouse wall and grit his teeth. He would need to tell Nancy that the poultice wasn't working.

When he'd caught his breath, he rose and ran to the door of the cabin. He laid his ear against it, and heard the creak of his mother's rocking chair. Was that Nancy, or someone else?

Ephraim tiptoed around the side of the cabin and peered out at the hitching post. When he saw Reverend Boggs's buckskin pony tethered there, quietly munching oats from a feedbag, his heart leaped. But if Boggs was here, where was Nancy?

He returned to the cabin door, took a deep breath, and pushed it open.

Reverend Boggs sat in the rocking chair next to Ma's bed, his Bible open in his lap. He looked at the door as it opened, then did a double take.

"Ephraim! Where have you been, son?"

Ephraim stepped inside and barred the door behind him. "I went to find Barefoot Nancy. I had to try to—" He was cut off when the reverend rose to embrace him.

"I wondered if that was what you'd done." Boggs held Ephraim by both shoulders and looked into his face. "You've arrived just in time. I don't think your mother is going to last much longer."

Ephraim felt like he'd been kicked in the gut. He rushed to the bed. His mother's face looked ashen, and the rise and fall of her chest was barely discernible. He knelt down and took her hand. It was cold and sweaty.

"Ma, I'm here."

She didn't respond.

Ephraim's mouth went dry. He turned to Boggs. "Where's Barefoot Nancy?"

The reverend frowned. "I thought you said you went to find her."

"I did. She's supposed to be here!"

Boggs shook his head. "Ephraim, I've been here all afternoon. A few people from town have stopped by, but I haven't seen Nancy."

Ephraim's mind raced. Where had she gone? She knew that Ma was dying. Had the old woman forgotten?

His mother squeezed his hand.

Ephraim looked down. Ma's eyes flickered behind their lids. She smiled feebly.

The signs of life sent a tiny ray of hope into the jumble of Ephraim's thoughts. Maybe they still had time. "Hang on, Ma. I'll go find Barefoot Nancy. I'll—"

Ma's eyes opened partway. She gripped Ephraim's hand tighter, pulling him toward her. Her lips parted.

Ephraim bent and put his ear next to her mouth. "What is it, Ma?"

Her tongue worked mutely.

Ephraim pulled back and looked at her again. Her eyes were fully open now, lucid. "That's it, Ma. Hang on! I'm goin' to find Nancy right now."

"Josiah?" The question escaped his mother's lips like a moth fluttering through the crack of a closing door. A name from the grave.

"No, Ma. It's me, Ephraim."

She closed her eyes. Her hand went limp in his.

"Ma?" Ephraim gripped his mother's shoulders and shook. "Ma. Wake up!"

He gathered her limp body into his arms. She felt lighter than he'd expected. He turned to Boggs. "You've got to help me! Let's get her to Nancy."

The preacher removed his hat and held it over his chest. "Ephraim, I think—"

"Just do it!"

Boggs lowered his gaze. "Your mother has passed, Ephraim."

Ephraim looked as his mother's still face, and he knew the reverend spoke the truth. Tears filled his eyes, running onto his cheeks.

Reverend Boggs put an arm around Ephraim's shoulders. "It was the Lord's will."

Ephraim hugged his mother close. His sobbing grew stronger, until his whole body shook. "Why didn't Nancy come?" he asked his mother's still form.

Boggs sighed. "I can't judge you for seeking help. In a time of weakness, we will look to any source for hope. It's human frailty, Ephraim."

Ephraim lowered his mother back onto the bed.

"I mourn for your loss, son, and as much as I'd like to leave you here to grieve, this town is crawling with people looking for you. When I came up here to look in on your mother, there were three of the Henson men watching the place. I asked them to respect a dying woman and leave."

"I don't care anymore," Ephraim said. The worst had already happened. His fears had come true. He was alone now, the last of the Cutler line.

"I won't listen to that kind of talk," Boggs said. "There are still people in this town who care about you, Ephraim, and I'm one of them. There's hope for you yet."

22

AN UNSETTLING NOTION

Nancy appeared in the clearing behind the store just as the sun disappeared beyond the mountains. Her gaze immediately fell on Isabel.

"Where's Ephraim?"

"He left to go see his ma a little before sundown," Isabel said. She had stayed as far from the dead finger as possible. If hadn't been for her promise to Ephraim, she would've left the woods immediately after discovering it.

Nancy shook her head. "That boy is a tomfool lunatic! He's goin' to get hisself hanged!"

"I told him not to go, but he was real worried about his ma."

"Those Hensons are watchin' the entire town. They saw me headed up to the Cutler place and asked all kinds of questions. It was like they knew he'd come to see me. I had to make up some cock 'n' bull story 'bout how I heard Lucretia needed doctorin'." Nancy sighed. "I best go try to find out what's become of that boy."

Isabel put a hand on the old woman's shoulder. "Nancy, before you go, there's something you should take a look at. I'm too scared to do it myself."

The granny woman's hazel eyes disappeared into the folds of a smile. She took Isabel's hand between her own. "Aw, honey, ye ain't the first young lady to come to ol' Nancy because you're afeared you're bleedin' to death."

Isabel's face reddened. "No, Nancy, I—"

"Why, I even knowed a few that took up sayin' extry prayers every day to get right with the Lord afore they passed on." Nancy chuckled. She patted Isabel's hand. "It ain't nothin' to worry 'bout, every woman since Eve has been afflicted with it. Just get yourself a rag to stop the flow, and it'll clear up soon enough."

"Nancy, I didn't mean... I wasn't talking about..." Isabel felt thoroughly flushed now. She closed her eyes and shook her head. "I think there's a body buried in the ground yonder."

Nancy's eyebrows shot up. "A body! Why didn't ye say so, dear?"

Isabel led the granny woman across the clearing. They stopped and peered down at the finger.

Nancy pushed up her sleeves and squatted by the lifeless appendage, her braids dangling as she examined it. She gnawed on her bottom lip, tugged on the finger, then brushed loose soil from around it until a pale hand was visible. "My dear, I believe you're right. Go get us some sticks so we can clear this dirt away."

"You want to dig it up?" Isabel's heart beat faster at the very thought.

"Ain't no other way to see who it is," Nancy said. She looked up. "Whoever this is, they cain't hurt us in the shape they're in, dear. Go on now, get them sticks."

Isabel fetched two long branches from the woods. Working together, the two women loosed the dirt and swept it away from the corpse. Once they'd unearthed it, they stood over the head for a closer look.

Jubal Early's face had been flattened. His nose was broken and his lips were thick and black.

Nancy gave a low whistle. "My lands! What happened to this

feller?" She lifted one of her bare feet and scratched at the sole. "I wonder who he ran afoul of."

Isabel stared at the body. A dark realization crept over her. "I think I know."

Nancy cocked an eyebrow. "Who?"

Isabel took a step back. "Reverend Boggs."

Nancy pursed her lips. "There ain't a doubt in my mind that somethin' ain't right with that preacher, but I never reckoned he was killin' folks in the woods between sermons. How do ye figure?"

Isabel took a deep breath. "Did Ephraim tell you that Reverend Boggs helped him get out of jail?"

"He did."

"Jubal was guarding the jail that night, but he went missin' along with Ephraim. Everybody in town thinks Jubal helped him escape."

Nancy looked back at the body. "That so?"

"Ephraim told me that Boggs drugged Jubal, put him to sleep, so he could get Ephraim out of the jailhouse."

"You're sayin' that the last folks to see this poor feller alive was Ephraim and the preacher?"

"Yes. Now, think about this. Who'd have a reason to kill Jubal? You could say Ephraim did, because he wanted to escape, but Boggs had drugged Jubal, so there was no need."

Nancy nodded slowly. "But Ol' Boggs wouldn't want nobody tellin' the town that he let Ephraim out."

"Exactly. So he took Ephraim home, then went back to the jail, dragged Jubal out here, and killed him."

Nancy rubbed her chin and looked toward Laurel Knob. "I ain't one to go and swaller an idea without chewin' on it some, but if this's true, then I just had me an unsettlin' notion."

"What?"

"When I was tendin' to Lucretia Cutler earlier, Boggs showed up. He told me to leave, started carryin' on 'bout witchery and the like. I didn't want the last thing poor Lucretia heard to be us fussin' at each other, so I left. Truth be told, there wasn't much I could do for her anyway."

"You think he's goin' to kill her?"

Nancy shook her head. "She's already dyin', bless her heart. What I meant was, if Ephraim left when ye said he did, he's probly with the preacher man right now."

23

THE FUNERAL

Ephraim sat at the table by the light of a candle, waiting for Boggs to return. After they'd arrived at the preacher's home, Boggs had gone to tell Polly Ewing of Ma's passing so funeral preparations could be made. He'd retrieved his old brogans from the cabin. His toes sought the familiar holes in the soles, tracing the outlines.

The cold pulse in Ephraim's arm began to build again. The bandage had started to come loose. *It ain't doin' much good anyway*, Ephraim thought. *Just like Nancy herself. She came all the way down here with me, and then what?* He pictured the old woman walking through town. Maybe she'd tried to find the Hensons; maybe she wanted the reward. He remembered Clabe Fletcher's words: *Two hundred dollars is two hundred dollars.* Still, he couldn't believe Nancy would do such a thing. Was the old granny woman's mind slipping? Had she forgotten?

He unwound the bandage, laid it on the table, and brought the candle close. The dark ring around each puncture had diffused outward, spreading through his skin like ink on a blotter. He ran his fingers over the blackened skin. It was cold to the touch, like the flesh of a corpse.

The door opened, and Boggs stepped in.

"Everything is taken care of—" The preacher caught sight of Ephraim's arm. "What happened to you?"

"A hellhound bit me."

Boggs walked over and peered down at the arm. "That looks like gangrene."

Ephraim shrugged. "It don't hurt right now."

"Who told you it was a hellhound? Nancy?"

Ephraim nodded. "She tried a few remedies on it, but I think it's gettin' worse."

Boggs sighed. "I'm surprised you haven't lost your faith in that woman. She failed you, and now she's failed your mother. I hope you've learned to trust my opinion of her."

Ephraim hung his head. "I should've listened to you from the beginnin'. I was just tryin' to save Ma, but I reckon you were right 'bout that stranger being the Devil. It had to have been him that turned the hellhound loose on me."

"The last thing I want to do is make you feel as if I'm passing judgment on you, son," Boggs said. "I'm here to help. Do you want me to heal your arm?"

Ephraim met the preacher's eyes. "You can do that?"

"I'm a man of God, Ephraim. That bite is the work of the Devil. Do you have faith?"

Ephraim swallowed and nodded.

Boggs unbuttoned his sleeves and rolled them up. He pulled out a chair and sat down. "All right, then. Lay it here on the table in front of me."

Ephraim did as he was told.

Reverend Boggs placed his fingertips over the wound. He sat quiet for a moment, then muttered something under his breath that sounded like a prayer.

Ephraim's arm remained unchanged.

Boggs looked up and placed a hand over Ephraim's eyes. "Do you believe your arm has been healed?"

"What? I don't know, I—"

"Pick your words carefully, boy. This is a question of faith."

Ephraim took a deep breath and summoned a picture of his arm, healed and whole. "Yes. Yes, I believe."

"As you believe, be it unto you."

Boggs removed his hand from Ephraim's eyes.

Ephraim held up his arm in amazement. The wound was completely gone. He ran his other hand over it. The flesh still felt slightly cold to the touch, but its appearance was nothing short of a miracle. For a moment, he forgot everything that had happened that day.

"How did you do that?"

The reverend's left eye glinted strangely in the candle-light. Boggs quickly reached up and rubbed it with a knuckle, then massaged his temples. "Belief is a powerful thing, Ephraim. But let me tell you, that was very tiring." He looked out the window. "Look, Ephraim, this is a poor time to talk about this, your mother having just passed and all, but we need to get you away from Sixmile Creek —far away."

He stood and moved to the stove. "I've found a man who will give you employment. In fact, he's made me a recruiter of sorts, and he will trust my judgment on anyone I deem worthy to enter his service." He picked up a potato and began slicing it into a skillet. "You'll have to sign a contract before you meet him; I'll prepare one, and we can take care of it tomorrow, after the funeral."

"What kind of work does he need done?"

"Evangelizing. Much like the work of a minister."

"So, I'd be a preacher, like you?"

Boggs turned around. "Yes, you can think of it that way."

Ephraim's brow furrowed. "But—I'm a murderer. That don't seem right."

"Don't worry over that." Boggs smiled. "This man knows the

value of a second chance. His employees are among the most devoted you'll ever see."

Ephraim sat silent as the reverend fried the potatoes. Boggs cooked them until they were crispy and brown, served some for Ephraim and himself, then put coffee in a pot to brew as they ate. Ephraim ate hungrily and finished well before the preacher.

The reverend pushed back his chair, still chewing. "You'll be needing sleep now. We have a lot to accomplish tomorrow. Please, use my bed. I'll be burning the midnight oil." He nodded to the coffee pot. "Preparing a eulogy takes time."

Ephraim didn't protest. He crawled into the reverend's bed. Through the window on the other side of the room, he saw the moon, nearly full, shining through the branches of the trees. Boggs cleaned up the dishes, then sat down at his desk and worked by the light of an oil lamp. Ephraim watched him. The reverend wasn't consulting the Bible; instead he had the strange book covered in golden stars and a moon open on his desk. He seemed totally engrossed in his reading, poring over the pages with a furrowed brow. His fountain pen scratched softly against the paper as he took notes.

The sound of the reverend's writing lulled Ephraim to sleep.

SNOWFLAKES FELL soft and gray against the sky. Ephraim huddled behind a tombstone, watching the scant crowd gathered around the freshly dug grave. Reverend Boggs's voice was muted with the distance, and Ephraim couldn't make out more than the occasional word. But he watched closely as Manson Owens and Leroy Coleman lowered the pine box into the ground and began to shovel dirt over it.

I'm the last Cutler.

The thought was accompanied by a terrible ache in Ephraim's chest.

When a mound of clumpy soil and dirty snow covered the casket, Manson and Leroy set down their shovels and the crowd dispersed. Only Reverend Boggs remained by the graveside, clutching a black Bible in his cold, white hands. When the last of the mourners had disappeared from the graveyard, Boggs turned toward Ephraim's hiding place and beckoned.

Ephraim stepped out from behind the gravestone and trudged over to his mother's resting place.

The two of them stood in silence. Ephraim removed his hat. A single hot tear traveled down the numbness of his cheek and dripped onto the disturbed earth.

Boggs clapped a hand on his shoulder and squeezed gently, but Ephraim could barely feel it. Though his arm was healed, the coldness in it almost seemed worse—or maybe that was just the weather. It might take time to fully heal.

"I wish to speak with you about the proposition I mentioned last night."

Ephraim took a deep breath and tried to collect himself. "Do you have the contract?"

"I do."

"How do I meet this man?"

"He will be visiting me soon, and if you've signed the contract, you'll meet him then."

"I'm ready to sign it."

Boggs opened his Bible and pulled out a folded sheet of paper that was tucked inside. He fished a penknife out of his pocket. "Ephraim, you didn't know me before I came to Sixmile Creek," he said, handing over the contract, "but you and I have more in common than you might imagine. This arrangement might sound strange to you, me asking you to sign an agreement with someone you've never met. It'll strike you as even stranger when I tell you that this contract must be signed in blood." He flicked open the penknife and offered it to Ephraim, handle first. "But in spite of my employer's eccentricities, I can't recommend him highly enough. He has a gift for helping people reconceptualize life, and their place in it."

Ephraim looked from Boggs to the knife. Then he grasped the knife handle and read the contract.

I, Ephraim Cutler, pledge my life—my might, mind, strength, and soul—to Scratch, Lord of Darkness. May he spare me from Death as I stay in his good graces. For the span of seven years I will. . .

Ephraim looked up, his brow furrowed. "Scratch? Reverend, this is a deal with the Devil!"

Boggs smiled. He held up the Bible and tapped it with a finger. "Thou shalt not kill, Ephraim. Do you think the Lord's going to save your soul?"

24

PHIDITY

I sabel picked her way through the woods to the place Nancy had said to meet. She found the old woman squatting by the edge of the graveyard.

"Did I miss anything?" Isabel said, crouching next to Nancy. Her breath came out as a white vapor, mixing with the falling snow.

Nancy pulled a dry weed from her mouth and pointed with its stem. Snowflakes dusted her black and gray braids. "Boggs has got Ephraim over by the grave, talkin' 'bout somethin'. Your folks tan your hide last night when you got home after dark?"

Isabel wrapped her arms around herself and shook her head. "I missed dinner. Ma said I was acting like a child, staying out too late and turning up with dirty clothes. Pa was angry that I left the store unattended."

"You tell 'em 'bout Jubal?"

"No. I didn't want them asking where I'd been. I'm willing to bet his death would be pinned on Ephraim if anyone heard about it. What do you think we ought to do?"

Nancy watched Boggs and Ephraim through squinted eyes.

"Well, we got to warn Ephraim. If Boggs killed Jubal, he ought to know."

Isabel watched as Boggs pulled a paper out of his Bible and pushed it toward Ephraim, along with a penknife. She glanced at Nancy. "What're they up to?"

The granny woman was getting to her feet. "I ain't sure, but I don't like the looks of it."

Dry leaves rustled and a twig snapped in the woods behind them. Isabel spun around.

A filthy-looking man crouched behind them, clutching a pistol, his mouth pinched into a hard line, his nostrils flared. He was wearing a wide-brimmed hat and had a ragged piece of paper clutched in one hand.

It was the stranger Isabel had seen at the church.

"Nancy!" she hissed. "The Devil!"

The stranger cursed and bolted forward to grab Isabel.

"Get behind me, child!" Nancy stepped between them with surprising speed. "I dare ye!" the granny woman said. "I dare ye to come one step closer!" Her eyes flashed, and one hand strayed to her apron pocket.

The man stopped, his eyes flicking from Nancy, to Isabel, to Ephraim and Boggs.

"Go on, Isabel," commanded Nancy. "Warn Ephraim." The old woman's hand emerged from her apron clutching a fistful of white powder. "I'll give him a taste of phidity."

Isabel's skirts flapped as she ran. Small flecks of snow pelted her face, melting as they touched her skin.

"Let's see what kind of devil ye are!" she heard Nancy say behind her.

The stranger let out a strangled yell.

25

RECKON WITH THE DEVIL

"Ephraim! The Devil's here!"

Ephraim looked up from the paper he had pinned against the Bible. Boggs's head snapped in the direction of the voice too.

Isabel was running toward him through the snow. She plowed straight into him, grabbing his arm and nearly knocking him to the ground.

"Isabel, what's goin' on?" he asked.

"The Devil's here!" she panted.

"Where?"

But before Isabel could answer, he saw.

Through the flakes of falling snow a figure appeared, wearing a broad-brimmed hat. The wind whipped his Confederate coat. Above his patchy beard, his eyes looked hard enough to have been knapped from flint. He gripped a tarnished pistol in one hand.

Ephraim's heart began to race. He pushed Isabel behind him and looked at Boggs.

The reverend's eyes were narrowed. He reached beneath his

coat, and when his hand reappeared, it was clutching his tomahawk.

The stranger stopped. His eyes were fixed on Boggs.

"Get back, Satan! You can't have Ephraim!" Isabel screamed.

The man stared past her, eyes locked on the reverend. He sneered, baring rotten, yellowed teeth. "I ain't no devil, girl." His voice was cold. "I'm here to reckon with the devil Bill Boggs."

Ephraim and Isabel looked at the reverend. He said nothing, studying the stranger, his face expressionless.

"What's the matter, Boggs?" the stranger said. "Don't you recognize Reuben Pierce no more? That's funny, because I haven't forgotten your face since you took Amos!" He raised his gun and aimed it straight at the reverend.

Boggs's face broke into a grin. "I remember you, Reuben, but I doubt your son cares to anymore."

Reuben gave a guttural roar and pulled the trigger on his revolver. Once. Twice. The gunshots echoed through the grave-yard. Reuben kept squeezing the trigger until his revolver clicked empty.

Isabel clutched Ephraim's arm in both hands. Boggs stumbled back into a tree, propelled by the force of the bullets. He dropped his tomahawk, clutched at his chest.

Reuben stood for a time, his gun still pointed at the preacher. He glanced at Ephraim and Isabel, then motioned with the pistol. "Go on. You two best get out of here."

Boggs slid down the length of the trunk, scarlet ribbons leaking between the fingers of the hand covering his heart. He stopped in a sitting position, closing his eyes with a groan. He brought his left hand to his mouth and began to cough, each hack more violent than the last. He wiped his mouth with the back of his fist.

Then he looked up at Reuben and bared crimson teeth in a cruel smile. With surprising ease, he got to his feet, retrieved the fallen tomahawk with his right hand, and opened his left, dropping six misshapen lumps of bloody lead onto the ground.

"Now why'd you go and do a fool thing like that, Reuben?"

Reuben took a step backward.

Boggs undid his cravat with his free hand, grasped the collar of his shirt, and ripped it open. "You probably heard your son talk about this. Take a look for yourself."

The reverend's chest was whole. Blood stained the skin, but there were no signs of bullet wounds.

Isabel gripped Ephraim's arm even tighter.

Reuben's shoulders sagged. He looked over at Ephraim. "Boy, that contract you're holdin', don't sign it. My son trusted Boggs, and now he's lost forever."

Isabel tugged on Ephraim's arm. "He's right, Ephraim. You can't trust the reverend. I found Jubal's body. Boggs killed him."

Ephraim stared at Isabel, uncomprehending. "What?"

"He killed Jubal Early, Ephraim. After he let you out of the jail."

Ephraim looked at Boggs.

"Rest assured I acted in your best interest, boy." Boggs's eyes never left Reuben.

"How was killin' Jubal Early in my best interest?" Ephraim's head spun. The reverend, a cold-blooded killer?

Boggs chuckled. "Now don't turn all holier-than-thou on me! The grass hasn't even grown over Silas Henson's grave yet." He took a step toward Reuben, tomahawk raised.

Reuben raised his fists. "Go on and kill me, Boggs. I'll die happy knowin' I ruined one of your deals."

Boggs snorted. "It'd take a lot more than your meddling to do that. This boy has been bitten by a hellhound." He pointed at Ephraim without looking, traced a sign in the air, and snapped his fingers.

The skin on Ephraim's arm prickled, and he pulled back his sleeve. The bite wound looked just as it had before Boggs healed it, except worse. The blackened holes now radiated an inky spiderweb of lines through his flesh. The coldness in his arm flared to life, sending daggers of ice toward his heart. He tried to breathe deeply through the pain, but felt unable to fill his lungs.

"I felt sure that granny witch would turn you against me," Boggs said. "That's why I sent it after you. Its venom is still in your veins."

"But last night you healed it."

Boggs laughed. "Belief is a powerful thing, even when it's misguided. By the setting of the next full moon it'll turn you into a ghost, a haint, damned to the realm between life and death. Your days are numbered." He and Reuben began circling each other, but he continued to address Ephraim. "You must turn to the Devil, son. He'll cure that bite and more. You saw me spit out that lead. I'm proof that the Devil rewards his own."

Ephraim let the contract fall to the ground. "I ain't signin' no deal with the Devil."

"Don't be stupid, boy."

A bullet whistled past Ephraim's head and clipped the edge of his ma's gravestone, spraying chips of rock.

Ephraim crouched, pulling Isabel down with him. He turned, searching through the snow, and saw Peyton, Ernest Williams, and several other men heading toward him on horseback.

"He's seen us, boys! Get him!"

Reuben took advantage of the distraction to swing at Boggs, landing a blow on the reverend's cheek. Boggs staggered back with a cry.

"Come on!" Reuben said. "Follow me!" He took off through the snow toward the woods.

The hoofbeats were fast approaching. Another rifle round slammed into a gravestone to Ephraim's left. He took off after Reuben, Isabel at his side.

Nancy appeared through the snow up ahead. Reuben wrapped an arm around her and threw her over his shoulder.

"Let go of me!" Nancy said. She slapped Reuben on the head. "Ye pistol-whip old ladies often?"

"Sorry, ma'am. I didn't know what you were goin' to pull out of that apron," Reuben said, panting.

Nancy wrapped her hands around his neck. "I seen ye hit that preacher man too, so we'll forget about it."

Peyton's voice rang through the graveyard. "Ernest! Put that down!"

Still running, Ephraim looked over his shoulder. Boggs was chasing after them, and behind him, Ernest Williams was holding a lit stick of dynamite. Ernest lobbed the dynamite and plugged his ears. The stick arced through the air.

Ephraim put on a burst of speed, pulling Isabel forward. "Run!"

An explosion rocked the ground behind them, sending bits of earth and gravestone flying. Chips of rock peppered Ephraim, stinging his unprotected ears and neck like a swarm of frozen hornets.

They reached the woods.

Reuben pointed through the trees to the creek. "We'll follow that up around the bend, and I'll take you to my camp."

Ephraim could barely hear over the ringing in his ears, but he nodded.

They ran to the creek and waded in. Reuben let Nancy down off his back.

Isabel gasped, lifting the skirt of her dress. "It's freezing!"

The chill took Ephraim's breath away, but it was nothing compared to the bone-deep ache he felt in his arm.

They reached the bend in the creek when the shouts of their pursuers echoed through the woods. There was no time to run; they needed to hide.

Ephraim spotted a broad shelf of rock sticking out from the bank. There was about a foot-high space between the underside of the rock and the top of the water. He sloshed over to it, motioning for the others to follow.

Taking a deep breath, he lowered himself into the water until it reached his chin. Then he slid under the rock. The others followed suit.

Moments later, they heard the splashing of horses in the creek.

"Ernest, what were you thinkin'?" Peyton sounded angry. "Isabel was with him! I don't know how Reverend Boggs survived that!"

"Aw, hush, Peyton. The reverend didn't come to no harm. I was just thinking 'bout that two hundred dollars is all."

"Yeah, well, if you're not more careful, you'll wind up hanging next to Cutler!"

Ephraim looked over at Isabel. Her teeth were chattering.

They waited until the sounds of the men faded into the woods before emerging from under the shelf. Reuben pointed to where a spring joined the creek, and they all followed him toward it, arms wrapped around their shivering bodies.

"How far away is your camp?" Ephraim asked.

"'Bout two miles up this way," Reuben said, pointing uphill. He shuddered as a breeze gusted across them. "I hope I still have a few coals burnin'."

26

TROTTER HEAD

Reuben's camp consisted of a small white square of canvas stretched over an A-frame of sticks. The remains of a cooking fire sent up a single curl of smoke, and a blackened pot sat on a rock next to it.

Ephraim helped Reuben gather sticks and rekindle the fire. Isabel and Nancy marched around the camp sniffling, rubbing their arms, and trying to stomp feeling back into their feet. When the fire was going, Reuben fetched a pair of blankets from his tent and offered them to Nancy and Isabel. The men turned their backs as the women removed their soaking clothes.

"That's a pretty dress ye got there," Nancy said to Isabel.

Isabel snorted. "I don't know how pretty it'll be after today."

"It's still a sight better'n mine!"

When they told the men it was once again safe to look, Ephraim and Reuben turned back around. Nancy and Isabel had wrapped the blankets around their sodden shifts. They spread the dresses on a rock and huddled, shoulder to shoulder, next to the flames. Reuben had no more blankets, so he and Ephraim just got as close to the fire as they dared, letting their clothes steam dry.

"Soon as I get rid of this chill, I'll get us some food," Reuben said to Ephraim. "I ain't got much, but I got a little of that cake you gave me."

"Anything sounds good to me," Isabel said.

Ephraim stared at Nancy, thinking about how she had failed to visit Ma. She must have read his expression, because she said, "Why ye squintin' up your eyes at me like that?"

"I trusted you," Ephraim said flatly. "You came all the way back to town with me, and you didn't save Ma. You didn't even look in on her. And now she's dead! Where were you?"

"I went to help her!" Nancy said. "There weren't nothin' to be done, the foxglove did its work." She stopped. "Wait, did Boggs tell ye I didn't come? He's the one that run me off!"

"She's telling the truth, Ephraim," Isabel said, wrapping her arm around Nancy. "You ought to know better by now than to believe anything Boggs told you."

Ephraim looked down. They lapsed into awkward silence.

Reuben cleared his throat and left the fire. He went to his pack and pulled out a hunk of the apple stack cake wrapped in oilcloth. He broke off a lump and passed it around.

When the cake came to Isabel, she examined it with curiosity. She seemed to recognize it, but didn't say anything. She broke off a piece and passed the rest to Ephraim. It was stale, and hard enough to hurt his jaw when he chewed it.

Nancy took a bite of her piece, crunched, and swallowed. She looked at Reuben. "I'm sorry I smacked ye, mister. We thought ye was the Devil."

Reuben looked up. "No harm done, ma'am. Any enemy of Bill Boggs is a friend of mine."

"So ye know that wicked preacher from somewheres else?"

Reuben nodded and stared off into the snow-dusted woods. "Unfortunately."

"Where from?"

"The war. I don't care to burden you folks with that story,

though. It's enough to say that I know Bill Boggs from the war, and that he took my son from me." He looked from Nancy, to Isabel, to Ephraim. "Any of you ever hear Boggs mention a boy named Amos?"

They looked at each other, and all of them shook their heads.

Reuben sighed. "I was so sure I'd find him if I tracked Boggs down. It's all been in vain."

"Did he get Amos to sign a deal with the Devil?" Ephraim asked.

Reuben nodded. "You saw what he did back there, spittin' up that lead like it was nothin'? Boggs can't be killed. Lot of boys in the war saw him do things like that and were mighty impressed. Near as I can figure, Amos was one of 'em."

They watched the fire burn as the sun sank behind the mountains. After a while, Nancy felt the dresses and declared them dry enough to wear. Ephraim and Reuben turned their backs again to let the ladies dress.

As darkness crept over the woods, Reuben and Nancy settled down to sleep. Reuben offered his tent to the old woman, but she wouldn't hear of it. She accepted his blanket, though, and bedded down by the fire. Soon she was snoring.

Ephraim stirred the embers with a stick, watching the moon rise. The glowing orb was nearly full. He thought he could feel the coldness stirring in his arm again. He rolled up his sleeve and held it to the firelight. The charred, deadened appearance had spread. When he held his arm closer to the flames, his entire forearm, from wrist to elbow, was numb to the heat. *So this is it*, he thought, staring vacantly into the fire. *I'll become a haint*. He thought of Wes Sherman, how the old man's ghost was rumored to haunt the woods around his cabin. He'd be like that, a story told to children at night, a thing spoken of in whispers around Sixmile Creek. It was a fate worse than death.

Isabel came over and sat down on the log next to him. She picked up his right arm and traced the outline of the bite marks.

"You don't deserve what's happened to you, Ephraim," she said. "You didn't mean to kill Silas."

"How do you know that?" Ephraim said. "Even I'm not sure."

"Because you're kind. You're the kindest man I know. I've always known that about you."

"Well, let me tell you, you don't have to be mean-spirited to be a murderer. I found that out."

Isabel slid her hand down his arm. "No, you didn't mean to do it. Or if you did, you meant it in a way that was good, like when you took that licking for Billy Cartwright at school."

Ephraim snorted. "You remember that?"

"Of course I do. It was the kindest thing I've ever seen anyone do. Miss Harmon accused you of stealing Rindy Sue's apple, but everybody knew that Billy did it."

"Billy didn't have anythin' to eat that day. He rarely did."

"You saved him from a licking, Ephraim. In a way, all this is you taking a licking for your ma. You. Have. A. Good. Heart." Isabel tapped the back of his hand, emphasizing each word. "And I believe this will all work out somehow, because of your goodness."

She grabbed his arm and held it up for a closer look. "Surely there's something we can do to draw out the venom. Isn't there?"

"If there is, I'm afraid I don't know it. Nancy tried a couple things, and none of 'em worked." Ephraim wanted to believe Isabel more than anything; he wanted to stay by the fire and enjoy her closeness. But as he looked at the moon, he felt the throb of venom in his veins. Goodness and kindness—even if he was those things—could not protect him from his doom.

He pulled his hand away from Isabel's. "I can't do this."

She sat up, looking hurt. "Why?"

He held her gaze, trying to find the right words. "No one died when I took a lickin' for Billy. Silas was a good man, Isabel, and he's buried now. Everyone says my pa was a good man, and he never made it home from the war. They were both better men than me—they never made the mistake I have. So how can I expect a fate better than theirs?"

Isabel's eyes filled with tears. She turned away.

"Look, Isabel, I wish I could pretend that all this is goin' to end well. I want to be with you. But I've hurt enough folks, and I ain't going to hurt no one else. Least of all you."

They sat there, side by side, separated by silence. Ephraim's heart pounded painfully. He wanted to take Isabel's hand and tell her everything was going to be all right, but this was how it had to be.

Reuben groaned and stumbled out of his tent, rubbing his eyes. He excused himself and walked off into the woods. Ephraim heard the rattle of dry leaves as the man urinated. He returned to the fire and squatted by it, hands outstretched to catch the warmth.

Nancy stood up suddenly. She tossed the blanket to Reuben, wrinkling her nose in disgust. "This blanket of your'n smells like a boar hog and a billy goat had themselves a pissin' contest in it. I reckon you could've used a lump of soap when we were down there in the crick."

Reuben scratched his beard and looked sheepish. "Sorry, ma'am. I been searchin' for my boy for so long, I guess I let everythin' else go. I ain't used to keepin' company of any kind." He reached into his coat, drew out the scrap of paper, and fiddled with it.

"What is that?" Isabel asked. "I saw you holding it when you came into the church."

"This?" Reuben held up the paper.

Isabel nodded.

Ephraim sat forward on the log. "Yeah, why were you lettin' it blow down the road ahead of you when I first saw you?"

Reuben smiled. "I don't reckon you'd believe me if I told you. It's the craziest thing."

"I'm ready to believe just about anythin' you tell me," Ephraim said, "after what I've seen over the past few days."

"To be honest with you, I don't really know what this is myself," Reuben said, turning the paper in the firelight. "My boy sent it to me. It came with the last letter I ever got from him. See, me and my boy both knew Boggs back before the war started." Reuben studied Ephraim. "Amos was about your age then, and Bill Boggs was the preacher in our town. When the war began, I joined up as soon as I could, thinking they'd leave my wife and son alone. I never reckoned Amos would've wound up a soldier. But pretty soon I got a letter from my wife saying conscript officers had come through. They took our mule, the hogs, emptied the corncrib, and told Amos he'd been drafted. My wife said not to worry though, she'd manage until I got home, and that Reverend Boggs had volunteered to join the army when he saw they were takin' Amos. But I did worry. I worried myself sick about him. The war ain't no place for a boy, and the fact that men have to fight them is somethin' I'll never understand."

Reuben grabbed a stick and prodded a log deeper into the fire. "Everythin' I heard 'bout Amos, I got from my wife. He was sendin' letters home to her, see. She wrote to me and said that a couple weeks in, he'd killed a Yankee boy 'bout his own age, and it had torn him up somethin' awful inside. He told her he couldn't quit thinkin' 'bout that boy's face, that he saw it every night before he went to sleep."

A lump rose in Ephraim's throat. He knew the feeling Reuben was describing all too well.

"His letters kept gettin' stranger and stranger. My wife started sendin' 'em to me so I could read 'em for myself. Amos said he wasn't plannin' on comin' home after the war. He told us that Boggs had shown him a better way to live, a way to live with your sins and be powerful. He said there wasn't a soldier alive that could kill Reverend Boggs. Said he'd seen Boggs kill ten Yankee soldiers usin' nothin' but a tomahawk, said it looked like a wildcat tearin' through a henhouse.

"I quit gettin' letters from home for a while, but after the war ended and I went back home, my wife showed me the last letter Amos ever sent her. He'd written that he wanted to come clean to us. Said he'd sold his soul to the Devil and was livin' after the manner of Cain—and that Boggs had showed him how to do it. He told us not to come lookin' for him, and that he wasn't our son no more."

Reuben gripped the paper tightly. "Way I see it, Boggs got into Amos's head somehow. He knew my son wasn't right after he shot that Yankee boy, and he used that to get him to sell his soul." He looked at the paper as if seeing it for the first time. "This was folded up inside that last letter. It's a page torn out of some book. I've read it several times, and I can't reckon what it's about. There's three lines on it." He passed the paper to Ephraim. "Have a look."

Ephraim held the page up to the firelight. It *had* been torn from a book, and part of the page had been left behind. From the torn edge, the three partial lines read:

L Eckerlin
   1757 and all years hence
   and the time for every purpose under heaven

"Can you make any sense of that?" Reuben asked.

Ephraim shook his head. "Not without the rest of the page." He passed the scrap to Isabel.

She examined it and passed it to Nancy. "So why do you toss it out in front of you?"

"That's the strangest part," Reuben said. "A year after the war, my wife died. I think her heart was broken over Amos; he was our

only child. After I buried her, I went home and I got real drunk."
He looked sheepishly at Isabel and Nancy. "I beg pardon 'cause I
know that ain't fit to say in the company of ladies, but it's the
honest truth. While I was drinkin' I got a fire goin', and I started
tossin' all of Amos's letters into it. Well, when I got to that scrap of
paper, try as I might, I couldn't get the blamed thing to go in! I'd
throw it in the fireplace, and it'd fly right back out and land by
the front door. Finally I left it there and went to bed.

"When I woke up sober, I remembered what'd happened, so I
picked it up and went outside to throw it into the hog pen. But it
wouldn't go in there neither! I noticed then that the paper always
flew the same direction, no matter which way the wind was
blowin'. I don't know why, but I realized that this thing was tryin'
to take me to Amos. So I got my pack ready, and I've been
followin' the blamed thing ever since."

Ephraim and Isabel glanced at each other, wide-eyed.

"Well it certainly brought you to Boggs," Ephraim said.
"There's no doubt about that."

"For certain," Reuben said. He inspected a hangnail, chewed
on it, and spat. "And it don't want to leave Sixmile Creek neither.
I've tried it out. It always goes back toward the church. I got no
idea where Amos is."

"I think I know somethin' 'bout this," Nancy said.

The granny woman had been uncharacteristically quiet
during Reuben's tale. Ephraim looked over at her now, and saw
that she was holding the scrap of paper in both hands, a somber
expression on her face.

"You can make sense out of that?" Reuben said.

Nancy nodded. "Some. Eckerlin's my family name."

Reuben straightened up. "Well, let's hear it!"

Nancy fiddled with the end of one braid, studying the paper
again. "I'll tell ye what I know. But first, we need to head back to
my place. I've got to talk with my pappy's shirt."

Reuben and Isabel looked confused.

Ephraim got to his feet. "Let's go," he said. "You'll see what she's talkin' 'bout."

~

THEY GOT to the Laura just as the sun peeked over the mountaintops. Earl rushed to meet Nancy as they approached. The goat was munching on what appeared to be the remains of a basket. The granny woman shook her head as she scratched him between the horns. "I wondered where that basket went. Must've left it outside." She went inside the hollow sycamore and came out holding a lump of soap, a straight razor, a bucket, an ax, and the folded cream-colored shirt.

She handed the soap and razor to Reuben. "The crick's that way," she said, pointing into the woods. "Go give yourself a good scrubbin'."

Reuben looked hurt. "Ma'am, that water's freezin' cold. Ain't no way I'm goin' to jump in it again unless I have to."

"Ye will if ye want to set foot inside my house!" Nancy declared. She passed the bucket to Isabel. "Fetch us some water to cook a proper meal, dear, and make sure ye stay upstream of him." She shot Reuben a narrow-eyed glance.

The ax she gave to Ephraim. "Ye can chop us some wood for the fire. And once you've finished, go inside and get a few apples out of the basket in there for Earl." She shook out the shirt. "Me 'n' pappy got to talk."

Despite receiving their orders, no one moved. They stayed to watch the granny woman. She walked to her clothesline, draped the shirt over it, then knelt down in front of it and started speaking in a low tone. Before long the garment was waving in answer, sleeves fluttering wildly in the barest hint of a breeze.

"Isn't it somethin'?" Ephraim said, looking at Reuben's and Isabel's slack-jawed expressions.

Earl moseyed over and began sniffing the hem of Isabel's dress.

"It reminds me of the paper," Reuben said. He drew it out of his coat and tossed it into the air. It spun and darted in the direction of Sixmile Creek before floating to the ground.

"Mr. Reuben, the crick awaits ye!" Nancy called from the clothesline. "Pappy says he can smell ye from here!" She pointed at Earl. "Careful, Isabel, that goat'll eat anythin'!"

By MIDMORNING, Ephraim had split a sizable stack of wood and had gotten a fire started in the stove. Isabel had cooked a round of cornbread and had a pot of beans boiling.

Nancy joined them in the Laura and said she had a long story to tell, but she wouldn't speak a word of it until Reuben returned. Fortunately it wasn't long before Reuben came back, Earl in tow. His scent had improved immensely, and he was clean-shaven, cheeks still red from the chilly creek water. His only complaint was that he'd lost his hat at the creek. Upon hearing this, Nancy shot Earl a withering glance. He stared back at her unabashed, jaw working suspiciously.

Isabel served the cornbread and beans, and they ate. Reuben and Ephraim sat at the table, while the women sat on Nancy's bed. When the last bite of beans had been cleaned from the pot, Nancy stood.

"I have a tale to tell ye. It begins with my pappy. His name was Abel Eckerlin, and he died afore I was borned. He was Dutch, and when he first came over from the Old Country, he lived in a place called Ephrata, up in Pennsylvany. He was one of them Dunker Brethren, but he took off into the wilderness to live by hisself. He lasted a few years as a hermit, then got friendly with a group of Cherokee that didn't live too far from him, and that's where he met my mammy."

Nancy stopped and held up a finger. "But the most important thing ye should know 'bout Pappy is that he had the gift of the cunning-folk. I got it from him. "

"What're cunning-folk?" Isabel asked.

Nancy smiled at Ephraim, then gave Isabel the same explanation she'd given him.

"Oh," Isabel said. "So what you're saying is, there's people born with magic gifts, and the ones who use it for good are like you—healing folks and protecting them. But those that use their magic for evil turn into witches."

Nancy nodded. "That's right, and ye know 'em by their evil eye." She cleared her throat. "Anyways, the reason my pappy left the church at Ephrata was, he'd made up his mind to study all of creation. He aimed to learn the power and purpose behind every time, season, plant, and critter. He wanted to write it all down in one book, like all the old almanacks rolled together. Accordin' to Mammy, he done it too, and then some." She looked over at Ephraim. "If there's a book out there that'd tell ye how to cure a hellhound bite, it'd be Pappy's."

Isabel grabbed Ephraim's hand and squeezed it. A flutter of hope stirred deep inside him.

Nancy looked at Reuben. "Can I see that paper of your'n?"

Reuben handed it to the granny woman.

Nancy held the paper up. "Near as I can reckon, this is a page out of my pappy's almanack."

"So where's the rest of it?" Ephraim asked.

"That's what I was talkin' to Pappy's shirt about. I asked it 'bout the way this piece of paper behaves. The shirt said, in not so many words, that it's charmed to find the book it belongs to."

Isabel's eyes grew wide, and she looked at Reuben. "You said that paper keeps trying to go to the church, didn't you?"

Reuben nodded.

"So Boggs has your pappy's almanack?" Isabel said to Nancy.

"I reckon that's right. But I can't figure how he come by it.

That book has been lost for over a hundred years. Nary a soul's seen it since Pappy was killed."

Ephraim stiffened. *The book with golden stars and a moon on its cover.* That had to be it. "I've seen it!" he said.

"Ye have?"

"Yes! Boggs keeps it on his desk. The first page in it is torn!" Ephraim closed his eyes, trying to summon the image of the page. What had it said? The year, 1757, and somethin' 'bout a calendar and seasons.

Reuben took the page back from Nancy and turned it over in his hands. "You say your pa was killed," he said. "Who done it?"

Nancy shrugged. "I don't know. I've asked the shirt to tell me many a time. It always says that the story of that day is too sad to bear tellin'. It says it can still feel the places where my pappy's blood stained it."

"Nancy," Isabel said, "if that shirt was your pappy's, is it his spirit you're talking to when you talk to it?"

Nancy pursed her lips. "Mmm, I don't reckon so. See, I've heard tell that the blood of the strongest cunning-folk is a powerful thing." She unfolded the shirt and placed it on the table. "Look here," she said, pointing to a hole in the shirtfront. "I reckon my pappy was wearin' this shirt the day he was cut down. Now this thing has been washed many a time since that day, so ye cain't see no bloodstains on it, but I reckon that when Pappy's blood soaked into the shirt, it passed some of his power into it."

The vision of Silas's blood soaking through his shirtfront flashed through Ephraim's mind. Guilt swelled inside him, and his wounded arm began to throb. He massaged it under the table. "So you think this almanack will tell me how to cure this bite?"

Nancy started to nod, then stopped. "Well, when I asked the shirt it said, 'To free the soul and claim the prize, evil must taint familiar eyes.'" She shook her head and folded the shirt back into a bundle. "I never was much good at understandin' this fool thing, but it sounds to me like Boggs has the prize that'll free your soul, Ephraim. If that ain't the almanack, then I don't know what it'd be. And if we're goin' after it, I think we best wait until Sunday and take it while he's preachin'."

WINTER TOOK hold of the mountains over the next few days. From the warmth of the Laura, Ephraim watched as snow covered the ground. The woods were silent beneath the thick white blanket, but his arm kept him from enjoying the peace. The venom was spreading; fingers of blackened flesh soon laced over his shoulder and onto his neck. Sideways glances from Isabel, Nancy, and even Reuben made him keenly aware that his condition was now visible above his collar. The coldness inside him was sharper than the winter nights.

They left the Laura at dawn on Sunday. It was snowing again. They waited in the woods on the far side of the church graveyard, watching the townsfolk enter the church. When the doors to the church were shut and the faint strains of singing reached their hiding place, Ephraim spoke.

"All right, let's go."

They stayed low, zigzagging from grave to grave, and made their way to Reverend Boggs's home. Ephraim darted up the stairs and tried the door. "It's locked."

"Move out of the way," Reuben said. He walked forward, wiped sweat from his face with a sleeve, and gave the door a powerful kick. The door swung open with the sound of splintering wood. "Go on," Reuben said. "You know where that book is. I'll keep watch."

Ephraim and Isabel stepped inside.

Ephraim made straight for the shelf that held the reverend's books. He scanned the titles. *The Higher Christian Life, Pilgrim's Progress, The Alhambra…*

The almanack wasn't there.

"I don't see it," Ephraim whispered. "Wait, it was on the desk when I saw it last." He threw himself at the reverend's desk, sliding aside papers and inkwells. He picked up an open tome, only to find that it was the Bible. "It's gone."

It has to be here somewhere.

He ran to the reverend's bed, looked under it, then stood and ripped off the blankets and shook them. "I can't find it," he said to Isabel, panic rising in his throat.

Then he remembered the cellar. He lifted the trap door and looked inside. The cellar was bare, just as it had been when he'd slept there.

He turned to Isabel, lifted his hands, and let them fall. "I don't know of anywhere else he could have hidden it. The almanack isn't here."

They walked outside. Reuben took one look at Ephraim's empty hands and said, "He must have it with him." He threw the scrap of paper in the air, and they all watched as it drifted a few feet toward the church.

Ephraim took his head in his hands. His only hope for a cure was slipping away. "There's no way we can get it away from him with the whole congregation in there," he said.

They stood in silence.

Nancy shut her eyes and took a deep breath. She opened them and gazed at the sky. "To free the soul and claim the prize, evil must taint familiar eyes," she whispered. Then she shook herself and looked at Ephraim, her face grim. "There's yet a way. I need ye to fetch some things for me." She looked at Isabel and Reuben. "All of ye."

"What? How?" Ephraim asked. "What are you goin' to do?"

"Don't worry 'bout the mules, just load the wagon," Nancy said briskly. "Isabel, I'll need ye to build me a good fire and get a pot of water a-boilin'. Ephraim and Reuben, go find me some hackberry leaves. I know the wind's blowed most of the leaves off the trees this time of year, but try to be quick about it." She scanned the reverend's home. "And I need to find a fire poker."

By the time Ephraim and Reuben made it back to the house with the hackberry leaves, the water in the pot was boiling, and Nancy had the tip of a poker shoved into the coals at the bottom of the hearth. She took it out and spat on the tip. The saliva bubbled and hissed.

She nodded in approval. "Go ahead and put them leaves in the water."

Ephraim obeyed, and they stood around the hearth watching the dry leaves ride the roiling water. After a moment, Nancy pulled a knife from her skirts and drew the blade across her palm in one swift motion. Isabel gasped, but Nancy shot her a sharp look as she held her curled fist over the pot and let a few drops of blood drip in.

"As soon as I say so, one of ye grab that pot and follow me."

"Wait a minute," Reuben said. "I think we all need to know what's goin' on here."

Nancy bent over the pot and studied the concoction boiling inside. "Witchery, that's what's goin' on here. I'm goin' to curse the preacher man, and the whole congregation. I'll hold this here poker, and when I give the signal, one of ye need to dump the potion over the hot end of it. It'll confuse 'em—addle their brains long enough for somebody to sneak in there and grab the almanack."

"I'll do it," Ephraim said.

"I reckon Reuben better do it," Nancy said to him. "That way ye can go after the almanack since you've seen it afore. Now, as soon as I'm done castin' this curse, y'all need to let me clear out. Don't none of ye follow me or go anywhere near the Laura till dawn tomorrow, ye hear?"

Ephraim and Isabel looked at each other, perplexed.

"Where should we go once we've got the almanack, then?" Ephraim asked.

Nancy looked up from the pot, and Ephraim was surprised to see tears in her eyes. "I don't know," she said, dabbing her eyes with her skirt.

Isabel rushed to Nancy's side. "What's wrong?" she asked, drawing the granny woman into a hug.

"The Black Madness," Nancy said. She pushed Isabel away and tried to compose herself.

"The what?"

"It's what happens when a person becomes a witch." Nancy wiped her eyes again. "All my life I've been a granny woman. My mammy raised me well—I ain't never used my power to hurt no one. I cure folks and undo the work of witches. If I use my gift to cast a curse, the Black Madness will come over me, and when it leaves I'll have the evil eye. I'll be a witch. My gift will turn sour, and it'll only be good for hexin'—I won't be able to heal and help folks no more. It was me the shirt was talkin' 'bout, 'evil must taint familiar eyes.'"

Ephraim stepped forward. "Nancy, I can't have you give up your gift on my account. I've ruined enough lives lately. I can't add yours to the list."

Nancy took a deep breath and drew herself up to her full height. "Ephraim Cutler, I'm an old woman and I can choose for myself. I've lived a long life, and I know what it takes. Ye done me a good turn that day when ye gave me half of your corn, and I'm a-goin' to do this thing for ye, and for everyone else that no-good preacher man has harmed."

She turned back to the fire and inspected the point of the poker, which was glowing a dull red. "We're ready. Everybody stay behind me, and don't be a-follerin' me once I've done this. I don't care if it starts snowin' oats and rainin' tomcats, you leave me alone! There ain't no tellin' what a witch'll do when the Black Madness is upon her. I won't be holdin' the reins on my actions till the sun comes up tomorrow mornin'. So stay clear!"

She held up the glowing fire poker, face hardening, and

nodded to Reuben, who grabbed a rag and lifted the pot from its hook over the fire.

"Come on," Nancy said. She strode toward the door, her baffled entourage in tow.

They rounded the side of the church and walked up to the double doors that led inside.

"Wait," Ephraim said. He turned to Isabel. "You shouldn't come in here with us. All of Sixmile Creek's in there."

Isabel folded her arms. "Ephraim, don't tell me—"

"He's right," Nancy cut in. "Ephraim, Reuben, 'n' me, this town don't think too highly of us. But you, Miss Isabel, you're different. You got a good family. Folks think the best of ye. If ye walk through these doors with us, it ain't gonna be that way no more."

Isabel looked from Nancy to Ephraim. "You think I haven't thought about this? I know what helping Ephraim is doing to my reputation. But you know what matters more than what this town thinks of me? What *I* think of me. I've come this far with you, and I'm not turning back."

"All right then," Nancy said. "The girl's made her choice."

Ephraim wanted to protest further, but the granny woman had already reached for the church door and yanked it open.

Boggs's sermon was in full swing. The reverend stood at the pulpit, Bible in one hand, the other punctuating his words.

"You and I, all of us," he said, sweeping an accusatory finger at the crowd. "We are able to hide so much. As a matter of fact, *most* of what is important to us, we're able to hide. But the Lord sees all. There's no escaping that all-seeing eye."

Nancy held the red-hot poker out in front of her like some hellish, sword-wielding general about to lead a charge. She stepped forward. Reuben stayed close behind her, ignoring the turning heads of the congregation. He locked eyes with Boggs.

The reverend trailed off as he saw the group entering at the rear of the church.

Ephraim's heart knocked against his ribs. All those eyes, eyes of folks ready to hang him. He swallowed hard and stepped up next to Reuben. Murmurs rippled through the congregation.

"Well, well," the reverend said. "A witch, a vagabond, and a murderer. And you, Miss Coleman?"

Nancy raised the fire poker and jabbed it toward the pulpit. "The day ye ran me out of this church, I told everyone the whirlwind was a-comin'. Well, now it's here! Your undoin' is at hand, preacher man!"

Ernest Williams and several other men got to their feet and started toward the granny woman, pulling pistols out of their belts.

Nancy closed her eyes and waved the poker. A fierce gust of wind whooshed into the church, rattling the open doors. "Ye wrongdoers, I conjure ye!" she said, her voice filling the chapel. "I seek refuge beneath the tree that bears twelvefold fruit, and conjure ye with the curse of the trotter head!"

Isabel looked at Ephraim, eyes wide.

"I bind your eyes that ye may hear, but not see! I bind your ears that ye may see, but not hear!" The wind blasted again, turning the pages of Boggs's Bible on the pulpit.

A shudder rocked the congregation. The standing men swayed as if caught in an earthquake. Ernest Williams convulsed, and a dazed look entered his eyes.

Reverend Boggs staggered, clutching the sides of the pulpit. His nostrils flared, and he bared his teeth.

"I cast your minds into darkness," Nancy finished quietly, lowering the poker. She nodded to Reuben.

He upended the contents of the pot on the poker's glowing tip, filling the air with a hiss.

Nancy groaned and doubled over. The poker dropped from her hand and hit the floorboards with a clang.

The standing men, including Boggs, collapsed to the floor. The others slumped forward and backward in the pews, eyes wild, mouths agape. But no one made a sound. The church was filled with an awful silence.

Ephraim felt weak in the knees. "I thought you said the curse would just confuse 'em."

"I did," Nancy said, still bent over, breathing deeply. She took her head in both hands.

"But they look like they're dead!" Ephraim said.

"What?" Nancy looked up at the still congregation and took a step backward. "Must've boiled them hackberry leaves a mite too long," she said, then gave a dreadful moan. "I got to clear out now. Remember, leave me be till sunrise!"

She stumbled out the door and disappeared.

"Get the book and let's go," Reuben said. "There's no tellin' how long this curse will hold."

Ephraim walked up the aisle to the pulpit. Reverend Boggs lay facedown on the floor behind it, arms reaching over his head. The muscles in Ephraim's stomach tightened; he imagined the man's head jerking up from the floor, his hand closing around Ephraim's leg. He shook his head to clear the image. *The almanack*, he thought. *I've got to get the almanack.*

It was on a shelf under the pulpit. Ephraim examined the stars embossed on its cover. "I've got it," he said, holding the volume aloft so Reuben and Isabel could see.

"Good," Isabel said. "Let's get out of here!"

THEY RAN BACK through the graveyard. As they crossed the creek, a roar of rage echoed from the church behind them, setting a startled flock of crows skyward.

Ephraim glanced over his shoulder, and to his horror, he saw Boggs stumbling through the tombstones. Just as Ephraim had feared, the preacher had overcome the curse.

Boggs stopped and lifted his arms to the sky, chanting something. The heavens began to darken as gray winter clouds gathered. Boggs then pointed toward Ephraim and the others. A lightning bolt ripped out of the sky and struck a tree to Ephraim's right. Shards of bark and splinters of wood sprayed. Ephraim, Isabel, and Reuben covered their faces as they ran.

Isabel cried out, and Ephraim turned to see that she had fallen behind, her skirt caught in a mess of briars. He ran back to her, Reuben on his heels.

"I think we should split up," Ephraim said as he tore the hem of Isabel's dress free. "Boggs can't track everyone."

"That's a good idea," Reuben said. "Where should we meet up?"

"At Nancy's place, tomorrow mornin'," Ephraim said. To Isabel he added, "It'll be cold tonight without fires, but as long as you keep movin' you'll stay warm. Only lay low if you have to."

"I'll run all night if I have to," Isabel said. She gathered her torn dress in her hands. "Looks like I won't be wearing this thing to any more funerals."

Ephraim grabbed Isabel by the shoulders. "I'm awful sorry 'bout gettin' you mixed up in this, Isabel. You and Nancy are the only friends I've got left around Sixmile Creek. I appreciate everythin' you've done to help me."

Isabel looked down. "I think the best of you, Ephraim Cutler. I don't want you to turn into a haint." She wiped her eyes with her hand, and Ephraim saw the gleam of tears. "If anyone deserves a second chance, it's you." She looked up and leaned in suddenly. Her lips pressed against Ephraim's.

A buzzing sensation filled Ephraim's brain. When Isabel released him, he felt warm in spite of the chill air.

"We'd best get going," Isabel said.

"Right," Ephraim said. "Get goin'."

Reuben tipped his hat and flashed Ephraim a grin. "See y'all at sunup," he said, and slipped off through the trees.

Ephraim found it hard to leave Isabel. "Why don't we stick together?"

Isabel shook her head. "You were right to begin with. We'll be harder to track if we take separate paths." She dabbed her eyes and smiled. "Don't worry about me. I'll be fine."

"All right. I'll see you in the mornin'."

"See you in the morning."

They set off in opposite directions.

27

A COUPLE OF SINNERS

Isabel had kept moving all day, never staying in one place for too long. She hadn't seen Boggs since they'd split up, which was both a relief and a concern. If the reverend wasn't chasing her, he was probably going after Ephraim.

Now the woods were growing dark, and despite her earlier determination, she doubted she could stay on the run all night. Her feet were numb from traipsing through the snow. She was exhausted, and she would need to rest soon.

Isabel gasped as her leg shot down a hidden groundhog hole. Her ankle twisted, sending a sharp pain up her leg. She pulled her foot out and dusted off the dirt and snow. Gently, she took another step—and winced. She'd sprained her ankle. She could hobble along, but there'd be no more running for her tonight. It was a good thing Boggs was busy elsewhere.

As if summoned by the thought, a light bobbed through the trees, piercing the darkness like an oversized lightning bug. A lantern. Isabel felt her heart being squeezed by fear's cold fingers. *Boggs.*

She looked around desperately for someplace to hide, and

spotted a dense thicket. She crawled over to it and forced her way inside, heedless of the scrubby branches scraping her skin and the disturbed snow showering down. She struggled to pull her dress in behind her. In the center of the thicket she found a little hollow. She curled up within it and did her best to calm her beating heart.

A minute later, she heard footsteps approaching, and then Boggs came into view, carrying a lantern and a whip. Only a few feet from her hiding place, he stopped. He held up the lantern and searched the trees. Then he whispered a few words, his hand tracing a pattern in the air. A small light, a spark, formed over his hand. Boggs blew on it, and it drifted away from him.

It moved toward Isabel.

Boggs looked toward the thicket.

Isabel covered her mouth, not daring to breathe.

The reverend walked to the thicket, lantern raised. He leaned down and parted the brush with his rifle barrel. He smiled.

Isabel tried to scramble away, but froze when she heard the hammer on the rifle click back.

"It's no use, Miss Coleman."

Isabel spun around. The reverend's left eye gleamed red in the lantern light. "If you touch me, my pa will have your hide!"

Boggs grinned. "Really? Your pa is none too happy about you gallivanting around the woods with a murderer and a thief." He let the whip uncoil. Several tails dangled from its end, each tipped with a small iron spike. "And after what you did at the church this morning, I doubt anyone in Sixmile Creek will come to your defense. That is, when they wake up. They're all still unconscious—including your pa." Boggs motioned with the lantern. "Now get out of there, turn around, and put your hands together behind your back."

Isabel's pulse raced. She felt around behind her. Something sharp pricked her finger, and she gripped it. It was a broken branch of thorns. She held it tightly as she crawled out of the thicket and slowly got to her feet.

Before the reverend could react, Isabel swung the thorn-covered branch at his face with all her might.

The thorns raked across Boggs's eyes. He howled and threw up his arms. The lantern fell to the ground and broke. Oil spilled out, igniting the briars of the thicket.

Isabel ran.

But not fast enough. Something sliced the air behind her, and she felt Boggs's whip wrap itself around her legs. As the iron spikes buried themselves in her calves, she screamed in pain. Boggs yanked on the whip, pulling her feet out from under her. Isabel's head connected with the ground, and stars blossomed in her vision as she rolled onto her back.

The thicket blazed behind the reverend as he walked toward her, casting him in a hellish yellow glow.

"Get up," he spat.

Summoning her remaining strength, Isabel kicked at him.

Boggs sidestepped her easily. "Fine," he said. "Let's do this my way." He knelt down and flipped Isabel over onto her stomach, pinning her to the ground with his knee. She struggled and screamed as he wrenched the whip from her legs and used it to bind her hands. When he'd cinched the knot tight, he hauled her to her feet.

"Where'd your friends go?" he asked.

Isabel glared at him, nostrils flared. But inside, her heart skipped a beat. *He hasn't found Ephraim or Reuben yet. They're still alive.*

"No matter, you'll serve nicely as bait," Boggs said. He reached into his coat and pulled out a tomahawk. "We need to get you back to my house... after one other stop. It would seem that this preacher has need for a couple sinners."

～

IN THE DARK, Isabel couldn't tell where Boggs was taking her. The preacher kept her ahead of him, prodding her with the tomahawk, and pausing every so often while he got his bearings. They continued like this for what seemed like hours, moving deeper into the snowy woods and uphill, until they came to a clearing. At its center sat a whiskey still.

Boggs stepped in front of Isabel for the first time, jerking the whip as he towed her behind him. "Where are they?" he muttered under his breath.

"Stop right there!"

Isabel looked up, trying to spot the source of the voice.

A length of rifle barrel gleamed in the moonlight, and then Jake Fletcher stepped out from behind a tree. Clabe followed him, holding a club.

"Reverend Boggs, is that you?"

Isabel's heart filled with dread.

"It is," Boggs said, turning to face the brothers.

"Well, it ain't every night we catch a preacher man stumblin' around in the dark," Clabe said. He motioned for Jake to keep his rifle trained on Boggs. "There something you want, Reverend, or did you just stop by to give us a temperance lecture?"

"Keep quiet, missy, or you'll regret it," Boggs whispered to Isabel.

He bent down and laid his tomahawk on the ground, then stood up, raised both hands in the air, and smiled broadly. "Hardly. I came up here to see if you boys want to make some money."

Clabe glanced at Jake. "What'd you have in mind?"

Boggs pushed Isabel forward. "I have an old enemy in town. I won't bore you two with the details, but this enemy of mine has allied himself with Ephraim Cutler, and the two of them, along with this young lady, broke into the church earlier today and stole something very valuable. As you can see, I've caught her, and I'd like to keep her under guard until I get my belongings back. In fact, I think Ephraim will turn himself in when he learns that I have the girl."

Clabe sniffed. "We've been huntin' Cutler ourselves. In fact we had him a couple days ago. What's the benefit if we help you?"

"I'll pay you each five dollars for every day you stand guard. I'll keep a tab and give it to you at the end. As far as the bounty on Ephraim's head, you two can keep it for yourselves if he turns himself in. I just want my possessions back."

Clabe folded his arms. "Ten dollars each, paid out every day, Preacher. That's our rate."

"Do you both have guns?" Boggs asked, eyeing Clabe's cudgel.

"No, only the one Jake's holdin'. We lost the other one a while back in the Hurricane Timber."

Boggs raised an eyebrow. "It'll be five dollars a day then." He held out a hand to Clabe.

Isabel's legs felt weak. She was trembling so much, she couldn't even feel the scratches and cuts from the briars and the whip. Boggs was right: if Ephraim heard that she'd been captured, he'd turn himself in. And the last thing she wanted was to be left alone with the Fletcher boys.

"Listen, Clabe, Jake," she said, "if it's money you're after, I'm sure my pa will—"

Boggs backhanded her in the mouth. She cried out, tasting blood on her tongue.

Jake and Clabe glanced at each other and grinned.

"Well, looky there. Reverend Boggs knows how to treat a mouthy woman. I like that." Clabe rubbed his chin, running an appraising eye up and down Isabel. "Now, when you say stand guard over her, you mean all we got to do is keep her alive and make sure she don't go nowhere, right, Reverend? You ain't opposed to anythin' else."

Behind her back, Isabel clenched her fists and strained

against the whip. If Clabe laid a hand on her, she would find a way to hurt him.

"Just don't let her wander off, boys. Do that, and you'll get your money."

28

EVIL EYE

E phraim had lost his way in the woods, something he never did. Isabel's kiss, the blanket of snow, and darkness all served to disorient him. He'd been traveling toward Flint Ridge since he'd left Isabel, but he couldn't identify his exact location.

A faint sound echoed through the still forest. Ephraim stopped walking and listened. Off in the shadows someone laughed. There was an eerie quality to it. Ephraim felt a shiver in his innards.

The cackling continued. Ephraim spun around, trying to pinpoint its source. It changed directions with inhuman speed—one second coming from the treetops above him, the next echoing from the forest to his left.

Ephraim crouched low to the ground. He wasn't sure if he'd been spotted yet. *It's dark. Maybe if I stay low and don't move...*

"I see ye!"

The voice chattered down Ephraim's spine like nails on slate. A moon shadow shifted among the trees—the slanting shadow of a woman. Ephraim saw bare feet in the snow. Nancy.

Ephraim cursed silently. He had been so preoccupied that

he'd unwittingly wandered too close to the Laura. And now he'd found Nancy, still in the throes of the Black Madness, and still hours before daybreak.

Nancy stepped forward into the moonlight. Her hair, usually tied into braids, was loose and sticking out at odd angles as if she had just violently shaken her head. Deep shadows pooled in the hollows of her cheeks, and her eyes looked cavernous.

The granny woman cocked her head and fixed Ephraim with her gaze. He felt paralyzed. He could no more turn away than a bird could shun the cold-eyed stare of a rattlesnake.

"Ye have the book," Nancy said. Her voice was a broken croak. She held out a hand. "Give it to me."

"N-no," Ephraim stammered. He'd faced a hellhound and a Devil-bound preacher over the last few days, but none of that was as unsettling as evil wearing a friend as a mask.

"Give it to me!"

Nancy vaulted into the air and flew straight at him, her tree-branch fingers extended like gnarled spears.

Ephraim dove out of the way, rolling through the snow. Nancy landed on all fours, snarled in his direction, and shot flealike into the air again.

Ephraim bolted like a scared rabbit. He zigzagged through the trees, trying to throw Nancy off his trail. Her cackles and shrieks echoed through the woods behind him, not gaining, but not falling behind either.

I need a place to hide.

Ephraim dodged an oak and nearly tripped over a log. He was about to carry on when he was halted by a thought. He turned around and investigated the log. At one end, he found what he was hoping for: the log was hollow. Adjusting the almanack under his shirt, he squirmed inside.

The log smelled musty. Ephraim's fingers sank into a layer of decayed wood and leaf mold along the bottom. His head scraped the rough roof, and a shower of debris fell around his ears. He wriggled onward until the space grew too tight for him to continue. Were his feet all the way inside? He drew them up for good measure.

Seconds later, he heard Nancy's muffled cackling. "Where are ye, boy?"

Ephraim could hear her feet dragging through the dry leaves outside. She sprang onto the log with a dull thump. Ephraim took a deep breath and held it.

"I ain't foolin', boy! Give me that book!"

Nancy shifted around on her perch, then climbed down. Ephraim slowly released the breath he'd been holding. He listened hard, trying to tell if she was gone. A minute passed, maybe more; he wasn't sure. Outside the log, nothing stirred. He tried to slow the crazed beating of his heart. After another minute had passed in silence, Ephraim reached up and dislodged a piece of rotten wood from behind his ear.

A prickly sensation spider-walked down his spine. Ephraim stiffened against it. The feeling spread, plunging roots deep into him, leaching his strength. His muscles gave way to a wave of jitters. Never in his life had he felt so shaky; it was overpowering.

"Found yourself a hidey-hole!" The words lanced through Ephraim. He lurched upward, banging his head against the inside of the log.

Nancy cackled. Her fingers clamped his ankle tighter than a robin's beak on an unfortunate nightcrawler. Before he could muster a kick, she wrenched him free of the log in a shower of splinters and punkwood.

Consternation mingled with fear as Ephraim realized that he was being dangled upside down by an old woman a head shorter than him. She gave him a violent shake, and the almanack tumbled out of his shirt and onto the ground. Ephraim snatched it up in both hands.

"I'll be havin' that," Nancy said, reaching for it with her free hand.

"Nancy, no!" Ephraim said. "You helped me get this, remember?"

Nancy's hand froze.

"Please. Put me down, Nancy. I'm your friend. You've got the Black Madness."

The granny woman studied him for a second, her face unreadable. "I know."

Ephraim gave a sigh of relief. "Nancy, I—"

She shook him again.

Ephraim kicked with his free leg. His boot connected with Nancy's hand, and he tumbled to the ground.

Nancy screeched and jumped on top of him, clawing at his face. Ephraim seized both wrists. They were small and frail, like an old woman's should be, yet he could hardly restrain them. Nancy bent over and bit Ephraim's knuckle. He yelled in surprise and pushed up with his knees, launching her off him.

Nancy sailed through the air and landed catlike on her hands and feet. Her left eye glinted red in the moonlight.

Words flooded into Ephraim's mind. *If a wicked glint you spy, you're under the gaze of the evil eye. Hang a horseshoe over the door, the eye will close forever more.* He thought of the horseshoe nailed to the tree above the door of the Laura. He had to make it there.

He ran, trying to orient himself as he went. If Nancy was here, the Laura couldn't be too far away.

The ground took on a downward grade, and Ephraim found himself in a creek bottom. He realized it was the same place where the hellhound had found him. That meant the Laura was upstream.

He turned and ran along the bank. A splash behind him announced Nancy's continued pursuit. He glanced over his shoulder and saw her dripping, bare feet slapping the creek water as she ran after him. *She must've leaped right into the creek*, he thought. He felt concern for the old woman's health on this frigid night even as he tried to escape her.

He rounded a bend in the creek, and up ahead, above the shorter trees, he saw the antlered branches of the Laura outlined against the moon. He put on a burst of speed, tearing through the woods toward safety, his lungs aching as he gulped the freezing air.

Nancy gave a screech when he entered the clearing surrounding the Laura. Ephraim didn't bother to slow his pace as he reached the door; he crashed right into it, falling inside.

Turning, he saw Nancy's face contorted in rage as he slammed the door shut in front of her. He fumbled with the bar, dropped it into the latch, then turned his back to the door and slid slowly to the floor, heart pounding, ticking away the seconds until daybreak.

THE GRAY LIGHT of dawn seeped through the gap beneath the door. Ephraim hadn't moved for the better part of an hour. After the night's events, he had lacked the will.

But when the light brightened, he rose and opened the door a crack.

There was no sign of Nancy. Snow fell in thick flakes. Earl was nowhere to be seen; hopefully the goat hadn't crossed paths with Nancy during the night.

Ephraim stepped outside and walked to the woodpile. Several minutes later he had a fire roaring in the stove. He fetched water, filled the iron pot, and added cornmeal.

When a knock sounded at the door, he jumped. "Who is it?" he called.

"It's me," came the sound of Reuben's voice.

Ephraim opened the door.

"You got the book?" Reuben asked.

Ephraim nodded and stepped aside, letting the man in.

Reuben sniffed the air. "Smells nice in here." He moved to the stove and opened the lid of the pot. "Cornmeal mush. Something hot sure does sound good. The cold is ten times worse on an empty gut." He patted his stomach. "Any sign of Isabel or Nancy?"

"I ran into Nancy last night." Ephraim related the night's events to Reuben as they waited for the cornmeal mush to finish cooking.

"Well, my night wasn't nearly as excitin' as yours," Reuben said, shaking his head. He moved to a shelf and took down two bowls, spoons, and a ladle. "After we separated, I thought I heard someone following me. So I found myself a nice thicket and holed up there until dawn." He took the pot from the stove and placed it on the table.

They each ladled steaming portions of the gruel into their bowls and fell upon their breakfast in silence. Ephraim wolfed his down, appreciating its warmth and the weight in his stomach. Reuben cleaned his bowl, licked the spoon, and sat back in his chair.

The sun was fully over the mountaintops now. With a sinking feeling, Ephraim wondered where Isabel was. If she didn't turn up soon, he'd go looking for her.

He got up from the table, opened the door, and peered out. Something moved among the trees—a person walking toward the Laura. Ephraim's heart leaped. Maybe Isabel was safe after all.

Reuben stood and moved to the doorway with Ephraim. He leaned his head out and looked around, drumming his fingers on the door. "Who's that?" he asked, squinting.

Ephraim studied the approaching figure. It was a woman hunched over, arms wrapped around her shoulders. She walked with her head bowed, loose hair obscuring her face. The excitement Ephraim had felt a moment before curdled to dread in the pit of his stomach. "Looks like Nancy."

His heart began to pound as the granny woman drew near. He

gulped. *She's fine now*, he told himself. *She said the Black Madness would be gone by dawn.*

Reuben stopped drumming his fingers and drew back from the doorway. "She look all right to you?" he whispered.

Ephraim shrugged. "Nancy," he called. "How are you?"

The old woman stopped walking and looked up, her right eye visible through the curtain of hair. She raised a hand in greeting and continued moving toward the Laura.

Reuben rested his hand on the butt of his revolver.

Nancy walked up to the doorway and stopped again.

"Mighty cold this mornin', ain't it?" Reuben said, tightening his grip on the pistol.

Nancy nodded. "It is."

"You haven't seen Isabel anywhere, have you?" Ephraim asked.

Nancy shook her head. "No."

They stood in silence for a moment.

"I've got some cornmeal mush on the table," Ephraim said. "Come on in and have some."

"I cain't," Nancy said. She pointed to a spot above the doorway.

Ephraim looked up and saw the horseshoe hanging there.

"You'll have to take that down afore I can come in," Nancy said.

Reuben shot Ephraim a sideways glance. He gave a slight nod to his gun.

"Y'all goin' to stand there lookin' spook-eyed, or are ye goin' to take down that horseshoe?" Nancy said, an impatient edge to her voice.

"I'll take it down," Ephraim said.

It took a moment to wiggle the shoe off the spike, but it came free. He tossed it out into the snow.

"Thank ye." Nancy came inside as Ephraim and Reuben backed away from the door. She moved silently over to a shelf and took down a hand mirror. Turning away from Reuben and Ephraim, she flipped the hair away from her face and looked at her reflection. "Lordy, they don't call it the evil eye for nothin'," she said, clicking her tongue. "It's as ugly as..." She looked up in the air as if searching for the right words. "Well, I don't reckon I ever seen one this ugly."

She turned around, and Ephraim suppressed a gasp. Her left eye was blood red. Its pupil had transformed into a horizontal black dash, like a goat's eye.

"What do ye think?" Nancy asked with a wry grin. "Me 'n' Earl got matchin' peepers now, don't we?" She reached up and tied her hair back into a bun. "I had to see it for myself first. There's nothin' worse than havin' folks gogglin'' at your face and not knowin' what the fuss is about."

Reuben was looking at her suspiciously.

"I'd feel better if ye wasn't a-squeezin' that pistol so tight, Reuben," Nancy said with a frown. "The Black Madness has left me. There ain't nothin' to be afeared of." She sat down at the table, pulled a bowl of cornmeal mush toward herself, and shoveled a spoonful into her mouth. "Not much taste, but I don't care. I'm as hungry as a fresh-waked bear."

The almanack lay on the table. Ephraim's hand twitched as her gaze fell upon it. "I see ye got the almanack," she said, "but no Isabel. What happened?"

When Ephraim and Reuben still hesitated to speak, she glared up at them from her bowl. "I'm a witch now, boys. You're bound to feel a tad jumpy 'round me, but best push it from your minds and be done with it."

Ephraim took a seat at the table but remained on the edge of the chair. He opened his mouth to speak, but found his gaze inexorably drawn to the goat's eye planted in Nancy's face. The granny woman now looked as if she were two beings rolled into one. The Nancy he'd grown to trust, and a caged demon staring out of a shared set of eyes.

"Ye goin' to tell me what happened, or sit there and ogle?"

Ephraim's ears grew hot. He stared down at the table and cleared his throat. "We all split up last night to throw Boggs off our trail. We agreed to meet up here in the mornin'. Neither one of us has seen Isabel since then. Reuben just got here, and I..." He paused. Did Nancy remember what she had done last night? He decided it would be best not to mention it. "I got here first," he finished.

"Well, no sense waitin' 'round for Isabel afore ye open that book. Go ahead," Nancy said. She shoveled another spoonful into her mouth.

"What if Boggs has her?"

"If he does, I reckon we'll hear 'bout it afore too long."

Ephraim glanced out the window. "We should still look for her. She might be lost out there."

Nancy shook her head. "All she has to do is head downhill to get back into Sixmile Creek. I'm sure folks will be glad to blame us for corruptin' her instead of throwin' her in jail. Besides." Nancy pointed to her evil eye. "Gettin' that there almanack cost us a hefty price. Go on and open it."

29

SELLOUT

I sabel sat in Boggs's kitchen, where Jake and Clabe had gagged her and bound her to a chair.

"I have some matters to attend to," Boggs said. "Clabe, I want you to stand guard while I'm gone. Jake, go find Ephraim. I can almost guarantee he's at the witch woman's home on the other side of Flint Ridge. Find him, tell him I have his girl, and that if he values her life, he'll meet me in Butcher Holler with my almanack at midnight, in two nights' time."

Isabel stiffened. Boggs was using her as bait to catch Ephraim. Her eyes prickled with tears of shame. They'd worked so hard to get the almanack. She couldn't allow Ephraim to sell his soul to the Devil on her account.

As Boggs walked to the door, a knock sounded.

Boggs cursed and spun around, fishing his tomahawk out of his coat. "Make sure she stays silent," he hissed, pointing to Isabel.

Clabe and Jake moved to Isabel's chair. Clabe pulled a knife from his belt and tested his thumb on its edge. He leaned in close to Isabel. "One sound out of you and I'll carve out that pretty little tongue of yours."

Isabel met his gaze with hatred. Once her daddy, Mason, or any other good man in this town heard what Clabe Fletcher did behind closed doors, he'd be lynched for sure. She hoped she lived to see that day.

She also knew that whoever was at the door was her only chance to escape. So she prepared herself to scream. It was worth the risk.

Boggs opened the door a crack and peered out.

"Time is growing short, William," a voice from outside said. It was deep, oily, and unfamiliar, but something about it told Isabel that this visitor wasn't going to be her savior.

"Master, please, come inside." Boggs tucked his tomahawk back into his coat and opened the door. He glanced at Clabe. "Put that knife away. It won't be necessary."

A man in a black suit and top hat stepped inside. He tapped his snake-headed cane on the floor as his dark eyes swept over the room. "Let see, who do we have here?" He scrutinized Isabel and the Fletcher boys in turn. "Clabe and Jake Fletcher, and Miss Isabel Coleman."

"How do you know my name?" Clabe said. "I ain't never seen you before."

The stranger raised an eyebrow. "Well then, Mr. Fletcher, allow me to introduce myself. I am the anger you felt the first time your father struck you. I am the greed in your belly. I'm every lustful, lecherous, covetous, vengeful thought you've ever had. And, I'm the reason that folks love the way your whiskey burns going down." He removed his hat and bowed. "I'm the Devil himself. At your service."

Behind the gag, Isabel's breath quickened.

Clabe snorted and took a step back. "The hell you are, mister!"

The Devil smiled. "The hell I am."

Clabe glanced at Isabel, wide-eyed.

She jerked her head toward Boggs. *I told you so.*

"William, forgive me for eavesdropping," the Devil said, turning to the reverend, "but did I hear you say that the Cutler boy has your almanack? That could be the end of you."

"I have survived longer than any other mortal man, Scratch. This will *not* be my undoing!" Boggs's voice quivered with rage.

"So what's your plan, William? You've got two days left. Should I start searching for your replacement?"

"You never asked to see my plan before," Boggs replied. "But if you must know, it's right here in front of you." He pointed to Isabel.

The Devil sauntered across the room and stood over Isabel. "Ah, yes. She's a hostage then."

Isabel's heart pounded beneath his gaze. She looked away, avoiding his eyes.

"Yes. Ephraim Cutler is quite close to her. If I know the boy well, and I do, he'll sacrifice anything to save her."

"It wouldn't be the first time a deal with me has been motivated by love," the Devil said. "I sincerely hope it works, and not just for your sake. I told you that Death is growing quite rebellious."

The Devil sighed and tapped his cane against his boots. "I'll leave you then. Don't let me down, William."

"You have no reason to doubt," answered Boggs. He offered a thin smile and walked the Devil to the door.

Isabel felt a wave of relief when Boggs shut the door behind his unexpected visitor. He turned back to the Fletcher boys, eyes blazing.

"You," he said, pointing to Jake, "find Ephraim, Reuben, and the granny woman." He looked at Clabe. "And you stay here and guard the girl. I have preparations to attend to. I will not be able to return here, so you two bring her to me in Butcher Holler in two days, at midnight."

∾

CLABE WAITED until the reverend had left, then spoke to his brother. "Do you think Boggs is goin' to pay us? He hasn't shown us a solitary dollar yet, and I bet he disappears if things don't go his way. Folks around here ain't goin' to take kindly to the idea of a preacher kidnappin' a girl."

"I reckon you're right," Jake said. "What do you figure we ought to do?"

"Well, he might still pay us, but I'm thinkin' we rustle up another payroll in case he don't. And if he does, we'll just have more money."

"You thinkin' of the Hensons?"

Clabe grinned. "Yes indeed. You run on along and deliver the message to Cutler, but get on back here quick. I'll arrange a meetin' for us and Peyton. We'll tell 'em where and when Ephraim's supposed to be meetin' the preacher—*if* he hands over the reward in advance."

It was Jake's turn to grin. "I like your thinkin', brother. All of a sudden, Louisville ain't lookin' so far away."

30

IRON BALLS FOR RUINATION

Reuben passed Ephraim the torn fragment of the title page, and Ephraim lined it up with its other half. As the torn edges touched, a bead of soft light ran along them, reuniting the fragments.

"Well don't that beat all you ever saw," Reuben said, leaning in to examine the healed page. The half that he had carried was still far dirtier than its mate.

The page read:

The Record of Abel Eckerlin
For the year of Christian Account 1757 and all years hence.
Containing a calendar of every season and the time for every purpose under heaven.

NANCY STOOD up and moved behind Ephraim to get a better look. The hair on the back of his neck prickled under her evil eye. He couldn't resist turning and glancing at it, then suppressed a shudder at the sight of that living, blinking goat's eye in the old woman's face.

"It's my pappy's book, sure enough," she said. She looked almost tearful.

Ephraim turned the page. The next page showed a drawing of a man, his arms and legs outstretched. Symbols were sketched around his body: a ram over his head, a bull by his neck, a lion and crab on either side of his chest.

"So... what exactly are we lookin' for?" Ephraim asked.

Nancy scowled. "What do ye think, boy? Find a page with 'Hellhound' written on it! You can read, can't ye?"

"Yeah, I can read."

Ephraim flipped through the book, page by page, until he found what he was looking for: the word "Hellhound" written in curly letters. The corner of the page had been folded down. "Here it is," he said.

Reuben and Nancy both leaned over him. "Read it for us," Nancy said. "My eyes ain't what they used to be."

Ephraim ran his finger down the page: "To create a hellhound, you must build a box of locust wood—"

Reuben snickered.

Nancy frowned. "A hellhound is hardly a critter to laugh at."

"No, it's not that," Reuben said. "Sorry. Go ahead and read it, Ephraim."

Ephraim cleared his throat. He skimmed over the rest of the instructions on creating hellhounds and settled on a paragraph detailing their nature. "The soul of a person bitten by a hellhound is slowly poisoned as the moon grows full."

Reuben erupted into laughter.

"What on earth has got ahold of ye?" Nancy asked.

Reuben doubled over, shoulders shaking, tears streaming down his cheeks. "I'm sorry," he wheezed, "but you just said your eyes ain't what they used to be!"

Nancy chuckled. "Well I'll be, that's what's got ye tickled. I s'pose that *is* pretty funny now, ain't it?"

Ephraim looked at the both of them and shook his head. "Are you two ready for me to read this?"

Reuben wiped his eyes. "Yes, Ephraim. I apologize. I ain't had enough sleep and I'm 'bout half crazy."

Ephraim tried to muster a smile but couldn't. The last line had left him sick with dread. His soul was being poisoned.

He turned back to the almanack. "With the settin' of the full moon, the spirit of a bitten person leaves the body and becomes trapped between the lands of the living and dead." Boggs had been telling the truth.

"The moon'll be full tomorrow night," Reuben said.

Ephraim continued reading. "Hellhounds are wild creatures, indestructible, and tamed only through the use of iron, which causes them great pain. And those that seek to be healed of their venom must also use iron. On the day of—" Ephraim paused to sound out the next word. "Ab-danns-dag?" He looked at Nancy.

The old lady shrugged. "Sounds like Dutch."

Ephraim looked back at the page. "On the day of Abdannsdag, they must pierce the heart of a hellhound with iron, and rub its blood over their wound."

Ephraim pushed back from the table. "So, I've got to kill this thing and rub its blood on my arm."

"You have to kill it on a special day," Reuben said, leaning over the almanack. "What was it called?"

"Abdannsdag," Ephraim said. "I've never heard of that before."

Nancy shook her head. "I cain't say I have either. Look around in there though. It *is* an almanack."

Ephraim thumbed through the pages until he found it. *Abdannsdag, The Cut Off Day.* "Looks like Boggs dog-eared this one too," he said.

He began reading. "The Cut Off Day was included in the

almanacks of old. It was originally discovered that weeds, thistles, and thorns cut off on this day wouldn't grow back. Evildoers found that much more than noxious plants could be killed on the Cut Off Day. Man, beast, and spirit alike could be pushed from this world into the land of death. On this day, supernatural adversaries, not usually vulnerable to the weapons of man, can be laid low through the use of iron.

"Since its removal from the almanacks, the knowledge to calculate the yearly Cut Off Day has been forgotten. However, using my knowledge of the stars, I have rediscovered the way to reckon the yearly date of Abdannsdag. I include it here, in hopes that it will help those faced with supernatural foes. I pray that this knowledge will not fall into the hands of those who would use it for dark purposes."

Nancy shook her head. "My pappy certainly was as learned as folks said he was."

Ephraim continued. "The Cut Off Day occurs between the rising and the setting of the full moon, when the signs are in the secrets." Ephraim looked up from the book. "We know we'll have a full moon tomorrow, but what does the rest of it mean? 'When the signs are in the secrets'?"

"That I can help ye with," Nancy said. She grabbed the almanack and flipped back to the diagram of the man. "The heavens are divided into twelve signs—ye can see 'em at night." She pointed to the symbols surrounding the man. "These are the signs."

"You talkin' 'bout the stars?" Ephraim asked.

"Them, along with other things in the sky. Each sign is linked to the body, and each sign rules a part of the year." She pointed to a symbol that resembled a scorpion. "This is the sign that's in the secrets."

Ephraim studied the sign. It was connected to the man's groin by a line. "What part of the year does it rule?"

"The signs are in the secrets right now," Nancy said. "The full moon that's a-comin' tomorrow night marks the Cut Off Day."

Ephraim sat back in his chair. "I haven't seen the hellhound since it chased me, and now I've got to find it before the full moon sets tomorrow."

"And you'll be needin' iron," Reuben said.

"What should I use?" Ephraim asked. "A knife would be near useless against that thing. There's no way I could get in close enough to stick it, not without it bitin' my head off."

Reuben rubbed his chin. "You any good with a bow and arrow?"

Ephraim shook his head. "I haven't played with one since I was little. I'm a good shot with a rifle, but even if I had mine, how would I get an iron bullet into it?"

Nancy walked over to her bed, got down on her knees, and reached under it. She pulled out a musket, a powder horn, and a worn leather bag. "I've shot creek stones out of Ruination afore. I used to have a sack of lead balls, until Earl ate 'em. I figured I could pick 'em up again once they came out the other end, but I never did find a single one." She looked from Ephraim to Reuben, who were both staring at her. "What I mean to say is: I reckon ye could ram just about anythin' down the barrel, long as ye got enough powder behind it."

Reuben took the musket from her and inspected it. "Smooth bore," he said. "It ought to work. But you'll need an iron ball." He handed Ephraim the gun.

"How are we goin' to get an iron ball?" Ephraim asked. "Manson Owens is the only one 'round here who could do it."

"He the blacksmith in town?" Reuben asked.

Ephraim nodded.

"Then we'll pay him a visit."

"I don't know 'bout that. He's the one who caught me after I killed Silas. He probably thinks I killed Jubal too."

Reuben patted his pistol in its holster. "I'll use this to make the blacksmith do the work for us. If everythin' you read about this Cut Off Day is true, I'm goin' to get me some iron, too, and cut down Bill Boggs."

"Ye won't be needin' that with Manson," Nancy said. "Just tell him what's been going on over the past few days. He'll hear ye out and help ye. Be careful not to be seen by someone else though. Oh, and Ephraim, I have somethin' for ye before ye go." She rummaged through a basket in the corner and came up holding the cream-colored shirt Ephraim had seen her talk to.

"Why are you givin' me this?" Ephraim asked, accepting the folded shirt.

"It was my pappy's, as you know," Nancy said. "The only thing I ever seen that belonged to him besides that almanack. I'd be ashamed to use it now that I'm a witch. I know ye ain't goin' to be stickin' 'round these parts after this is all over, and I want ye to take it."

"Thank you, Nancy, but I'm not cunning-folk. I wouldn't know how to use this."

Nancy smiled. "I may be old, Ephraim, but I ain't no fool. This'll help ye, and when the time is right, you'll learn how to use it. And I want ye to keep the almanack too."

"But—"

The old woman held up her hand. "My doctorin' days are over. The only thing that book could teach me now is how to work evil. It'd be best if it weren't nowhere near me."

Ephraim tucked the almanack and the shirt into the bag.

"Go on now, you two," Nancy said. "I'll stay here in case Isabel shows up. There ain't no time to be wastin'."

A knock sounded at the door.

"I bet that's Isabel," Ephraim said, his heart leaping in his chest. He ran to the door and flung it open. "Isa—"

Jake Fletcher stood outside in the snow, rifle at the ready.

Ephraim jumped away. Reuben pulled out his pistol.

"Easy now!" Jake said, taking a step backward. "I just come up here to deliver a message from Reverend Boggs."

"What does he want?" Ephraim said.

"He wants you to know that he's got your girl. Caught her last night. She ain't been harmed, and if you want her to stay that way, the reverend says you need to meet him tomorrow at midnight in Butcher Holler, at Wes Sherman's old place. He said to bring his book with you."

Jake turned and ran back into the woods.

"Coward," Ephraim said. He slammed his fist on the wall. "We've got to go after her. We got distracted by the almanack; we should've been looking for her."

Nancy shook her head. "Jake said they caught her last night, Ephraim. It wouldn't have done no good."

Ephraim's whole body felt tense. He paced back and forth in front of the open door, oblivious to the snow blowing in around him. "Silas is dead. Ma is dead." He looked at Nancy. "You're a witch. And now Isabel is a hostage, all on my account." Tears of self-loathing sprang to his eyes. "All because I shot a man who didn't deserve it."

He threw the musket on the floor. "I don't want to kill anymore! I don't want anybody or anythin' else to have to die, or get hurt, so that I can live. I should go dig myself a grave and sit in it until this poison finishes its job."

Reuben laid a hand on Ephraim's shoulder. "Don't lose your head. Remember, Boggs is behind this." He looked Ephraim in the eyes. "It's true: you killed an innocent man. You're right to regret it, and I imagine you'll spend the rest of your days regretting it. Remember, though, this has all been Boggs trying to play you right into the Devil's hands, just like he did with my boy, Amos. Don't give up now. We have to work together to stop him, so he doesn't do this to someone else."

Ephraim lowered his head. "All right," he said. "But forget the hellhound. We need to go after Isabel."

"And what if ye cain't find her?" Nancy put her hands on her hips. "I'm sure Boggs is guarding her well. By midnight tomorrow ye won't be in no shape to deal with him. Go deal with the hellhound first. Once that poison is drawn out of ye, ye can square off with Boggs. Besides, that Isabel is clever. She can take care of herself."

Ephraim was quiet. He knew Nancy was right. He stooped and retrieved Ruination.

Reuben patted him on the back. "Let's go get our iron," he said.

EPHRAIM AND REUBEN crouched on a thin blanket of snow, ears pressed to the back door of Manson's forge. Ephraim heard the rhythmic clink of the hammer against the anvil as the blacksmith worked. Someone else was in there, too; Ephraim caught stray words and phrases.

"—killed my prize boar hog," the visitor said.

CLANK.

"Same bear that tore up my bee gums, bet you a dollar," Manson said. *CLANK.* "Caught his toenails a while back." There was the hiss of hot metal being quenched. "That's why I'm fixing this here trap."

Ephraim listened hard, willing the visitor to leave quickly. The banging of the hammer resumed, and he caught the words "piece of my hog left" and "bait." Another few minutes passed before at last Manson bid the visitor goodbye and the front door of the shop opened and closed.

Ephraim looked at Reuben, who nodded. They eased the back door open and slipped inside.

A partially repaired buckboard wagon sat immediately in front of them, propped up on blocks of wood. Ephraim looked underneath it and saw Manson hammering at the anvil through the spokes of the wheel on the far side.

He leaned toward Reuben and whispered, "I'll talk to him. You guard the front door. Lock it so no one comes in."

Reuben nodded.

Ephraim took a deep breath, leaned Nancy's musket against the wall, and stepped out from behind the buckboard. Manson had his back turned and didn't see him. "Mr. Owens," Ephraim said.

Manson stopped hammering, raised his head, and looked toward the front door.

"Mr. Owens, back here," Ephraim said.

Manson turned around. The hammer dropped from his fingers. "Ephraim! What are you doin' here?"

Ephraim held out his hands in a peaceful gesture. "I want to talk to you," he said, stepping aside so that Reuben could make his way to the front door. "This is my friend, Reuben. He's goin' to watch the door so that no one steps in on us."

Manson folded his arms and studied Reuben. "All right then," he said. "Be careful when you drop the crossbar—it's heavy. Smashed more fingers than I can count." The old blacksmith turned to Ephraim and motioned to a bench by the forge. "Sit down, Ephraim. Tell me what this is all about."

Ephraim breathed a sigh of relief and moved to the seat. "You've probably been wonderin' where I've been," he said.

Manson simply nodded.

"Well, I'm goin' to tell you," Ephraim said. "There's a lot goin' on in Sixmile that folks don't know about."

He began with the night he'd killed Silas Henson and told the story in mostly sequential order from there, explaining about the hellhound, Boggs's pact with the Devil, the almanack, and Abdannsdag.

Manson remained quiet throughout the entire tale, listening

intently, not moving from the anvil. When Ephraim finished, the smith turned and stared at the coals glowing in the forge.

"I believe you," he said, stroking his beard. "Every word. But I fear there ain't many in the town who will. I ain't been much of a church-goin' man since Reverend Boggs came to Sixmile. Truth is, there's somethin' 'bout him that just don't sit right with me. The missus thought I was losin' my faith." He chuckled. "I must say, I never figured Boggs for a servant of the Devil, but that ought to get her off my back when I tell her that." He shifted off the anvil and looked at Ephraim. "You got that old musket with you?"

"It's in the back," Ephraim said. "I didn't want you to think I'd come to shoot you or anythin'."

Manson smiled. "Let me have a look, and we'll make you some iron balls." He snorted. "Though it sounds like you already got a pair, takin' on a hellhound in the woods at night."

Ephraim grinned.

Reuben cleared his throat, and Manson looked to the front door. "Somethin' you need, mister?"

"I was wondering if you had anythin' else, a weapon forged out of iron. I aim to settle a quarrel with the reverend."

Manson moved to a corner of the shop and began sorting through various tools and implements. "I got an old iron corn knife here," he said, holding it up.

The corn knife was about as long as a man's arm, with one edge sharpened.

Reuben examined it. "That'll do."

"I'll put a fresh edge on it for you," Manson said, producing a whetstone from his apron pocket. He took a few minutes, honing the blade and testing it on his arm until it shaved off a patch of hair. "There you go," he said, handing the weapon to Reuben. "Now"—he turned to Ephraim—"let's see that musket."

Ephraim handed the weapon over. The blacksmith inspected the gun and stuck a grime-blackened finger into the end of the barrel. "Looks to be .75 caliber. You'll be needin' an iron pumpkin ball." He sat the gun down and scratched his chin. "Question is, how am I goin' to make it for you?"

"Can't you cast some, like you would a lead ball?" Ephraim asked.

Manson shook his head. "I can forge iron, not cast it. There's too much air in my fire. If I got it hot enough to melt the iron, it'd just burn it up." He walked over to a bench and rummaged through a pile of iron scraps. "I think I know what we can do," he said, holding up several chunks of iron shaped roughly like cubes.

Manson piled charcoal into the forge and pumped the bellows. He picked up one of the iron chunks in a pair of tongs and shoved it into the fire. Yellow flames spat out from under it. Then he took a splayed cigar stub from his apron pocket and lit it with a coal from the forge.

Manson pumped the bellows a few more times. "You want to keep your fire hot, but not too hot," he said, turning the chunk of iron in the coals. The metal was glowing a cherry red. "Got to watch the colors."

Gradually the iron began to glow a translucent yellow. The heat made the surface of the metal shimmer. "There she is." Manson drew the metal from the fire and laid it on the anvil. "Now to make it round."

He took up the hammer and swung it down on one of the chunk's corners. The soft iron gave under the blow with a dull ring. Manson turned the chunk, knocking the corners and edges in. "Now we take another heat," he said, plunging the iron back into the fire. "Put that musket barrel up here where I can look at its diameter."

Ephraim picked up the gun and leaned the end of the barrel against the anvil.

Manson took the iron to the anvil again. He hammered faster this time, pausing every few hammer strokes to squint at the barrel. "That ought to do it," he said, scooting the rough orb to one side of the anvil. "But we'll make you a few."

By the time Ephraim and Reuben left the smithy by the back door—with a "thank you" for Manson and a "good luck" in return—Ephraim had three iron pumpkin balls. It was snowing again, and they used the cover to slip unnoticed back into the forest.

Reuben turned to Ephraim and stuck out a hand. "I think we'll part ways here for a while," he said. "If Boggs is goin' to be in Butcher Holler tomorrow night, I want to get there before him. Get the lay of the land and get the jump on him."

"I'll see you there at midnight tomorrow," Ephraim said. "Don't let him hurt Isabel."

"I'll do my best. You just find that hellhound. You're ready for him."

I hope so.

Ephraim watched Reuben slip off between the trees. He remembered the last spot he'd seen the hound, on the bank of the creek downstream from the Laura. He might as well start his search there.

He sighed, shouldered the musket, and set his jaw. *Let the hunt begin.*

31

PEYTON

C labe didn't wait for Jake to return before seeking out the Hensons. A few minutes after Jake's departure, he tightened the cords that held Isabel to the chair.

"You best stay still, missy. I ain't goin' to be gone long, and if I come back and find you tryin' to run for it, I'll beat you silly. You hear?" He scooted her away from the window, then left, locking the door behind him.

Isabel's fingers and toes soon grew numb from the tightness of the rope. Beneath the gag she moaned in discomfort. She tugged against the ropes, wincing when they cut deeper into her flesh. The knots were firm, and Isabel knew she'd never loosen them without help. She closed her eyes and offered up a silent prayer.

Minutes passed slowly into hours. The sun sank past the window, and the parsonage grew colder. Isabel sat in her chair, her head drooping in a semi-stupor.

Her head snapped back up again when voices from the yard reached her ears, muffled by the walls and distance. Her heart leaped at the possibility that there was someone outside who might be able to help her.

She threw her weight forward in the chair. It moved no more than an inch. But she repeated the motion, again and again, inching the chair toward the window until she was right next to it, her head level with the bottom pane. Her nose touched the cold glass as she peered out into the yard, searching for the source of the voices. Down by the garden, barely within her field of vision, stood two men.

She turned her head and pressed her ear to the window.

"... told me you said for me to meet you here," one of the men was saying. Isabel recognized the voice. *Peyton!*

"I did," the other man said. It was Clabe. "I got a deal to cut with you."

"What kind of deal?"

"You still offerin' two hundred dollars for Ephraim Cutler?"

"Yes, I am," Peyton said slowly. "Do you have him?"

"Is it worth two hundred dollars to you if I tell you where he'll be tomorrow night?"

"Of course it is—assumin' you're tellin' the truth."

"Oh, I know where he'll be," Clabe said. "Fetch that two hundred dollars and I'll tell you."

"Now wait a minute..."

Isabel pulled her ear away. She wanted to hear more, but this might be her only chance to get free. She reared back and slammed her forehead into the glass. It didn't break, and Isabel grimaced in pain. She tried again, and this time it shattered. Isabel felt one of the cold shards slice her skin.

Out in the yard, the men stopped talking.

"What was that?" Peyton said. He looked up the bank toward the cottage.

Clabe cocked the lever action on his rifle. "Stay where you are, Peyton!"

"What's this all about?" Peyton asked. "Who are you hidin' in there? Is it Ephraim?"

"Afraid I can't say. Reverend Boggs hired me to keep that a secret."

Isabel leaned toward the window. She could barely make out the top of Peyton's head. He was quartering away from her.

"Fine," he said. "I'll go and get the money. I'll give you half now, and half once I've got Cutler."

Isabel's heart fell. Peyton was leaving her.

She peered down through the broken glass. Clabe and Peyton were shaking hands. As she watched, Peyton glanced in her direction, and for an instant, their eyes met. Isabel shook her head in warning. *Please, don't let Clabe know you saw me.* She willed Peyton to hear her thoughts. She feared Clabe would shoot Peyton if he got any more curious.

Peyton blinked and turned back to Clabe, his expression unchanged.

"Should I meet you back here?"

32

OL' REELFOOT

Hunger burned in Sampson's belly. He'd scrounged a few mice and other rodents in the winter woods, morsels just large enough to whet his appetite. He'd even circled back to the graveyard on the off chance that his master had dropped anything edible there. He'd found nothing. Now Sampson padded through the snowy woodlands, a predator too large to be sustained by the available prey. The pain in his gut grew. Hunger overwhelmed him. He wandered aimlessly, crossing over paths he had already taken.

Fevered thoughts of cornbread, gravy, and raw meat danced through his mind. When he slept, he dreamed of the boy he'd failed to catch, the scorching odor of his trail. His world had become a jumble of instincts—domesticated, feral, and supernatural. He lay in the snow, conquered by the pangs in his shriveling stomach. He closed his eyes and wished for sleep.

The wind carried a scent to him—metallic, rich, and sharp in the cold air. Without opening his eyes, he lifted his nose. The scent was no dream. *Blood.* And judging by the strength of the smell, lots of it. Saliva pooled in Sampson's mouth, and in his gut, digestive juices gurgled in anticipation.

The wind was blowing up from lower in the valley, close to the settlement where the people lived. He rose and trotted toward it, his nose leading him to the slaughter.

Sampson emerged from the woods at the edge of a cornfield where a few stray stalks still stood, dry, brittle and iced with snow. He skirted the field and found the source of the scent: a gut pile, left over from the butchering of a hog. He ran for it eagerly, raising his tail as high as it would go.

The moment he set foot in the gut pile, he felt and heard a bone-crunching snap. Excruciating pain lanced up his leg. He leaped back with a yelp, then yelped again as his movement was cut short by a vicious yank. An iron contraption was fastened firmly to his leg. Its sharp, triangular teeth pierced his flesh, and the pressure the trap exerted was unbearable. Sampson snapped at the trap, shook his leg, and howled in pain, but the trap showed no signs of loosening.

Exhaustion set in within minutes. Weakened by both hunger and pain, Sampson crouched miserably in the snow.

He sensed movement along the tree line. A massive bear lumbered out of the shelter of the trees. The brute shuffled past Sampson without a single glance. Warily, it investigated the gut pile, taking care to step over several other traps obscured along its periphery. The bear lowered its snout into the mound of entrails and began to feast, smacking noisily.

Sampson licked his chops and whined.

33

CUT OFF DAY

I t took Ephraim most of the day to reach the place where he had last seen the hellhound. In the waning light he combed the area, sweeping away snow from the creek bank until he located faint tracks in the frozen mud. Finding them beneath the snow was quite a feat in itself, unlike anything Ephraim had ever accomplished in all his days of hunting—yet it did him little good. He now knew what the creature's footprints looked like, but he could see that it hadn't revisited this place since it had pursued him, which meant he was no closer to finding it. As he kindled a fire against the encroaching dark, the woods had never seemed vaster.

The wound in his forearm pulsed along with his heart. He could feel the poison tingling in his veins like needles of ice, growing stronger by the hour, inching toward his heart. *One day left*, he thought.

An odd resignation filled him. *Maybe it won't be so bad*, he thought. Perhaps the slip into the spirit world would be peaceful.

He lay back and looked at the starry heavens above. He wondered if he would still appreciate their beauty as a haint.

THE NEXT THING EPHRAIM KNEW, the sun was rising. He sat up stiffly and poked at the coals in his fire. There was nothing strange about the day, but the knowledge that this was the Cut Off Day—the last day he had to either kill the hellhound or die— gave every passing second the weight of a dying breath. He rose and shouldered Ruination. He had nothing to begin his search with, but he decided to start working in circles out from this place where he'd last seen the hound.

By midmorning, he was only halfheartedly searching for tracks. He hadn't come across anything in his circling, and the farther he searched, the less hope he had. At a loss, he decided to revisit the Hurricane Timber, the place the hellhound had found him.

He set off for it, running through the woods, wading through snowdrifts with Ruination held high. The sun was overhead when he came to the clear-cut. The ground was treacherous beneath the snow. Gnarled roots and holes waited to snag a care-less foot. Ephraim worked his way to the lone standing tree where he and the Fletchers had taken shelter during the storm. It seemed like a lifetime ago now. He didn't venture too close to the base of the tree. A snow-covered mound beneath it looked suspi-ciously like Frank's remains. He searched along the path he had taken when he'd run from the hound.

But there were no tracks in the snow.

Ephraim had hoped the hellhound might have returned here —the same way deer often traveled on familiar trails, or perhaps because some unearthly magic caused it to haunt this forsaken region. Those hopes, he could see now, had been unfounded.

His heart sank.

He didn't even bother to scrape the snow from around the grave. Even if he found tracks in the dirt, it'd be impossible to follow a trail beneath the snow. He leaned Ruination against a fallen tree, sat down next to it, and sighed.

Ephraim reached into his leather bag and pulled out the almanack. He studied the section about hellhounds again, hoping he'd overlooked some useful information that might help him track the animal, but found nothing. With a sigh, he pushed the book back into the bag.

His fingers met the rough wool fabric of the shirt Nancy had given him. He pulled it out of the bag and held it up, remembering how Nancy had spoken to it, discerning messages in its answering movements. An idea struck him.

I wonder if this thing knows where the hellhound is.

A sapling stood nearby, a child of one of the storm-felled giants. Ephraim walked over to it, hooked the neck of the shirt over two twigs that projected from a forked limb, then stepped back.

The shirt dangled lifelessly.

Ephraim cleared his throat. "Where is the hellhound?"

He waited, studying the shirt.

Nothing happened.

Ephraim lifted his hat and scratched his head. This was a pointless endeavor; he wasn't cunning-folk like Nancy. Maybe there was a spell or something that had to be cast to bring the shirt to life. Still, he had no other options. And why would Nancy have given him something he couldn't use?

Ephraim thought for a moment. Nancy had knelt when she'd spoken with the shirt.

He lowered himself to his knees. The snowy ground was cold through his pants. He looked up at the shirt. It bobbed gently on the branches. Had a slight breeze disturbed it, or was it trying to encourage him?

Ephraim took a deep breath. "Where is the hellhound?"

The bobbing subsided, and the shirt hung still again.

Ephraim sighed. This wasn't going anywhere. He stood up

and turned his back on the shirt. As he looked over the snowy woodlands, he was struck by the thought that his last hours would be best served by forgetting this fruitless search. Yes, that was the best course of action. No more worry, no more struggle.

He turned to retrieve the shirt.

Its arms were folded.

Ephraim's breath stalled.

The arms of the shirt slid free of each other and dangled limply at its sides. But for a moment it had looked... well, cross, like a mother scolding her child. The message was clear: Ephraim was doing something wrong.

He racked his brain. Nancy had knelt in front of the shirt, but what had she said? He closed his eyes. He didn't remember her exact words, but it had seemed like she was talking to another person. He swallowed, realizing his mistake.

"I'm sorry. Let me start over." Ephraim knelt and removed his hat. "My name's Ephraim; I'm a friend of Nancy's. You may have seen me up at the Laura, that is, uh, if you can see." He hoped the shirt wasn't offended by that. How sensitive was this thing?

The shirt didn't move.

Ephraim continued. "So here's the thing. I've been bitten by a hellhound, and if I can't find it by the time the moon sets tonight, I'm goin' to turn into a haint. I don't know if you care about any of that, but Nancy does. She turned herself into a witch just to save me. In fact, that's why she gave me you. So if you could help me, I'd really appreciate it, and I'm sure she would too."

The shirt stirred. Its movements were subtle at first, but grew slowly. It fluttered in intricate patterns for a few seconds, then fell still again.

Ephraim had no idea how to decipher the shirt's language, but he was making progress. His heart hammered with excitement.

"I didn't mean to sound all demandin'," he said. "This is the first time I ever talked to a shirt."

One arm of the shirt rose, moved in a circle, and dropped.

"Does that mean you forgive me?"

The shirt repeated the gesture. It seemed to Ephraim like an affirmative.

"So, about that hellhound..."

A breeze pushed through the trees. Both arms of the shirt lifted upward and drifted to one side, fluttering like twin flags. The direction was unmistakable.

Ephraim needed to go southeast.

34

HORSE THIEF

As soon as Peyton had left, Clabe returned to the parsonage. He slammed the door behind him.

"I thought I done told you I'd knock you silly if you tried to get away!"

He strode across the floor and dealt Isabel a backhand to the face that flipped the chair onto its side. Isabel gasped as the air was forced from her lungs.

Clabe stood over her, glaring. "We'll see if you try somethin' like that again!" He hauled her roughly back into an upright position.

Fresh tears mixed with the blood from Isabel's cut forehead, dampening her disheveled hair and the cloth of her gag.

Clabe leveled a finger at her. "I'm going back out to wait on my money. I don't want to hear a peep from you while I'm out there. If I do, that slap I gave you will feel like a granny did it compared to what I'll give you next." He stormed out.

It wasn't long before Isabel heard Peyton's voice again. "I got your hundred, Clabe," he said.

"Give it here then."

"I brought somethin' else for you too."

Isabel heard the sound of a fist striking flesh, and Clabe bellowed in pain. A scuffle ensued, both men grunting. Peyton cried out. A series of sickening thuds followed—one man raining blows on the other.

Then silence.

Labored footsteps ascended the stairs to the front door. Isabel held her breath. A key scraped in the lock, the knob turned, and the door creaked open, letting in a gust of snowy air. A tangle of limbs, boots, and bloody faces stood in the doorway.

Isabel recoiled, then realized what she was looking at. Peyton stepped inside and tossed Clabe's limp form from his shoulders onto the floor.

He pulled a knife from his belt and rushed to Isabel's side. His hands shook as he untied her gag and cut the cords that bound her wrists and feet.

Isabel began to sob. She embraced Peyton in a hug.

He stiffened, then tentatively patted her on the back. "It's all right," he said. "You're free now."

She released him and stepped past him, moving around the table to where Clabe lay. She gripped the back of a chair in one hand and raised her foot, then brought it down on Clabe's gut. She stomped again and again until she was out of breath, then turned. Peyton was standing dumbfounded by the chair she'd been tied to.

"Did you kill him?" she asked.

"I laid him out," Peyton said, moving to stand beside her. "But you just might've finished him off." He pulled a handkerchief from his pocket and dabbed at Isabel's forehead.

"Don't worry about that," Isabel said. "You need it more than I do. Your face is all bloody. So are your knuckles."

Peyton smiled. "Let me clean you up. Truth be told, I don't care for the sight of other folk's blood."

Isabel snorted. "I don't see you cleaning Clabe's face, and it's a bloody mess." She closed her eyes and let Peyton finish wiping her forehead.

"Yeah, well I guess I didn't look at him too hard then," Peyton said. "He wasn't too pretty to begin with, either. Why was he keepin' you up here anyhow?"

Isabel opened her mouth, then paused, remembering Peyton's quest for justice.

"And why'd you run off with Ephraim in the graveyard?"

Isabel swallowed. "Let's get out of here," she said, "and then I'll tell you."

They tied Clabe up and locked him in the cellar before leaving.

Peyton's horse stood down the hill, head bowed against the snow. Peyton helped Isabel onto the saddle, then climbed up in front of her. She wrapped her arms around him as they rode toward her father's store.

"You goin' to tell me now?" Peyton asked over the wind.

"I was helping Ephraim," Isabel said. "He doesn't deserve to die."

Peyton yanked back on the reins, bringing his horse to a stop. "You were helpin' him?"

"Listen, Peyton, there's a lot more going on here than you realize."

"Maybe I should have left you with Clabe Fletcher!"

Isabel clamped her mouth shut and let go of Peyton. "Say that again, Peyton Henson, and I won't speak another word to you!"

"Fine. What else is goin' on then?" Peyton looked over his shoulder at her.

"Reverend Boggs is responsible for Ephraim killing your brother."

Peyton snorted. "So the preacher is a killer, is that what you're sayin'?"

Isabel nodded. "He's in league with the Devil. I saw him myself—the Devil, that is. He came to call on Boggs while I was tied up in there."

"You saw the Devil, in the flesh?"

Isabel nodded.

"You really expect me to believe that?"

"It's true. The Devil's after Ephraim, he wants him as a servant, so he sent Boggs to corrupt Ephraim's ma. She got Ephraim's mind all turned around—told him she'd kill herself if he didn't kill a Yankee."

Peyton shook his head. "This is the biggest bunch of hogwash I've ever heard. I bet Ephraim told you all this. And now I knocked out Clabe before he told me where Ephraim's goin' to be tonight."

With a sigh, he flicked the reins, and the horse started forward again.

Isabel's heart clenched tight as she thought of Ephraim. She had to find him before he went to Butcher Holler tonight. If he didn't know she was free, he might sell his soul to save her from Boggs. But where was he?

They rounded a bend in the road, and far up ahead, they could see Isabel's father's store. Several men were gathered outside: Ernest Williams, Lester Ewing wearing the hat she'd sold him, Hebe Washburne, and many more. All of them held the reins of their horses. Some also held torches.

"Peyton," Isabel said, "get us off the road."

"Isabel, what are you—"

"Just do it!"

Peyton guided the horse off the road into a thicket of trees.

Isabel leaned around Peyton, watching the men at the store. Ernest Williams climbed the stairs to the porch.

"You think they're after you or somethin'?" Peyton asked. "Because your pa's been lookin' all over for you. Everyone reckoned Ephraim forced you to go with him and the witch-woman."

"Shhh!"

Ernest turned around and addressed the group. "I think you all know what brings us here tonight," he said, raising his voice above the hubbub. "My Francis still ain't right after what that old woman done to us in the church. We was expectin' another young'un, and she says she ain't felt the baby move since she woke up from that curse. For several years now, many of us have suspected that there's been a witch among us, and now we know. Well, it's time to put a stop to the Devil's work in Sixmile Creek. And I, for one, am ready to do away with Barefoot Nancy. How 'bout you'uns?"

A cheer went up from those gathered around.

"It's about time somebody did somethin' about that witch," Peyton muttered.

Isabel wanted to slap him.

"Well then," Ernest said, "let's not waste any time gettin' it done. Who here knows the best way up to her place?"

A hand shot up.

"Hebe, I figured you did. Lead the way."

The men mounted their horses and wheeled off down the road, heading for Flint Ridge.

Isabel's throat clenched. The idea of the old granny woman single-handedly facing down a mob of armed men made her blood run cold. She knew she had to intervene, but how could she hope to warn Nancy and find Ephraim in time? She couldn't get ahead of Ernest's gang without a horse of her own, and even if she had one, she couldn't beat them to the Laura *and* find Ephraim.

She glared at the back of Peyton's head—then an idea came to her. *If I have a horse and Peyton doesn't...*

She took a deep breath and shoved Peyton with all her might.

Peyton yelped in surprise as he fell from the saddle and landed on his back. Isabel leap-frogged into the middle of the saddle, dug her heels into the horse's flanks, and slapped the reins, urging the horse into a gallop.

Behind her, she heard Peyton's angry shout. "So this is how you thank me for savin' your life?" he yelled.

35

THE BEAR TRAP

Ephraim followed the shirt's directions throughout the afternoon, and kept his eyes peeled for any sign of the hellhound. As the sun sank low, the wind kicked up, howling through the trees. Snow fell thick and fast. In the deepening gloom and the swirling snowflakes, he found it increasingly difficult to maintain his bearings.

He pulled the shirt out of his bag and held it out in front of him. He didn't dare hang it from a branch in wind like this. "Am I goin' the right way?" he yelled over the wind.

The shirt flapped one way then the other. In this wind, it was impossible to tell which of its movements were its own.

Ephraim stuffed it back in his bag and pressed on, trying to hold to the course he'd been taking.

But the weather only worsened, and he was soon surrounded by an incomprehensible blur of half-seen trees and billowing white. At this rate, he wasn't sure he'd spot the hellhound if it walked right in front of him. The search was hopeless.

At last he slumped against a tree, defeated. This was it. Night had fallen, and in a few hours he'd be a haint. He felt his heart pounding, pumping the poison through his veins. He watched his breath ghost out of him and fade away on the winter wind.

And then, through the blizzard, Ephraim caught the faint gleam of a lantern. It blinked out, then reappeared a few moments later, closer. And this time it illuminated the outline of a figure bowed against the storm.

The sight of another human being brought Ephraim a feeling of warmth. He threw caution to the wind. "Hello there!"

The figure stopped and turned sharply to face Ephraim. "Ephraim? Is that you?"

The figure approached, and in the lantern light Ephraim made out the bearded face of Manson Owens.

"You got your gun with you, son?"

"I do. Manson, what's—"

The blacksmith didn't wait for Ephraim to finish. "I was out checkin' some of the traps I set for that bear. And I've got a critter caught in one the likes of which I've never seen. I reckon it's that devil-dog you're after. I shot at it, emptied my rifle, but the crazy thing didn't even flinch. It looked at me and—"

Now it was Ephraim's turn to cut off the old man. "Manson, just take me to it."

THE TRAP WAS near the edge of Manson's cornfield. As they drew near, both men slowed their pace and took care to muffle each step—caution born of habit and instinct.

Manson pointed across the open ground to a dark form hunched low. No sooner did Ephraim spot the hellhound than it emitted a low growl. It rose, accompanied by the clanking of an iron chain, and its red eyes fixed on Ephraim. Its lips curled back, baring fangs that dripped with black drool.

The hound tried to lurch toward the men, but one foot was weighed down by a massive trap. Manson and Ephraim approached until they were only a few feet from the snarling beast.

Ephraim raised Ruination to his shoulder and sighted down the barrel. The hound slunk away from him as if it could smell the iron ball inside waiting to pierce its heart. A cold wind blew across the field, a cloud shifted in the sky, and suddenly the hound was bathed in a halo of pale moonlight. Ephraim could see the creature clearer than he ever had before: it was the hide-bound skeleton of a bear hound, its oversized eyes glowing with an inner fire.

"Good Lord protect us!" Manson said. "That thing looks like it's got the hydrophoby!"

Ephraim shifted his face away from the gun. The hellhound's back was crisscrossed with a network of scars and wounds. Some were open and oozing dark blood.

Something deep within Ephraim stirred. He lowered the musket.

"I know you used to just be a dog," he said.

The hellhound snarled and shifted. The chain clanked.

"Boggs buried you, didn't he? He turned you into a hellhound."

The red eyes regarded Ephraim with a cold intelligence. The hound whined and lowered its head to lick its wounded leg.

"He whipped you." Memories boiled in Ephraim's mind. His mother handing him the pistol. A mug of foxglove tea. The flash of a pistol discharging.

He dropped the musket to the ground and crouched down until he was level with the hound's face. "I can't kill you." A tear trailed down his cheek. "I'm goin' to turn you loose. If that means I'll be a haint, so be it. I ain't killin' another thing that don't deserve it just to make my miserable life longer."

He took a step toward the beast.

"Ephraim, have you lost your ever-lovin' mind?" Mason

looked at him in utter bewilderment. "Why'd you have me make them iron balls for you? Shoot it!"

The hellhound growled. Its ears flattened.

"Manson, I'm not going to kill it. It doesn't deserve to die any more than Silas did." Ephraim took another step forward.

The hound didn't move.

"Hold on now! You fixin' to turn that thing loose?"

Ephraim nodded.

"Then you give me that gun, and I'll shoot it when it tries to tear you to ribbons."

Ephraim looked down at Ruination.

"For cryin' out loud, boy! If you're set on savin' this crazy thing, at least give a gun to an old man so he can protect hisself!"

Ephraim handed the musket to Manson, then took a deep breath and turned back to the hellhound.

Gingerly, Ephraim reached forward and took hold of the entrapped leg. The muscles beneath the dark fur were taut and quivering. Ephraim placed his foot on the spring and leaned his weight onto it. The spring depressed, and the jaws of the trap loosened. Ephraim pulled the jaws open, removing the teeth from the hellhound's flesh.

With a snarl, the hound lunged at Ephraim, jaws open wide.

Manson yelled, and the roar of Ruination's barrel shook the night.

Ephraim heard the iron ball whistle overhead, flying into the trees. In his panic, the old blacksmith had missed by at least five feet.

The hellhound lowered its head to the ground, cowering. It looked from Ephraim to Manson. Slowly it straightened up, its wounded paw held close to its body.

Ephraim held stock still, barely breathing. The red-eyed beast gazed at him as if deciding its next course of action. And suddenly, a feeling of calm washed over Ephraim. He felt peace, relief at having finally made his decision. He had not killed this poor animal. The poison in his veins was finishing its work, and he would pass into the spirit world, but not with more blood on his hands.

The hellhound took a limping step forward. Its nose was level with Ephraim's face, and it took a tentative sniff. The hound's hot breath washed over Ephraim, thick with the scent of decay. The hound sniffed again, moving to Ephraim's left shoulder. Inch by inch it explored the length of his arm, snuffling in short, powerful bursts. The dog honed in on Ephraim's forearm, the place it had bitten him. It nuzzled the area and began to lick it.

"You want to see what you did to me?" Ephraim shrugged off his jacket and rolled up his sleeve. In the moonlight he could see the dark wounds where the teeth had punctured his skin. They weren't red or swollen, but cold and sunken—not infection, but creeping death.

The hound licked the wounds, leaving traces of black saliva on Ephraim's skin.

"I can't watch this!" Manson said. Ephraim heard the scrape of the ramrod as the old man seated another load.

The hound raised its wounded foot and pawed at Ephraim's arm. Ephraim lowered it.

The hound licked the gashes on its own leg, then nuzzled Ephraim's arm. It repeated the process again, then yet again. Curious, Ephraim looked closer. He saw that the hound was leaving bloody nose prints around the wounds on his arm—and that the areas where the blood touched were growing pink and warm, losing the gray, lifeless tone. Warmth blossomed beneath his skin.

Ephraim was amazed. Hope surged through him. He reached down and rubbed his hand on the hound's trap-wound. His hand came away sticky and wet. He rubbed the blood all over his forearm.

The wounds healed instantaneously.

Ephraim looked deep into the red eyes of the hellhound. His cheeks were wet. "Thank you," he whispered.

The hound licked its chops and stood, favoring the wounded limb. It turned and limped off into the woods.

"What was that all about?" Manson removed his hands from his eyes and watched the hound go, slack-jawed.

"I wish I had time to tell you," Ephraim said, getting to his feet. "But I need to get to Butcher Holler before midnight." He took Ruination from the old man's trembling hands.

36

A THING SO OLD

Riding a horse over Flint Ridge was no easy task. The trail that left the main road was narrow, and hard to follow in the blizzard. Its only regular travelers had been Nancy and Earl.

Isabel gritted her teeth. She wanted to goad Peyton's horse into an all-out gallop, but she knew that to do so was folly. Her only consolation was the knowledge that the men ahead of her couldn't be moving much faster.

She lost the trail in the snowstorm several times, but knew she was close when she heard whoops echoing down the slope.

Oh no. I'm too late.

She sank her heels into her horse's flanks, but it was still a few minutes before she arrived at Nancy's home. Or what had once been her home.

The Laura was burning, sending tongues of fire up into the night sky. The snow, melted by the heat of the blaze, fell from the Laura in a halo of steaming rain. Men rode around the burning sycamore, whooping. A board had been nailed across the door, barring it shut—and no doubt trapping Nancy inside. Earl lay dead near the tree's base.

Isabel leaped from the saddle and ran forward. The heat hit her face like something solid. But before she could reach the door, it exploded outward, throwing burning splinters. Nancy emerged from the blaze, a being made of smoke and ash. Her face and hair were black with soot.

Ernest Williams and several of the other men drew pistols and rifles. The air filled with gunshots.

Nancy stumbled back, step after step, her body taking the force of each bullet, puffs of ash dusting off her. She stopped and doubled over. The men quit firing. With horror and disgust, Isabel recognized the eagerness on Ernest's face. He wanted to see the damage they had done to the old woman.

"Ye all have been callin' me a witch ever since that preacher come 'round." Nancy's voice carried across the hollow even though she was bent over, her hair obscuring her face. "And yet every one of ye knows that I have delivered your babes, I've tended to ye all in sickness, and I've done it all for a ham hock here, a string of beans there, sometimes nothin' at all. But that weren't enough for ye. This town wants a *witch*."

Nancy straightened. Isabel hardly recognized her face. Her left eye blazed sulfur yellow and blood red. She raised her hands over her head, mirroring the pose of the sycamore burning behind her. The flames in the tree whooshed higher into the night in a towering column of flame.

"Well, ye done *got* yourselves a witch!" She brought her hands down toward the men, and the column of fire roared forward, engulfing them.

Shrieks and the scent of burning hair and flesh filled the air. Isabel was farther away than any of the men, yet still had to throw herself to the ground as the wave of broiling heat washed over her. Ernest Williams rode out of the flames frantically beating at his shirt and his horse's tail, both of which smoldered.

Nancy launched herself into the air and collided with him, knocking him out of the saddle. She landed on his chest. Cackling, she plunged her hand through his ribs and tore out his heart.

Isabel averted her eyes as Nancy dispatched the other men who'd survived the flames. She was terrified, and at the same time it seemed wrong to abandon Nancy in this, the darkest hour of the old woman's life.

Only when the clearing grew silent, except for the crackle of flames, did Isabel turn back to face the scene. Nancy was standing still, watching her. Isabel held her breath, not daring to speak.

The granny woman took a few steps forward. Her shoulders sagged, and the light blazing in her left eye dimmed. Patches of the old woman's skin and hair had been burned away. Ash and blood—her own, and that of her victims—covered her hands and arms.

A tear fell from Nancy's normal eye, cutting a furrow in the soot that coated her face. "I came to Sixmile Creek to help folks, not hurt 'em," she said, her voice a dry rasp.

A lump rose in Isabel's throat. "But that doesn't mean you have to let them kill you," she said.

"I know that." Nancy turned around and spread her arms, encompassing the carnage and ruin strewn about the clearing. "But this ain't just me protecting myself. It's more'n that. Much more."

Isabel didn't know what to say. The old woman's honest admission was undeniable. At least seven families in Sixmile Creek were now fatherless, maybe more. She didn't know if any of the men had escaped Nancy's wrath.

"I wasn't made for witchery, Miss Isabel. But I'm afraid that's all I'm good for now," Nancy said. "I cain't stay here no more. I ain't fit to be near folks."

Tears welled up in Isabel's eyes and flowed onto her cheeks. She ran to Nancy and wrapped the old woman in a hug. "Where will you go?"

Nancy closed her eyes and almost smiled. She looked like she was soaking up the kindness, filling a canteen before a journey through a desolate land. "There's a place I know, way up in the mountains. I seen it once when I was younger. I don't reckon folks have made it out that far." Her gaze traveled down the Laura from crown to base. The snow around the old tree had receded, leaving behind a steaming ring of damp earth. "It's a shame, ain't it? Seein' a thing so old go up in flames."

They stood in silence for a moment.

"Go on now," Nancy said, not taking her eyes off the burning tree. "Ephraim will have need of ye."

Fortunately, Peyton's horse hadn't strayed far. Isabel climbed back in the saddle and pulled on the reins, wheeling it around. She had lost one friend this night, but there still might be time to save another.

37

EARTH AND WORM

The veil between the worlds thinned as Death urged Isham toward the land of the living. They pushed through, emerging into a dark, snowy woodland.

Scratch stepped out into the moonlight, twirling his hat on a finger. "I don't know why mortals ever refer to you as untimely. In my experience, Death, you are a punctual creature."

"Where are they?" Death asked, scanning the trees.

"I'm sorry, who exactly are you referring to?"

Death gave Scratch his coldest stare. A gust of wind and snow swirled around him. "Your servants."

"I'm afraid you'll have to be more specific than that. I have many servants. Which ones are you looking for?"

"Don't fool with me, Scratch. You know that two of them have contracts that end tonight. Hand them over."

Scratch laughed. "You never were one for names and faces, were you? Please tell me you can name at least one other mortal besides dear Maude."

Death pulled his reaping hook from its sheath. Clouds of vapor puffed from his nostrils like the breath of an enraged bull. "I'm not in the habit of being mocked."

"No, I suppose you're not. But even so, I don't know what you think you're going to do with your farming implement."

"You're playing games with me, Devil! I'm after the two mortals who made a pact with you on this night, seven years ago. The man and the boy. I know their faces; names mean little to me."

"Shame. If they were all the same to you, I was going to hand over someone besides William. I'm quite partial to him."

"Where is he?"

Scratch pointed into the forest. "Over that way. Surely you're capable of finding him."

"You show me. I had to track the last one clear across Arkansas, remember?"

"Fine. Do you prefer that I ride in front and hold the reins, or would you rather I sit behind you and whisper directions in your ear?"

Death scowled. "You walk."

Scratch sighed and put on his hat. "Just because things are going your way tonight doesn't mean you need to rub salt in my wounds. I insist on riding to find Amos after this; he's up north in the lumber camps."

The Devil led Death through the forest. They passed through an overgrown graveyard at the bottom of the hollow, then climbed the slope to a cabin. William was crouched on the porch, sharpening the edge of a tomahawk with a whetstone.

As they approached, he got to his feet and walked stiffly to meet them. He was gripping the tomahawk's handle so tightly that his knuckles blanched.

"The night isn't over yet!" William said. His voice had a shrill edge.

Scratch shook his head. "William, do you really think—"

"The boy is coming, Scratch! I told him to meet me here. You saw the girl I'm baiting him with. She's being brought here as we speak—I'm sure of it!"

Death almost smiled at the sight of the mortal fool babbling. He raised a hand.

William stopped speaking.

"You have until the moon sets," Death said. "Then I will claim your soul. Earth and worm will claim your flesh."

William blinked.

Something moved in the shadows behind William, and a moment later the sharp end of a knife sprouted from William's stomach, pushed through from behind.

William looked down at it, unmoving, mild surprise on his face.

The assailant shoved the blade in further and stepped into the light. He looked up at Death and Scratch. "Which one of you's the Devil? I'm looking for my boy, Amos!"

Scratch chuckled. "So, you're Amos's father? He never mentioned you."

"Reuben?" A young man's voice echoed down from the head of the hollow.

Death turned. A figure was silhouetted against the moon at the top of the ridge.

William lifted his head, like an impaled scarecrow coming to life, and a smile spread across his face. "Ephraim's here," he said, chuckling. He reached up and loosened his cravat with one hand and twirled the tomahawk with the other. In one swift movement, he turned and buried his tomahawk in the chest of his assailant.

The man gasped. His knees buckled.

William reached behind him, grasped the handle of the knife sticking out of his back, and wrenched it free. He cast it aside and grabbed his would-be-murderer by the shirtfront, hauling him up until their faces were separated by mere inches.

"You read my almanack, didn't you?" he hissed through bared teeth. "You thought iron would kill me this night. You went through all the trouble of finding me, Reuben. You picked the right weapon, and you picked the right night—but in the end, you didn't stick me in the heart." He wrenched the tomahawk free and pushed Reuben to the ground.

Death watched Reuben's soul trickle out of his body.

William gazed at the man for a moment, chest heaving. Then he ran a hand through his hair and wiped the blade of the tomahawk on his pants. He turned to Scratch with a smirk. "I told you the night wasn't over. You'll have your prize, and I'll have mine."

The Devil grinned and shook his head. "William, you never cease to amaze me."

"Hands up, Reverend!" shouted a new voice.

Death turned to see a young man kneeling in the snow, aiming down the barrel of an old-time musket. "I've got this loaded with an iron ball!" he yelled. "Where's Isabel?"

38

BUTCHER HOLLER

The moon illuminated Butcher Holler with a ghastly light. Ephraim kept the barrel of Ruination on Boggs's chest as he surveyed the scene. Reuben's lifeless form made him feel sick. His eyes flicked to the two figures behind Boggs: a man in a black cloak on a white horse, and a small man wearing a suit and top hat. The back of his neck prickled.

"Ephraim! Ephraim!" Isabel's voice rang across the hollow. "I'm over here! Boggs doesn't have me!"

Ephraim lost his focus for a split second. Isabel? Where was she?

The moment's hesitation was all Boggs needed. He bounded forward in a blur of motion and swatted the musket from Ephraim's hands. The gun pinwheeled into a thicket, and Boggs threw an elbow into Ephraim's face.

Stars exploded across Ephraim's vision. He fell back in the snow, stunned, and his ears were filled with a ringing. But Boggs didn't press his advantage, and as Ephraim sat up, blinking away the pain, he saw why. Boggs had gone after Isabel instead. He held her by the hair and dragged her closer, stopping a few feet from Ephraim.

He pulled a tomahawk from his belt and showed it to Ephraim. "If you move from where you lie, I'll split her skull with this before you can blink!"

Ephraim didn't move.

"Now boy, I've given you just about every chance to join me and Scratch willingly. And here we are, fast approaching midnight on the Cut Off Day. So this is your last chance. Sign yourself over, or the girl dies."

Ephraim's heart sank. "All right. I'll do it!" he said.

"I thought you'd see things my way," Boggs said, smiling. He released Isabel's hair and motioned to Scratch. "What did I tell you? The boy's ready to sign the contract."

Ephraim locked eyes with Isabel, who motioned downward with her head slightly. He looked down and saw that she had her fingers curled around a stick. Understanding what she planned, he nodded.

Isabel threw the stick into the woods. It struck the trunk of a tree with a thunk.

Everything happened in a blur. Boggs spun toward the sound, tomahawk at the ready. Ephraim didn't hesitate, didn't even think —he launched himself at the preacher from behind, catching the man by both knees. Boggs tumbled forward, the tomahawk falling from his grasp, and Isabel snatched it up. Ephraim threw himself onto Boggs's back with a ferocity borne of true desperation. He grabbed the back of the preacher's collar, lifted Boggs's head, and slammed it violently onto the frozen ground. The preacher went limp.

"Well done, Ephraim!"

Ephraim looked up. The man with the top hat clapped his hands in obvious glee.

"You are truly vicious. A man after my own heart!" The man folded his hands behind him and walked over to where Ephraim sat straddling Boggs's prone form. He stuck out a hand. "Allow me to introduce myself. I am Scratch. I'm sure you've heard of me."

Ephraim stared at Scratch's outstretched hand. An involuntary shudder ran through him.

Scratch shrugged and let his hand fall to his side. "I'm thinking the two of us should dispense with this intermediary; he won't be around for much longer anyway. Let's strike a deal, boy!"

"I ain't strikin' no deal with you," Ephraim said.

Scratch laughed. "At least hear me out, son. This is an opportunity most will never get." He crouched down, so he looked Ephraim straight in the face. "Listen—to prove to you how willing I am to negotiate, why don't *you* name the terms? You serve me, and I'll give you whatever you want."

Ephraim said nothing.

"All right then, how about I propose a few things for your consideration? I have a knack for finding offers that are quite enticing." Scratch rose and squinted pensively at Ephraim for a few moments. "You don't strike me as a young man with an unquenchable desire to be a legendary fiddle player—I'll forego that offer." He glanced at Isabel, who still clutched the tomahawk. "But love...? Ah, yes. If you agree to serve me, I'll cut her in on the deal. Immortality for the both of you, and we'll piece it out in fifty-year segments, plenty of time for unending love. How does that sound?"

Ephraim looked at Isabel.

She shook her head.

Scratch pulled out a pen and a piece of parchment. "Just a moment," he said, scribbling. "I'll draw up something here, we can review it, and if it's agreeable, we'll all sign." He turned and motioned to the pale man. "Death, come over here."

"Why me?" Ephraim asked.

Scratch looked up from the paper. "Pardon?"

"Why did you send Boggs after me? Why do you want *me* to serve you so much?"

Scratch folded the parchment and tucked it back into his coat. He motioned for Ephraim to stand. "Walk with me."

It was the last thing Ephraim wanted to do, yet somehow he found himself striding through the snow alongside the Devil. They stopped out of earshot of Isabel and Death. Scratch faced Ephraim and cleared his throat.

"Ephraim, if there's one thing God and I have in common, it's that we both can sense great potential." He stuck out a finger. "And you, my boy, have it. Just like your father before you."

"What do you mean?"

"I mean that you have a gift. People trust you, even when you've committed horrible crimes." Scratch pointed at Isabel. "Does she know that you're a murderer?"

Ephraim nodded.

"And she's here, trying to save you! Ephraim, I've been around for a long time, so believe me when I say that the girl loves you. Look at her!"

Ephraim looked at her.

"She's a churchgoing, hardworking girl, the daughter of good parents, and yet she's in the middle of the woods at night, risking her life to be with a criminal, a man worthy of the gallows! Why?"

Ephraim hung his head.

"I'll tell you why," Scratch said. "You can kill, you can steal, you can run off with an honest man's daughter, but when people look at you they see goodness. Most men are tainted by their sins, and people sense that—they *recoil* from it. It's a gift to be able to do the wrong things for the right reasons. Even with blood on your hands, you can look people in the eye. You could be a tempter without guile, Ephraim. You could reach souls I never could. And I will reward you handsomely for it."

The weight of Scratch's words was more than Ephraim could bear. Self-loathing enveloped him. He wanted to be with Isabel more than anything. She was the one ray of sunshine in a life that had been clouded over since the death of his father. Yet through his longing, he knew that she deserved better.

"You're right," he said. "I ain't worthy of her."

"That's beside the point, boy. What red-blooded man would turn away a woman like that? She wants you! You want her! Take what's yours to claim. The courage to act *makes* you worthy of it!"

Visions of a life with Isabel flickered through Ephraim's mind, promising untold sweetness, like the smell of a baking pie. He remembered the feel of her hand in his, the way his heart beat faster every time she sat next to him.

Scratch produced the pen and parchment again, and pushed them into Ephraim's hands. "Go on. Sign, boy. You're almost there."

Ephraim's gaze flicked to Reuben's lifeless body. *He was just a father who loved his son.* How many boys like Amos had Boggs corrupted?

Ephraim thought of the desperate evil glinting in the preacher's eyes as he'd held the tomahawk over Isabel's head. *If I sign this, that's what I'll become.* He shuddered. Isabel could never love someone that evil. Surely a pact with the Devil would end in bitterness far worse than any he'd experienced.

With a deep breath, he turned to Scratch. "I made a mistake that ruined everythin' I care about, but servin' you ain't goin' to set things right."

Scratch's smile disappeared. "Think about your decision, Ephraim. I never begin negotiations with threats, but hear me out now: all murderers are eventually mine. You *will* be mine. Serve me now, and I will remember your obedience for eternity. Deny me, and I will make sure that Hell lives up to its reputation."

Ephraim's heart beat so fast he thought it would burst. He shook his head. "I'll never do it."

Scratch scowled. "So be it. But know that the Devil gives no second chances."

"Ephraim!" Isabel yelled.

An explosion of black powder shook the night.

Ephraim spun around.

Boggs was on his feet, Ruination clutched in his hands, the end of its barrel weeping smoke.

Ephraim instinctively looked to Isabel. Was she all right?

Isabel covered her mouth with her hand. Both she and Boggs were gazing at Death.

The pale man had an odd expression on his face. He raised a hand to his chest, coughed, and toppled off his horse. When he hit the ground, he lay still, his black cloak a disembodied shadow against the whiteness of the moonlit snow.

Boggs charged forward and leaped onto Death's steed. It reared, trying to throw him, but Boggs hung on grimly. He gained his seat and seized the reins. The horse wheeled and bucked. Boggs jerked the reins viciously, bringing the horse under his control. He dug his heels into the steed's pearly flanks and flogged it with the reins.

Ephraim watched in disbelief as Boggs galloped off down the hollow.

"Well, I never..." Scratch looked at the still form of Death, then up at the spot where Boggs had disappeared among the trees. He opened his mouth as if to say something, then closed it and shook his head slowly. A grin crept across his face, and he started to laugh. "Oh my, Death's going to have quite the time sorting this out!" His laughing grew louder, filling the hollow.

And as Ephraim watched, the Devil's form began to fade. Just before he vanished, Scratch tipped his hat. "It's a shame we couldn't do business. I'll be waiting for you at the Judgment, boy!"

39

THE PALE HORSEMAN

E phraim crumpled the Devil's contract into a ball and dropped it on the ground.

"Is he dead?" Isabel asked as Ephraim joined her by the fallen figure of Death.

"Sure looks like it."

"But...I thought he was Death."

"That iron ball must've killed him. Look, Boggs hit him right in the heart."

"Iron ball?"

"Yeah, today you can kill any supernatural thing with iron, least that's what the almanac said. I was goin' to use it on the hellhound."

Isabel looked alarmed. "How's the bite? Tonight's the full moon."

Ephraim rolled up his sleeve and showed her his arm.

Isabel seized his arm and examined it. "Ephraim, you're healed!" She drew him into a hug. "Thank the Lord! It's over!" She took a step back and looked into his face.

But Ephraim couldn't meet her gaze. "No," he said softly. "This isn't over. It'll never be over."

"What do you mean?"

Ephraim remained silent for a moment, unsure if he could speak over the breaking of his own heart. "I have to leave Sixmile Creek. I can't see you anymore. I'm damned."

Isabel studied him. "I knew you couldn't stay here, Ephraim. Not with Peyton and everyone hunting you. That's why I made up my mind." She wrapped her hand in his. "I'm coming with you."

"No, Isabel. Didn't you hear me? I'm damned. I'm still a murderer. The Devil said I'll be his when I die."

"I don't care. I love you."

Ephraim looked into Isabel's eyes. "I love you too, and that's why I can't do this to you. You deserve better."

Tears filled Isabel's eyes. "Don't say that, I—"

The crack of a rifle echoed down the hollow, and Ephraim felt a sharp pain in his shoulder. The impact drove him back a pace, and he realized he'd been shot.

Peyton Henson stepped out from behind a tree, racking the lever on his rifle.

Isabel screamed.

Peyton walked toward Ephraim, his rifle raised.

Isabel stepped in front of him. "No! Peyton, don't!"

"Out of my way, Isabel! This ain't your fight. I beat Jake Fletcher till he told me where y'all were, and I ain't about to let you stop me."

"You'll have to shoot me too!" Isabel said. She stood tall, though she was shaking.

Ephraim watched Peyton with an odd sense of calm. His shoulder burned with pain from the rifle shot, but it felt purifying in a way—a clean agony, cauterizing the ulcer of guilt in his soul. "Move, Isabel," he said. "Let him through."

Isabel looked back at him, and Peyton stepped past her, sighting down the rifle. "There's no mercy for you here, Cutler! I've come to settle this."

"I ain't goin' to ask you for mercy," Ephraim said. "You deserve justice." He spread his uninjured arm wide. "Hit me in the heart this time." He felt empty, numb, unable to mourn his own demise.

Peyton's eyes were black with hatred. He laughed. "You think I'm goin' to make it that quick? I want to watch you hurt!" He lowered the barrel of his gun and shot Ephraim in the leg.

Ephraim gasped and collapsed to the ground.

"I'm going to stretch this out!" Peyton yelled into the night, racking the lever of his rifle.

"Stop!" Isabel stepped in front of Peyton again, this time grabbing the end of the barrel.

"Let go," Peyton hissed.

"No! You both deserve better than this!" Isabel started sobbing. "Look!" She pointed to Reuben's body, cooling in the snow. "It's not justice you're after," she said, "it's revenge! That man spent his life on revenge, every day of it since the war. Look at what it got him—nothing! Killing Ephraim isn't going to bring Silas back. The only thing it will do is turn you into a murderer too."

Peyton bit his lower lip, staring at Reuben's body.

"Revenge won't make anything better," Isabel said quietly. "But forgiveness will."

Peyton's eyes flashed at Ephraim. "I can't forgive the scum that cut my brother down!"

"Then just let him go," whispered Isabel. "And give it time." Her eyes sparkled with tears.

Peyton shifted uncomfortably. The barrel of the rifle dropped slightly.

Death moaned and shifted in the snow.

Isabel and Peyton jumped back.

The pale figure groaned. He rubbed his chest, shook snow from his beard, and got to his feet. He scowled as he looked around the clearing. "Where's Isham?" His ice-cold eyes seemed to pierce the young folk. "Where's my horse?"

Ephraim and Isabel glanced at each other.

"Boggs took him," Ephraim said.

Death spat in the snow. "They've gone and done it this time, Scratch and his blasted servants!" He looked around the clearing again. "Scratch left, didn't he? He never stays around to clean up after himself."

Ephraim nodded.

"I thought you were dead," Isabel said.

Death snorted. "Dead? That iron sure stung, it knocked me into the netherworld, but I'm no more dead than a rabbit thrown into a briar patch." He studied the ground, his eyes settling on the path of hoofprints in the snow. "I swear I'll make Scratch pay for this," he muttered to himself, walking in the direction Boggs had taken.

"Wait," Ephraim said.

Death turned around. "Yes?"

"Before Scratch left, he said that all murderers would eventually be his. Is that true?"

Death shrugged. "I reckon so. The judgment of souls is no concern of mine."

Ephraim thought of Isabel's words to Peyton. *Forgiveness can make things better.*

"You said you travel the path between this world and the netherworld. Could you let me ask the man I killed to forgive me?"

Death's eyes narrowed.

"He was an innocent man," Ephraim said. "I want to make things right with him."

The pale man shook his head. "That's impossible. The dead have no business with the living. I've never allowed such a meeting. It goes against the natural order."

"But, you *could* do it?"

Death eyed Ephraim warily. "I don't know. Doing so would require the full exercise of my power. I would need my reaping hook and horse, both of which are currently missing."

"Oh." Ephraim hung his head.

Death turned and continued to follow Isham's tracks. Then he stopped, bent down, and retrieved a crumpled wad of paper from the snow. The contract Scratch had written. Death unfolded it and scanned the page.

He turned back toward Ephraim, a pensive look in his eyes. "Scratch offered you this deal?"

"Yes."

Death looked down at the paper again, his brow furrowed. "He offered you fifty years free from death in exchange for your service?"

"Yes."

Death looked toward the forest. "I've never seen him offer anything more than seven years."

"He said he really wanted me, so he tried to negotiate."

Death shook his head. "The Devil just doesn't do that. Everything always has to be on his terms." He studied Ephraim as if really seeing the boy for the first time. "If I were to aid you, in the way that you ask, there'd have to be a price."

Ephraim swallowed. His heart was thumping. "What kind of... price?"

"A deal." Death was speaking slowly, his voice filling with confidence. "Yes, a deal. Like Scratch and his countless servants. I will let you speak with the man you murdered, to seek his forgiveness, if you agree to serve *me* for a time. Help me even the score with Scratch."

Ephraim couldn't believe this was happening. "For how long?"

Death considered. "One hundred and fifty years."

Ephraim was dumbfounded. "What? Why so long?"

Death regarded him somberly. "It is the price I require. You ask for something I have never granted a mortal."

This is it, Ephraim thought. *This is my one chance to set things right.* He looked at Isabel, then back at Death, and an ache spread through his chest. "I'll do it."

"Choose in all solemnity, boy. I will bind you into my service, and that cannot be undone. If you ride with me, I guarantee there will be days when you *long* for the peace of the grave. Understand that by agreeing to this deal, you are surrendering that peace."

"I'll do it," Ephraim repeated.

"Then come." Death held out a pale hand.

Ephraim limped forward.

Death placed his hand on Ephraim's shoulder. A chill swept over him. The pulsing of his heart slowed. He felt as if his blood had turned to clay, dense and cool. His ears filled with the sound of rushing water. He felt the current and realized that it wasn't water that flowed around him, but time. His bones defied it, standing strong like rocks in a river.

Death released him, and Ephraim gasped as if he had surfaced from a plunge into an icy lake. He flexed his wounded shoulder. It was healed. His leg was, too.

"Let's go then," Death said.

"Wait."

Ephraim turned to Isabel. Tears were streaming down her face.

His heart grew leaden. *One hundred and fifty years.* He'd never see her again. She'd grow old and... He couldn't bear the thought. He swallowed, but the knot in his throat wouldn't go down.

He took her hands in his. "Goodbye," he said.

She wiped her eyes. "Goodbye, Ephraim."

"Are you ready to leave, boy?"

Ephraim turned to Death. He thought he detected a flicker of sympathy in the ice blue eyes.

"I am."

Death gathered his cloak around him. "Very well. Let's go find my horse."

<<<<>>>>

Follow Ephraim's continuing story in November Witch, *coming in spring 2018.*

ENJOYED SOME DARK HOLLER?

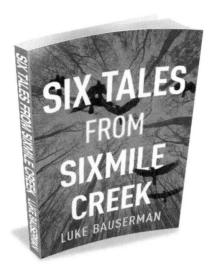

Read the fascinating history and folklore that inspired Some Dark Holler in, *Six Tales from Sixmile Creek*. You can get a copy FOR FREE when you sign up to join my Reader's Group. To get started, go to: www.lukebauserman.com/sixtales

ACKNOWLEDGMENTS

For Nyla. Sambatra izay fitoerany na ny handalovany aza mamendrofendro.

Thank you to everyone who has encouraged me during the writing of this book, especially to all the enthusiastic readers on my blog, TheWeeklyHoller.com.

A special thank you to the Third Sunday Club: Austin Rehl, Jordan Allen, and Sadie Bauserman. Your feedback was instrumental in shaping this story.

The readers at BetaBooks also provided crucial feedback as this story was refined.

Thank you to David Farland who showed me how to "rewrite to greatness."

This story owes a debt to other Appalachian authors whose stories inspire me, namely Manly Wade Wellman and James Still.

In the process of creating this novel I've had the privilege to work with a number of talented professionals. David Gatewood edited the manuscript. Cody Tilson designed the cover. Proofreading was done by Stephanie Parent and Polgarus Studio.

ABOUT THE AUTHOR

Luke Bauserman is an author, adventurer, and explorer from the Appalachian foothills of southeastern Ohio. He writes about rural history, American folklore, and backwoods strangeness on his blog, The Weekly Holler (www.theweeklyholler.com).

You can sign up for Luke's newsletter, with giveaways and the latest releases, here: www.lukebauserman.com/news

Connect with Luke:

www.lukebauserman.com

luke@lukebauserman.com

Made in the USA
Columbia, SC
04 January 2019